COLORS OF THE NIGHT

SPIRIT WARRIOR – VOL. 2

PETER H. ZINDLER

Colors of the Night

For information, contact
　　Pete Zindler
　　peterhzindler@gmail.com

Cover art and chapter art by Mark Rudge, San Diego, California

Cover design and layout by Sarah and James Gardiner, Mission Viejo, California

Text design and layout by John Whiteman, La Jolla, California

Cover inspiration by Adrielle Zindler, Ramona, California

ISBN 978-0-9797119-4-7

To HIM

With HIM

For HIM

Other books by Peter H. Zindler:

Enoch the Elephant – a children's classic.

Spirit Warrior – the first in the Spirit Warrior's Series.

Seeds of Greatness Sown in the Heartland – a devotional.

Waterfront Rats – a modern military fictional novel.

Self-Publishing and Marketing from the Trenches –
        a non-fiction work.

"Excellent! This incredible story captures readers with suspenseful action, romance, evil, and the awesome power of the Almighty. An absolute Masterpiece."

Elijah Hollinger
Ramona Teen Creative Writer's Group

ACKNOWLEDGEMENTS

I would like to thank the many people that are involved in the writing, editing, critiquing, and production of this novel. First of all my wife, Adelaide, my son, Terance and my daughter, Adrielle who are my greatest fans and constant inspiration to continue writing.

A special thanks to Adrielle for helping Daddy with the cover – you are awesome and remember a Daddy's love has a lifetime guarantee – but not at K-Mart.

Thanks to Sarah and James for the cover art work.

Monica – thanks for help in the trial scene.

Bob Ward – great job of editing.

The members of the Ramona Christian Writers Critique Group have been invaluable. Thanks Byron, Joe, Mike, Gail, Stacey, and Pam, who have expended many hours guiding me along the word journey of writing a novel.

A special thanks to John Whiteman and Asenith Dixon for their efforts in layout and editing.

Sean, thanks for help with the fight scenes – Hoo-rah!

Dave Hebron, you've always been Spirit Warrior's champion!

Thanks to Spirit Warrior's other champion, Thaddeus Tague, for reading it 13 times. Thanks for your comments on "Colors"

A very special thanks to the Ramona Teen Creative Writer's Group: Julianne, Allison Boulton, Georgia Phipps, Katrina, Austin Koch, Robert Hayes, Elijah Hollinger, Julie, Kat, James, Trevor, Catherine McCarthy, and Emily. I'm most proud of you all and expect to see you in print very soon.

CONTENTS

PROLOGUE 13
CHAPTER ONE...15
CHAPTER TWO 21
CHAPTER THREE 29
CHAPTER FOUR 35
CHAPTER FIVE 39
CHAPTER SIX 47
CHAPTER SEVEN 57
CHAPTER EIGHT..63
CHAPTER NINE..71
CHAPTER TEN 75
CHAPTER ELEVEN...81
CHAPTER TWELVE 87
CHAPTER THIRTEEN..95
CHAPTER FOURTEEN..103
CHAPTER FIFTEEN...107
CHAPTER SIXTEEN 113
CHAPTER SEVENTEEN 119
CHAPTER EIGHTEEN...127
CHAPTER NINETEEN 135
CHAPTER TWENTY-ONE 145
CHAPTER TWENTY-TWO...151
CHAPTER TWENTY-FOUR..169
CHAPTER TWENTY-FIVE 177
CHAPTER TWENTY-SEVEN 191
CHAPTER TWENTY-EIGHT...199
CHAPTER TWENTY-NINE 205
CHAPTER THIRTY..213
CHAPTER THIRTY-ONE 217
CHAPTER THIRTY-TWO..223
CHAPTER THIRTY-FIVE..237
CHAPTER THIRTY-SIX...247
CHAPTER THIRTY-SEVEN..255
CHAPTER THIRTY-EIGHT 261
CHAPTER THIRTY-NINE 273

CHAPTER FORTY 279
CHAPTER FORTY-ONE 287
CHAPTER FORTY-TWO 291
CHAPTER FORTY-THREE 295
CHAPTER FORTY-FOUR 300

THE BEAT OF WAR

by Michael Hundley

Faintly it begins,
A call for which there is no end.
The sound it echoes in your heart,
Compelling you, one set apart.
Louder now, thump the drums,
An invitation not heard by some.
A call to serve, to face the fight,
To stand against the foe of right.

A chill falls down, your muscles tense,
Your soul awakes, with heightened sense.
Your eyes look to the coming storm,
And see the faces, battle worn.
A hesitation, a paused respite,
Sneaks in your mind, a stirring fright.
Then powerfully, as never before,
A thunderous refrain, the Beat of War.

Any doubt is gone, any fears have let,
Your path is clear and your way is set.
A vision now appears to you,
Oh warrior brave and soldier true
You see a child, innocent and pure,
Smiling, laughing, safe and secure.
A passion, a drive, this picture does implant,
To be strong and strive for those who can't.
This calling you feel, has a familiar ring,
Like One who lived and loved, the Servant King.

PROLOGUE

"Destroy his reputation," demanded the bald headed man with a permanent scowl saddled on his face, sitting on his golden throne in the City beneath the Sea. "If I'm going to reclaim my empire in the Blue Ring Galaxy, I must obliterate the holier than thou image set in people's minds."

"No. Kill him!" his nephew exclaimed, clenching his fists, rippling the sculpted muscles and corded veins in his thick forearms and ham-like biceps. The Herculean man with a wash board stomach towered above most men. Five years ago, Megog had lost his Crown Championship in the ultimate fighting ring to Vying, the commander of the forces of the Realm. Venom from that loss relentlessly scourged his soul every day.

"What a simpleton you are, Megog. If it were that easy, I would be serving you. Remember that!"

"I'm sorry, Emperor Og. What is your plan?" Megog asked obsequiously.

"Go to Binery! Get Scarface and the others and bring them here. It is time for my revenge."

Megog hurried out of his uncle's presence while the rest of the slaves bowed down and chanted, "Worthy is Emperor Og. Great and powerful is our King."

Og's face flushed from their worship. He closed his eyes and listened deeply to their adulation.

"Leave me!" he suddenly bellowed, his fiery eyes flashing uncontrolled anger. Getting up, he slammed his palm into the back of a female slave propelling her across the room. "Back to work you worthless beings. I want the prototype Cyverex-6 tested immediately!"

PETER H. ZINDLER

Chapter One

Sudden movement flashed in the woods. It didn't belong. I looked again, but everything was serene and quite beautiful. Stately pines stretched their scented limbs toward the rich azure sky, rejoicing at the warm gentle breeze flowing through their leafy branches, cloaking the thick dark underbrush. Maybe my eyes had deceived me. No, I saw something, something dark and big, moving in the shadows of the forest.

The blue sun radiated warmth, shining brightly. It was good to be on the surface of Planet Micron. For many years, we had lived in the hollowed out old city, Vardo, beneath the sea, hidden from the surface attacks of planet Za-Kar. Traveling in the open on Micron's surface used to be very dangerous, but we were finally free from the Og's tyranny that had ruled and corrupted the Blue Ring Galaxy for twenty-two years.

Dropping to one knee, I examined the rich dark soil, slowly sifting it with my fingers. Covertly I watched for movement in the darkened trees. My spirit was troubled, uneasy. Evil was watching, boldly coming closer.

My old friend and brother in battle, Dax, walked over to me with a wary look on his face. He'd grown into a fine soldier and recently had achieved the rank of Warrior, elected by his superiors.

"Vying, what is it? Why have you stopped?"

"Be still! I saw movement in the brush. Something's out there. Look to where my finger is pointing. My spirit is uneasy, tingling. Something is out there, watching, waiting."

Dax kneeled down and scooped a handful of dirt. "Should we call off the training and return to New Vardo?"

"No, the knights have done well this week here in the outback. They'd be disappointed if we returned early. By staying longer, we demonstrate to the senior military leadership that just because we're at peace doesn't mean we should shorten their training cycle."

"Perhaps we should post a watch tonight. I could tell them that standing watch is an integral part of their training."

I liked it when leaders around me used their minds, but it especially pleased me that Dax had grown to be a competent soldier. His ruddy complexion, framed by dark eyebrows had drawn many a second glance from the fair maidens on Micron, both young and old. The intense physical discipline of military life had honed his athletic body, stripping him of any excess body fat.

"Good idea. Post the watch. When we break from this exercise, have the knights set up my tent along the tree line, away from the others."

"Why would you want to be outside the perimeter?"

"Being out here in the fresh air takes me away from the stress of military politics and stimulates creative thoughts. I have an idea for a new ship of the line. I want to make some conceptual drawings in the quiet of the night. You know how noisy the young men can be."

"I understand. So ordered, Commander."

The knights set up camp in the clearing placing my tent near the trees so later I could slip out into the woods, unnoticed. I knew I had to enter the forested darkness and hunt for the intruder.

Pulling out their swords, they practiced their thrusts and parries. Half-heartedly, I demonstrated some moves, but my mind was on the danger that lurked in the growing darkness. I kept a constant vigil on the woods knowing that whatever it was, it was well-trained in concealment.

With chow almost ready, Dax dismissed the young knights. They went to their tents to drink water and recount the day's experience. They were the best class that had come out of the Academy in five years. After this two-week training experience, the young men would be ready to join the warriors on interplanetary exploratory missions.

One of the knights brought me part of a roasted three-footed dinga that had been snared earlier in the day. Though the marbled meat smelled good, I had no appetite. I took the plate into my tent and set it down on a canvas chair. I peered out of the breezeway flap angled toward the woods. Standing still, I strained my ears for any unusual sound, perhaps a twig being snapped or a sudden flight of birds. Nothing.

Silently I waited as time ground to a halt. Hungry birds should have been flying about in search of their evening meal, yet all was quiet, much too quiet. Something had put them on alert as they roosted on empty bellies. The gnawing feeling in my stomach wouldn't leave. The eerie stillness told me a threat was out there. Waiting. Watching.

Figure 1: A Hoon Stalking

Mark Rowe 02/24/03

The cloak of night covered our camp. Feeling hungry, I finally ate the flavorful meat, still tuning my ears to the sounds of the nocturnal woods. I picked up an electronic drawing pad and sketched a few lines, but creativity wouldn't come. I extinguished my light and lay on the cot. It felt good after a long day tramping about the hills. I wanted to close my eyes and envision the new ship, but that was impossible. Whatever was stalking us, occupied my mind, preventing the release of creative ideas.

I couldn't wait any longer. Slowly I eased my body off the cot, grabbed my sword, and crouched at the flaps of my tent. I heard the camaraderie of the young men and remembered the talks my great friend Wolks and I used to have after sparring in the battle ring. There was always a deep satisfying feeling at the end of a hard workout. The cool water we drank afterwards was better than Milo wine. Many things had changed since that time and now Wolks was king of Micron.

Quietly I slipped under the flap and slow crawled to the tree line. Getting up, I eased through the brush and into the woods. Just as I slid behind a big tree, a twig snapped under my foot, shattering the silence. Instantly I froze. If there was someone or something nearby, he knew I was stalking him. Controlling my impatience, I waited until the birds began chirping their evening songs again. Noises from the camp diminished as the young men retired to their tents. A lone sentry was leaning up against a tree. I wondered if he would stay alert. Standing guard was the most boring of all military duty, especially in times of peace.

My eyes adjusted to the blackened trees as midnight approached. Slowly I stepped away from the tree line going deeper into the shadows.

A faint metallic clink pierced the night. Instantly I raised my sword. Where was it? I held my breath and strained my ears. Nothing. Slowly and patiently I advanced toward the noise, hoping to catch a glimpse of its owner. I stopped and waited for another telltale sound. But none came. Was he stalking me?

Was I being too cautious, overly paranoid? No, I'd seen something earlier, something that didn't belong, something hiding in the trees. I'd heard the sound of steel hitting stone. My spirit was again tingling, jumping up and down in my stomach, bearing witness that danger lurked nearby. I continued walking, my eyes adjusting to the growing darkness, my ears fully alert. My anxiety increased. Quietly I surveyed the trees and bushes. I sensed an eerie presence. I could feel its aura, but I couldn't see anything. Where was it hiding? I raised my weapon with both hands, braced my feet and prepared to render a devastating strike.

Suddenly an explosion ripped the night! Searing flames backlit the clearing. Instinctively I sliced the air with a powerful sweeping blow, hitting nothing. Quickly, I sheathed my weapon and dashed back to the camp.

Two steps out of the woods, I froze. A brilliant flash illuminated a huge hairy, muscular figure running from the camp to the other side of the forest. It couldn't be! They were all dead. I'd seen the last of them swallowed up by an open earth. I searched the shadows again, but saw no sign of the creature. I ran to the tents.

At the edge of the clearing, I stopped. Only one tent was burning. Mine! He had come to kill me.

Knights were swatting burning embers of what was left of my tent with branches from trees and throwing water on the smoldering canvas.

"Where's his body?" shouted Dax as they beat the fire with branches. "Where's Commander Vying? I saw him enter his tent."

"Relax, Dax. I'm right here."

He whirled around, stunned and relieved. "You couldn't be alive. There's nothing left of your tent."

"The Almighty was watching over me. I felt uneasy and took a stroll in the woods."

Relieved, Dax looked at me. "I thought you died."

"What caused the explosion?"

"Perhaps it was the glow light," he offered as the knights had all gathered around us.

"Dax, post a watch on the remains of my tent and order the others to return to their tents."

"Cappy, you've got the first watch over Commander Vying's tent. Lito, you will relieve him just before dawn," Dax ordered.

The knights returned to their tents as Cappy dashed off to retrieve his gear.

"I'll move out my tent and you can have it."

"No, don't bother."

"Where are you going to sleep?" Dax asked.

"Do you have room for an extra bedroll in your tent?"

"Yes, Commander."

"Good."

The fleeting image of the escaping Hoon wouldn't leave my mind. He had tracked us all day and torched my tent. Somehow these beasts, gorillas with the implants of criminal brains, had survived the Great War. How was that possible? Why were they on Micron? And why was he hunting me?

Chapter Two

"Push yourself beyond what your mind thinks you can do," I encouraged. "In battle you must overcome fatigue or it will cost you your life."

One of the knights gasped dropping to his knees, gulping in air, unable to take another step. The incline he and the others were running up was quite steep and was made even more arduous with rock-filled packs strapped to their backs. I reached down and helped him to his feet, then gave him a cool drink of water. "I can't go any further!"

"You must stay hydrated. You've been working hard, but you can make it. Remember the race is not to the fastest runner, but to those who persevere. How do you feel?"

"Much better, sir."

"Good. Sometimes we have to shoulder each others burdens. Turn around."

I took his backpack and strapped it onto my pack. The weight almost took me to my knees, but I adjusted.

"Now, how do you feel?"

"Much better, sir."

"Here's what we'll do. We'll climb up to that ridge over there." I pointed to an overhang that the other knights were just approaching. "When we get there, I'll give you your pack and you can go the rest of the way."

In the distance I could see Dax leading the knights up the hill as we followed.

The blue sun was again shining brightly. The mountain air was cool, refreshing, and filled with the sweet aroma of fresh pine. The pristine evergreens drew my constant attention as my guard was up. We took our time. At every opportunity I carefully studied the woods.

The knights worked hard with little dissension under Dax's leadership. He joked with the young men, but when it came time to push, he was always at the front leading the charge.

Shadows began forming as the sun slipped past the horizon. Dax walked up to me.

"Where should we make camp?"

"Stay away from the tree line. Stake the tents over there in the open."

"That's what I was thinking," Dax replied.

"You were? Why's that?"

"I checked your campsite early this morning and found your glow light. There was nothing wrong with it."

"What are you saying, Dax?"

"Something's still out there! Whatever came after you is still around. I noticed that you've been looking into the woods all day."

"Yesterday, I saw a Hoon," I whispered.

"What!" Dax exclaimed.

"By now they know I survived the attack."

"Do you want an evening patrol?"

"No, but I want my own tent again. If they're after me, I don't want to endanger the knights."

Respectfully, Cappy slowly walked up to us. "Excuse me, Warrior Dax, will there be any training before chow?"

"No, the knights have worked hard today. Tell them to relax and enjoy their meal. Post an evening watch."

The frosty night air seeped into the campsite but the warm fire held it in abeyance. The knights sat in a circle on fallen tree branches.

"Commander, were you afraid when you faced Megog in the battle ring for the Crown Championship?" one of the young men asked.

"Sure I was, but I trained hard and put my trust in the Almighty."

"Was Og as big as they say?" another asked.

"Bigger. He's a giant, over seven feet tall and with his bald head, he looks even taller."

"What happened to Og and Megog?" Cappy asked.

"They escaped justice. We've had intel gatherers looking for them, but neither has been spotted."

"Did you get to meet Queen Zelestar? Is she as beautiful as they say?"

I thought for a moment reflecting on her true beauty, beauty that only comes from a selfless heart. "Without question! A finer lady doesn't exist," I answered immediately missing her, remembering the warm moments we shared together. I wondered when I would see her again. Although, I knew she was needed on planet Milo.

"Drink plenty of water tonight," I quickly added before they could ask any more questions. "Tomorrow will be another tough day. Stay hydrated."

I got up from the fire and went to my tent. That Hoon had come to kill me and would try again. I knew Og had sent him and I would be more than ready for his return. Closing the tent flap, I sat in my chair wearing body armor and a sword at my side. I listened carefully for the beat of war.

Sometime during the evening, I drifted off, but was awakened by a faint noise and the smell of sulfur. Something was very close. Quietly, I eased the folds of the tent back and looked around. Clouds blanketed the darkened sky. I waited until my eyes adjusted to the night and slipped out. Standing in front of my tent, I heard a snort come from behind. Silently I unsheathed my sword and quietly stepped around the rubberized canvas.

With furious eyes and razor sharp teeth, the beast attacked. I dodged to the left and rolled to the ground. Springing to my feet, I swung my sword deflecting its tail as it tried to impale me. To my amazement, steel hit steel and sparks exploded. The hybrid mechanical beast landed on its hind feet, turned and faced me. I'd never seen anything like it. It was three leeds long. It folded its translucent wings and marched straight at me, unafraid. With piercing unwavering eyes, I knew it would attack. I circled to my right not wanting to be a stationary target while looking for an opening. Its bright gleaming silver fangs, stretched wings and huge tail were ready for a fight. Instead of feathers, it had smooth metallic scales stretching across its body.

Figure 2: Cyverex-6

Curiously, it stopped and looked me over. Two bright red lights flickered in its left ear as if it were receiving a transmission. The reptilian machine paused for a moment, raised its head to the sky and let out a deep guttural groan and flew straight at me. I dropped to my back and thrust my sword upward at its belly. My blow missed.

Flapping its massive wings and looking skyward, the big beast leapt into the sky as if launched from a photon cannon.

The powerful raptor was quickly out of sight. I stood by my tent with my sword drawn. Re-sheathing it, I dropped to my knees, bowed my head and thanked the Almighty for protecting me.

After a moment, I walked to the edge of the camp and saw the sentry fast asleep. I looked at the dying embers of the fire and added tree bark and a few thick branches to it. The dry wood caught quickly and soon a glowing fire radiated a soothing heat reminding me of the love of the Almighty Father. Quietly I thanked Him for awakening me once again. I felt the Great Holy Spirit envelop me and I was overjoyed to feel His presence. He filled me with His peace and I felt complete in Him.

A thought rose up in me, that I must return to the Sea of the Moon and retrieve the Almighty's Book. A sense of urgency filled my spirit and I realized the Almighty was calling me on a special mission.

The shuffling of the sentry's feet snapped my eyes open. I looked at the young man.

"You're up early, Commander," he commented.

"The cool night air awakened me. Have you noticed anything unusual on your watch, Cappy?"

"No sir. All is quiet and the camp is secure."

"That's true for now, but I want you to check the perimeter and report back to me."

"Yes sir," he replied, with raised eyebrows concerned that he had missed something in the night.

I was anticipating the discussion we would have as I tossed a log on the fire. The sun's rays glowed brightly against the blue horizon, igniting a myriad of ever-changing colors. Bright orange hues chased wisps of gray as a column of slow moving clouds trekked across the early morning sky, changing colors along the way. I delighted in the Almighty's skyscape and reflected on His glory. Perhaps the Almighty had sent this strange beast to awaken me and prophetically unveil the second coming of His Son utilizing an artistic tapestry of brush strokes on a canvas of cumulus clouds.

Two knights drifted out of their tents to share the warmth of the fire. I filled a kettle with water and began brewing herbal tea.

Dax came over to me. "What's the training exercise for today?"

"Divide the knights into two squads. Do you see that peak over there?" I asked pointing to a rock formation.

"The jagged one without trees?"

"That's it. I want each of the squads to approach from that canyon.

Halfway up the mountain set up separate combat outposts. This exercise will test their mountain mobility."

"Are the squads to engage each other?"

"No. After they set their camps, climb up the mountain to the peak to increase their fortitude and endurance. Make sure they keep hydrated. I want them fully acclimated to mountain warfare."

"Where will you be?"

"I have to go to the Sea of the Moon. The Almighty has given me an urgent task. I'll be back tomorrow evening. Keep an eye open for any unusual activity. Tell the knights to be on the alert and to help one another in their squads. This outback has never been settled and may have some very strange creatures."

"When we finish the climb do you have any other training for us?"

"No, reset your camp out here in the open. Stay the night and then we'll head back to New Vardo. Lead from the front and put Cappy in charge of the other squad. Drive them, but don't break them. Remember you're building warriors for difficult missions. Teach them that facing impossible odds is often what we face in battle. This exercise is to build dependence on one another and your leadership will be tested."

"Is it wise that you should leave?"

"The art of leadership must be developed in you. If I stay, you won't have that opportunity. Now go. Take command."

I watched in delight as Dax called the knights together and explained the training exercise. With a lowered head, Cappy finally reported to me.

"I saw some strange footprints around your tent, Commander."

"That's correct. While you were on watch did you see anything unusual?"

"No, sir."

"How could that be? An intruder entered our camp this morning and you never saw or heard anything?"

"I must have fallen asleep for a brief period," he answered painfully, his shoulders slumping bracing for a firm rebuke.

I just nodded my head. "Normally I would render severe punishment for dereliction of duty, but because you immediately told the truth I will keep this between us. If an enemy had attacked the camp, we might all be dead. You compromised camp security and the safety of the others. Don't let this happen again!"

"I won't Commander."

"I believe you," I said sincerely.

"What entered the camp? Did you see it?"

"Yes. It was some kind of winged beast. Keep your eyes open. Tonight I want you to take the third watch again. When you feel sleep overtaking you, walk around, do some exercises, but don't lean against a tree. Push your squad today. Challenge the others by leading from the front. If Dax gives me a good report of your leadership, I will completely forget this matter."

"Thank you, sir, you won't be disappointed."

"I hope not. You're a fine young knight."

Dax walked up to us.

"Are you ready, Cappy?"

"Yes sir."

"Take your squad and lead them into the canyon and up the north side of the peak. I'll see you at the top."

"Yes sir," Cappy said as he walked toward his squad and prepared them to go.

"The Sea of the Moon sounds intriguing. Are you sure you don't need any help?" Dax asked.

I marveled at his youthful enthusiasm as I strapped my backpack to my shoulders. "Sure, I could use your help, but you're here training knights to be warriors."

"Could you delay your mission?"

"No, I must obey the Almighty's leading. Keep an eye out for anything unusual. Something or someone is watching us.

Mark Rudge 03/26/08

Figure 3-1: Vying Riding an Air Glider

Chapter Three

With both feet on my air glider, I flew weaving through the trees at a rapid pace, testing my reactions. It was very dangerous, yet exhilarating. I felt free and so alive. Standing upright, I cruised up and over the mountains and through the valleys, heading towards the ocean. At intervals, I slowed down and turned around to see if I was being followed, but saw nothing. I crossed over the last mountain pass and headed down to the Sea of the Moon. Its waves, sparkling like brilliant diamonds, greeted me like an old friend. Twenty-eight years of light had passed since Crusader, the deep space ship from Earth, had carried me to the Blue Ring Galaxy and crashed into the sea, sinking quickly. I was anxious, but somewhat afraid to find the remains of my natural parents entombed in the ship. Pushing emotions aside, I knew in my heart the Almighty wanted me to retrieve His Book. The people on Micron desperately needed it to guide their lives. Peace in the Blue Ring Galaxy bought many freedoms, but without guidance, some of those freedoms were destructive.

I slowed the glider with pressure from my right heel and descended to the beach. I piloted it to a brush nearby and landed. De-energizing it, I stepped off and hid the glider under some bushes behind a tree. The pungent salt air and rolling waves brought fond memories of my surrogate parents Tor and Tia, and the other crewmembers who had survived the crash. They'd often quoted the Almighty's Book, but I'd never seen it. No copy of His Book had been taken off the ship. Deep within me, I knew it was still aboard.

In a dream one night, the Almighty had given me a design for a special underwater breather that split water molecules into oxygen and hydrogen, venting the hydrogen and allowing me to breathe the oxygen. As long as it worked, I wouldn't run out of air, but this was the first time I'd tried my new design for an extended period. Keeping my body armor on, I attached a buoyancy belt, when inflated neutralized my body weight.

Tia, Tor's beautiful Polynesian wife, raised and loved me as her own. She taught me to swim in this sea before planet Za-Kar's forces invaded Micron and destroyed our shore side tree dwellings. Along with the other crewmembers from the Crusader, we lived peacefully for ten years before evil invaded the Blue Ring Galaxy. My old shipmates, Og and Megog — purveyors of evil - rose up and seized control of Za-Kar turning the planet into a war machine bent on greed and enslavement of the peace-loving citizens in the Blue Ring Galaxy.

I donned my breathing apparatus and slowly and waded out into the cool shallow water. Sudden rippling of the water caught my attention. Quickly, I pulled my dive knife and waited to see if something would rise from the deep and attack. I stood firm. A large tenfibian rose out of the water and swam near me. I remembered as a child, before the evil times, how I swam amongst a pod of the creatures. Their gentle nature and keen intelligence always drew me to them.

Not long after the first tenfibian passed by, two more of the large amphibious mammals with ten yellow spots on their backs surfaced and walked past me to the beach. I relaxed for a moment, fascinated by these huge docile creatures. A curling rogue wave crashed into me knocking me off balance. Quickly, I dove beneath the cascading water and headed for the bottom.

I had a good idea where Crusader was resting on the ocean floor because Tia and I had visited it often, but had never gone inside. I kept swimming in the general area, but couldn't spot the ship. As I dove deeper, the pressure increased and I cleared my ears by moving my jaws in a chewing motion. I looked all around before reaching the sandy bottom, but couldn't spot Crusader's hull. It was a big vessel and I remembered that half of the upper deck was visible.

Out of the corner of my eye, I saw a brown flat fish with white spots all over its body rise up. It lunged at me. Instantly I dropped to my knees and drew my knife, but it was too late. With its blunt nose, the heavy fish hammered me to my back, knocking my breather out of my mouth. Quickly I snatched the apparatus back before it floated away. The fish, two leeds in length, turned and attacked again.

I ducked under its large nose and thrust up with my knife, ripping its belly open. Blood and white guts clouded the water around me. I knew that I'd better leave in a hurry. It wouldn't be long before carnivorous sea serpents with a keen nose for the smell of fresh blood would come and fill the area. Quickly I swam away.

Straining my eyes, I noticed a white object on a ledge. I kicked with all my might and swam toward it. Could it be? Had a back eddy shifted

Crusader's final resting point or had I forgotten its location? An underwater current suddenly drove me back. Immediately, I looked toward the water's surface wondering if an unexpected surface storm had agitated the water. A deep divine calm enveloped me and for the second time on this mission, I felt at peace with what I was doing. I was following the Almighty's plan. He had led me to the ship. Maybe the fish were sent for a course correction.

I swam toward Crusader. The closer I got, the more it came into focus. Barnacles and sea growth covered its darkened hull. The wreck, though several stories high, was smaller than I remembered. Where on this massive ship was the Almighty's Book? I knew He would have to show me. I was rescued from the ship as an infant and it was with morbid fear that I wondered if I would find the remains of my parents somewhere on the vessel.

Figure 3-2: SS Crusader

Crusader was broad at the bow and narrow at the stern. I swam on the starboard side, but didn't see any opening or damage to the ship's plating. Another camouflaged fish exploded out of the sand. I grabbed an outcropping of shell plating and slipped beneath the curve of the hull. I didn't want to fillet another one and bring more sea serpents to the area. Why were these strange blunt hammer-nosed fish attacking? Were they territorial? In the many times Tia and I had swum in the Sea of the Moon, we'd never seen them. What were they?

Suddenly ten more of the flat brown fish appeared and joined the other. I was in serious trouble. In a school, they attacked. I reached further under the hull and tried to push myself into the sand. Pressing down under the keel, I spotted a jagged opening in the ship. It was twenty leeds away, but the angry fish blocked my path.

Before I could make a move, one of them pummeled me in the stomach. Oxygen exploded from my lungs as I floated away from the Crusader. I couldn't breath, but looked toward the opening as the fish turned around and got ready to make another run at me. Had I not kept my body armor on, I would have been finished by now. I had only one thought, but it was insane. The school of fish might pound me before I ever made it to the opening, but I had no choice.

I swam straight at the aggressive fish and just as we were about to collide I dropped to the bottom and pushed my breather into the sand and turned it on full. Sand came swirling up from the floor and created a huge underwater cloud. For an instant, the fish were disoriented. I quickly headed to the rip in the underside of the hull. The opening was too small for me to get through. Instinctively, I grabbed for my sword, but it wasn't there. I could sense the sea attackers readying for another strike. I pulled at the plating with all my might, but it still wouldn't budge.

The first blunt-nosed attackers came at me and I waited until the last possible moment before ducking. The fish couldn't stop and slammed into the shell plating of the ship. Praise be to the Almighty! The hole got bigger. The second wave hit right next to the first. Dazed, they floated upward. Quickly I squeezed through the opening, not waiting for the rest to attack.

It was murky and dark inside. I could feel sand floating across my arms. I needed to see if my breather was working although I was still getting oxygen.

Again the thought of seeing the remains of my natural parents overwhelmed me. All I knew about them was what Tor and Tia had told me.

I pulled a glow light from my belt, activated it and there, curled up in the corner, was a giant sea cobra, ready to strike!

Chapter Four

The gargantuan snake shot forward baring his deadly fangs. In the watery depths, I couldn't move as quickly as on dry land. I barely shifted to the right. The serpent struck hard, hitting my armor plating with a glancing blow.

Reaching for my knife, I momentarily took my eye off him as his cold clammy skin slid across my body. I thrust my knife up. But my arm wouldn't move. The serpent was tightly winding himself around me. I couldn't see his massive head as I became enveloped by his slippery skin. I struggled, but couldn't free myself. He began to squeeze tighter and tighter, forcing the air out of my lungs.

Suddenly from nowhere his head arose and he looked at me with a sense of curiosity. He moved his head from side to side, savoring his next meal. I thrashed against his body, but it made no difference. My lungs couldn't expand. My breath was short and labored. The metal bracket of my breather dug into my spine causing excruciating pain.

"Lord Jesus!" I cried before the serpent wrapped himself around my neck, cutting off all flow of oxygen. My life flashed before me. I always thought I'd die on the battlefield with sword in hand fighting an enemy of the Realm. I remembered this ship and the moment my paternal mother passed me through a small opening to Tia. My mother's pained expression was still with me, even after all of these years. I remembered her flowing red hair and delicate hands that bid me farewell. She was trapped in a compartment and couldn't get out. How ironic. I too was trapped beneath the Sea of the Moon only to join my parents in their final resting place.

My thoughts became fuzzy and I thought I'd breathed my last, when suddenly the pressure was released. I gulped a deep breath of air and opened my eyes. I was still loosely encircled by the snake, but his attention was focused elsewhere. Another giant sea serpent, bigger than the first, had entered the ship and was eyeing me as the prize.

With lightning quickness, it struck a vicious blow at the first snake's neck. Immediately, I swam away as fast as I could. Searching desperately for an escape, I noticed a hatch in the corner with a round handle in the center. Using my knife as an extension, I turned the handle counterclockwise and felt the mechanism disengaging. I pushed on the hatch, but it wouldn't budge. I looked back at the sea serpents. They were fighting, trying to squeeze the life out of each other as they traded blows with their heads like two boxers, each trying to sink their deadly fangs in the other.

I wedged my knife between the frame and the hatch and pried with all my might. It moved slightly. Though the ship had been underwater for years, the material used for hinges hadn't rusted and the hatch slowly opened. Quickly, I darted through the opening and resealed the hatch from the other side as I looked back and saw the larger snake swallowing his adversary.

"Thank you, Almighty," I said to myself, hoping there was another way out of the ship.

I swam up a ladderway to the next hatch and pried it open. A long corridor opened before me. I wondered what part of the ship I was in. Before I could move, a school of small fish swam out of a room. Their pink coloring glowed brightly. Instantly I stopped all movement, not wanting to attract their attention, especially if they thought I was their next meal. Uninterested, they swam by. I waited until they were gone and entered the room they'd just vacated. From what I remembered, this couldn't be my parent's room. I wondered what kind of electronic equipment the ship had and if it could be activated. On a desk in the room, I noticed a screen and a clear sealed tube with amber fluid floating near it. I grabbed the tube, having no idea what it was, and put it in the dive bag strapped to my waist. The rest of the room was nearly empty. I touched the screen hoping, it might activate, but nothing. I turned and headed to the passageway.

Swimming through the dark and narrow corridor, I hoped it was the centerline of the ship. I came upon another ladderway and swam up. The next deck revealed an open area strewn with metal boxes. I pried one open, then another, but they held nothing. Excitement built within me as I continued my hunt for the Almighty's Book, hoping to find it.

I left the large open bay to continue down another corridor, searching for the stateroom shared by my natural mother and father. The passageway opened to a maze of doors, some open, some shut.

The first room contained a bed frame, desk, and shelves. On the desk was a screen with a small box next to it containing a few data pads. Wondering what they held and leaving nothing to chance, I put them in my dive bag.

I remembered Tia telling me that my mother had been trapped in her stateroom. Something deep inside me told me that I was on the right deck. I began swimming forward meticulously examining every hatch and frame.

Suddenly, without warning, my breather stopped! Fierce panic gripped me. I pulled it off my back and discovered a large dent in it. I adjusted the valve and was rewarded with a surge of oxygen. Normally, I'd have plenty of time to deploy the backup system, but I couldn't be sure because of the damage. I needed to finish the search quickly and get out. Images of the giant sea serpent flooded my mind. Would it be waiting for my return? My glow light dimmed as I swam back the way I came. Underwater darkness entombed me. Hand over hand I came to a split in the passageway. Which way had I come? I couldn't remember.

"Lord Jesus, help me find my way out," I quickly prayed. I knew my life hung in the balance of that prayer and remembered the many times the Almighty had rescued me from the hands of my enemies.

As I swam forward the lights of my breather flickered. Without air and light, I was doomed. My lungs began convulsing and felt like they were on fire. The glow light dimmed even more. I banged it on my palm hoping to get more light. Then a strange peace settled over me and I knew the Almighty was present even in this watery depth. I spotted a smashed door and quickly swam toward it. Could this be my mother's room?

I squeezed through the small opening and noticed a green metallic bottle on the bulkhead. I pulled it off the bulkhead and fitted my mask tube to the spout. I turned the valve counterclockwise. To my horror water came out. I gagged and pulled it away from my face. Then I noticed air bubbles floating up from the mask. I grabbed it again, jammed it in my face and opened the valve wide trusting Jesus. I inhaled what came and instantly the burning in my lungs ceased. My head cleared. Reluctantly, I closed the valve and held my breath not knowing how much oxygen the bottle contained.

Time was running out and I saw an inner room with a door that had been smashed with a small opening. The cracked door beckoned me and I peered inside, noticing a desk and a picture frame hanging on the wall. On the desk were more data pads. Could they be the Almighty's Book?

I pried on the door, but my knife was useless. Returning to the passageway I saw what looked to be a battle axe. I quickly grabbed it, but the handle disintegrated and the metal axe head sank to the deck. I put the mask to my face and turned the valve again, taking in three long breaths of air. I had to get into that room.

Picking up the axe head, I returned to the room and began hammering away at the opening. Surprisingly the steel door gave way and the opening increased enough to swim through. I quickly took another long breath of air. Kelp had grown over a shelf above the desk. I swiped it away with my hand. Enclosed behind glass on the shelf were several shiny disks. Each was encased in a sealed container. I used the axe head to smash the glass.

Taking all the disks and data pads and shoving them into my dive bag, I looked at the picture. As I brushed the barnacles from it my world stopped!

Chapter Five

There before me was a picture of two people holding a baby. Excitement made my heart want to burst, but my lungs called me back to reality. Using my knife, I took the picture from the bulkhead. Swimming down the corridor, with a little visibility, I found the ladder-way that led to the open bay. As I swam toward the ladder, my light was growing dimmer eventually going out. With my mind's eye I visualized the ship remembering how to get back to the final stairway, Feeling the bulkhead, I blindly swam down it toward the hatch. Taking another long breath of air, I slowly turned the wheel counterclockwise and opened the hatch.

Dim light penetrated the hold through the hole in the hull and I saw hungry eyes glaring at me, tracking my every move. When I moved, the engorged serpent moved. The only way out was straight ahead and I was running out of oxygen. I couldn't wait any longer! I had to act or die. Strangely, I noticed the outline of the other snake in its belly. How could he still be hungry? I had to attack, but my knife was useless against this giant water snake. It was still hungry. I could see it in his eyes. Patiently, it waited.

"Feed the serpent," came the Almighty's thought. What could I feed him with? Then another thought came to me.

I pushed off the bulkhead with the oxygen bottle out in front of me, I swam toward it. His mouth opened as if by cue. He lunged at me. Turning the valve on, I slammed the bottle between his fangs, deep into his mouth. Immediately I dove down and swam for the opening never looking back, not knowing if my plan had worked. I reached the rip in the hull plating and quickly pulled myself through. Just before I was completely out, something grabbed my breather and pulled me back. I fought with all my might, but the serpent wouldn't let go. My lungs were burning and I snapped my head around to face the giant serpent one more time, but he wasn't there. I discovered the strap of my dive bracket had caught the edge of the jagged opening. Reaching back, I released it and swam straight up, desperate for air.

With my lungs on fire, screaming for oxygen, I finally broke the surface and took a deep gulp of fresh air. I thanked the Almighty for delivering me from the deep. I hoped His Book was on the disks. Now I needed someone to extract the data from them.

With renewed strength, my overhead strokes powered me to the shore. Emerging from the water, I collapsed, physically, emotionally, and mentally drained. I lay there and rested. Dusk was settling in and I changed out of my wet clothes and built a fire on the beach of the Sea of the Moon. Navigating through the trees and mountains at night wasn't safe, so I rested by the warm embers and ate some dried fruit. I opened the dive bag pulling out my treasure, memorizing every detail of my red haired mother smiling sweetly. I could feel her love flow to me. I looked at the bespectacled man next to her and saw a keen sense of intelligence. I wished that I could have known them. I closed my eyes thinking of them.

Chirping birds awakened me with a cheerful cacophony of notes. I felt better than I had in a long time. I could feel the Almighty's exhilarating love. Carefully I put the picture of my parents into the dive bag. Finally I arose, packed my things, and jumped on the air glider, heading for the mountain pass. I scanned the countryside hoping to spot the strange flying creature that I had encountered before.

Returning to the outback took most of the day. But, once I arrived, I found the camp deserted. Cooking pots and equipment were scattered everywhere as if a tornado had stormed the area. My heart plunged. What had happened? I searched for a blood trail on the ground, but all I found was Cappy's sword and Hoon footprints. How could they be here? Where had they come from?

How could I have been following the Almighty's will and yet have this happen? I began to doubt my motives for going back to the Crusader, but then realized it was never my intention before I left for this training. I remembered the thoughts the Holy Spirit had imparted to me before leaving New Vardo. When we left the city, I'd taken my breather, not knowing why. I searched my heart to see if I'd done wrong, but I knew it was His plan. Still, how could He have let this happen?

Hurrying to the air glider I hopped aboard and began to follow their spoor out of the camp. I noticed the grass bent over and I could see their trail led back toward the capital, New Vardo. I was relieved, but puzzled. If the Hoons had attacked, something terrible must have happened. Dreadfully, I circled the area hoping that I wouldn't see my worst fear — a dead body!

Figure 5: New Vardo

Thankfully there was none, so I following the tracks looking for any telltale sign that would indicate why they'd disappeared. As the day drew to a close, I arrived on the outskirts of New Vardo and got off the glider and walked to the city gates. Kaldor, a battle tested veteran from the Great War and member of the Council of Peers, was waiting for me.

"Vying, where have you been? Everyone's looking for you," the tall wiry warrior asked. We had fought together in the last few battles of the Great War. Kaldor was something of a mystery because he never mentioned his home planet, but his loyalty to the Realm had been battle-proven. I remembered the speed and accuracy of his punches and powerful leg kicks. In the final battle to overthrow Og's palace against Za-Kar's crack troops, he used his skills effectively and without tiring. His furious attack left scores of enemy troops incapacitated.

"I had to check an area out in the outback," I said, not wanting to lie, but not wanting to tell him that I'd left the knights in Dax's command. I replied feeling the urgency of his questions. Sometimes when I was around him, I felt uneasy, but I couldn't figure out what it was.

He shook his head. "You really messed up," he said, his normally carefree attitude and easy smile gone. His emerald green eyes captured the last bit of sunshine and twinkled in the fading sunlight. A subdued smile escaped his mouth as if he was enjoying my plight.

"What happened?"

"You don't know?"

Normally it was impossible not to like Caldor's and he had gained the confidence of my two great friends, King Wolks and Queen Sera. I was envious at the end of the war when I saw both Zelestar and Sera sharing a moment of laughter with him on the beach. I don't know what he said, but they enjoyed his company just a little too much for me and I wanted to be with Zelestar. Women were drawn to him and he once told me he'd never get married. There were just too many females begging for his company.

"Tell me, Kaldor, what happened."

"The King told me to keep a lookout for you. He said the Council of Peers is convening tomorrow morning for an emergency inquest."

"Why?"

"Cappy died on the way back."

"What?" I gasped.

"Dax said you had to go find something. Cappy collapsed on the climb up the peak. As they got ready to leave they were attacked."

"By whom?"

"This is where it gets really strange. Remember, I was with you on Mercus when the ground opened up and swallowed the Hoons."

"Yeah."

"Well, Dax reported that they had been attacked by Hoons."

They were watching us the whole time and picked their moment to attack, when the knights were most vulnerable. How could I have been so stupid?

"It gets worse, Vying."

"What do you mean?"

"You're being charged with dereliction of duty resulting in the loss of life."

"What? That's insane!"

"I know Vying, but Cappy's mother has filed charges against you, claiming that if you hadn't left the knights in Dax's command, none of this would have happened."

"Where's Dax? I've got to talk to him."

"You can't."

"What do you mean I can't talk to him? What's going on?"

"Dax has been sequestered until the trial. The prosecutor doesn't want you to have any contact with him. She may bring charges against him, as well."

"But we were on a military training mission! You know anything can happen."

"You and I know that, Vying, but the peacetime element has slowly eroded the warrior ways. Most of those on the Council have little taste for war. They want to ensure peace and with tight controls. Cappy's death greatly disturbs them. Wolks wants to see you."

"Good, let's go," I said as we entered the palace and went to the King's chamber. Two rather large knights stood guard outside of his room and, with a nod from Kaldor, they allowed us to pass.

"Where were you?" King Wolks demanded without greeting me. He was a strong man with powerful shoulders and thick biceps. His red beard and long hair looked enflamed by his emotions while he sat at his desk scrutinizing me.

"I just got back."

"You know what I mean, Vying. I've had warriors out looking for you, so I could talk to you before tomorrow's Council session. Where did you go yesterday?" he asked standing up from behind his desk. He was taller than me and, in his aggravated state, he appeared even taller.

"I left the training camp for a day. Dax was in charge and he was doing a great job."

"Where did you go?"

"To the Sea of the Moon to dive the wreck," I said leaving out the part about the Almighty's leading. I knew he wouldn't understand how the Almighty speaks to me in thoughts, showing me what to do. "You know Dax is ready to lead."

"Vying, he just achieved the rank of Warrior."

"And he fought side-by-side with us during the war or have you forgotten?"

Wolks' face flared red matching the color of his beard. "Old friend, this isn't about you and me, nor even Dax. Cappy's mother sits on the Council of Peers and is very influential. They've already convened and have issued a warrant for your arrest."

"Can't you do anything? You used to be on the Council."

"I was out-voted. We're no longer at war and they want peace at all cost."

"You know that sometimes people die in training exercises and certainly during war."

"Yes, but that's the problem. There is peace in the Blue Ring Galaxy and Cappy's mother wants revenge. Her husband was killed during the Great War and now her only son is dead. She's been robbed of her two loved ones. She wants your head!"

The full effect of what could happen sank in. I was speechless.

"I've contacted Tor and Tia. They'll be coming from Za-Kar, but this doesn't look good. I've heard rumors that the Council may call for the death sentence."

"What!" I exploded.

"Cappy's mother is quite beautiful," Kaldor said speaking up for the first time.

"And what's that supposed to mean?" I asked in a surly tone.

"All I'm saying, Vying, is that she has been without a man for a while and has made alliances with certain men on the Council."

"Oh, that's great."

"Vying, you and I have been through many things and have gotten out of some tight spots, so don't lose hope. I'm still the King here on Micron."

"Thanks, old friend. The Almighty has gotten us out of many tough situations."

"I took the liberty of appointing Admiral Monka as your defense. I hope you don't mind, but he's the only one with trial experience that I knew you could trust."

"No, that's fine."

"Now I've got to do something that I don't like, but I hope you'll understand. This isn't about you and me. I'm truly sorry, Vying. I wish there was more I could do."

Wolks turned to Kaldor. "Take the prisoner to his cell."

Chapter Six

Incarcerated, I couldn't sleep all night. In the morning, guards came to my cell and handcuffed me. They escorted me to the Seat of Judgment. The lonely walk down the long sterile corridor to the Council chamber reminded me of my walk in the underground tunnel leading to the battle ring on Mercus where I defeated Megog for the Crown Championship. I took hope that the Almighty would bring a similar victory.

Unfortunately, this battle was much different. Instead of a robe and fighting trunks, I wore my uniform. The two guards guided me to the docket in the middle of a cylindrical room that opened up to seat the Council members five leeds above me. I looked at the overflowing crowd in the upper level. The guards and I were separated from them by one level as the Council took their seats on the edge of above us.

"Murderer! There's the murderer!" Cappy's mother screamed at the top of her lungs jumping up and pointing at me from her seat. The Council occupied the first circular row, higher up in the gallery, spectators eagerly grabbed the few vacant seats that rose to the top of the building. President Sorrl occupied an imposing throne that was extended into the arena from the side. He looked across the room to the Council of Peers who formed an elevated circle around the pit where I sat. It was all very intimidating.

"He's the one responsible for the death of my Cappy! He's the one who abandoned his post!" she sobbed and broke out into uncontrolled tears. Her voice echoed throughout the building.

I looked up as the rest of the Council began taking their seats. They refused to look at me, which I knew wasn't good. Some of them I knew, but, at some point while I was away, a shift had taken place on Micron. The Great Interplanetary War was forgotten and those who disturbed the peace were dealt with harshly. My comrades in arms, the warriors, had been replaced by those who loved the pleasures of peace and prosperity devoid of any conflict. How quickly they had forgotten the bloodied price we had paid for freedom in the Blue Ring Galaxy. President Sorrl arose and the audience came to a hush.

"Citizens of New Vardo, this special meeting of the Council of Peers has been convened to judge a very serious matter. Death reached out and took the life of a young knight during a training exercise. This Council will determine whether negligence and dereliction of duty by their leader, Commander Vying, led to Knight Cappy's death. The Council will listen to testimony and render judgment. Their ruling will be final. The prosecution will call its first witness."

Ariel, a petite chestnut haired woman, walked forward from the shadows of the ground floor and took her place as the Prosecution at the podium facing me. Admiral Monka, in full dress uniform, slowly walked up to his podium beside Ariel.

"The prosecution may begin," Sorrl announced.

"The prosecution calls Warrior Dax to the stand," Ariel said.

I was surprised she called Dax, beginning the assault with someone I considered a brother and a key character witnesses for my defense. The young man walked in with a look of despair on his face as he sat down on the side of the Chamber. I wanted to tell him it wasn't his fault, but I just nodded at him when our eyes met.

Figure 6: Dax in the Witness Box

"Have you ever testified before the Council?" Ariel asked sweetly, smiling at him in a disarming way.

"No ma'am," he answered stoically.

"Do you understand that you must answer all questions truthfully?"

"Yes ma'am, but I would do that anyway. Commander Vying has taught me that truth is the warrior's way of honor."

She paused for a moment gathering attention in her silence and then looked up at the Council members. "I ask that the Council discount the second part of Warrior Dax's statement. What Vying may have taught him does not preclude the fact that he must answer with truth at all times."

Skillfully she had deflected the first bit of support for me. I wondered if Admiral Monka would be up for this battle of wits. Then she looked to President Sorrl, demanding his concurrence.

"Warrior Dax, just answer the questions. Please refrain from giving your opinion of the prisoner, unless specifically asked."

"Yes sir."

"I'm sure you meant well, Dax, but this tribunal is weighing a very serious matter," she said sweetly turning up the charm.

She was good, very good. I hoped my proconsul would be equally good, but somehow in my heart I felt that the only person available at such short notice was the wrong choice. I wished my parents, the ones who had raised me, could be here. Admiral Monka had a formidable record as a warrior and was no stranger to tribunals, but he was elderly and not as quick as Ariel.

"Have you ever been on a mission when Commander Vying has placed your life in danger?"

Dax looked at me and didn't want to answer.

"Warrior Dax, please refrain from looking at the prisoner for your answer. Has Commander Vying ever placed your life in danger?"

"Many times," he mumbled as the crowd murmured their harsh disapproval.

"I'm sorry, Warrior Dax, I didn't hear what you said," she said.

"Yes," he replied loudly.

"How many times did this occur?"

"We were at...."

"Warrior Dax," she quickly cut in anticipating his answer, "please keep your answers in line with the question. How many times did he put you in harm's way?"

"Several times, but we..."

She cut him off and delivered a furious verbal barrage. "Several times Commander Vying has placed this boy's life in jeopardy! This is not the first time. It was inevitable that someone would have to die for his recklessness."

"Objection, your Honor," droned Admiral Monka like an ancient foghorn on a dreary misty morning.

Ariel glared at Monka.

"The prosecution must remember that we were at war in those days."

"Thank you for pointing that out, Admiral," she answered cunningly. "Are we at war now?" she asked firing a direct salvo at Monka as if he was the one being judged.

"No, we are not," he replied.

"Precisely my point, Council," she said looking up at them. "During peacetime Commander Vying gave orders to drive young men to the point of exhaustion and ultimately death and for what reason? Where is the enemy? Are we to tolerate this kind of sadistic behavior?"

"Objection your honor, the prosecutor is now giving her opinion, not facts," Monka retorted.

But I could see that the damage had already been done. Members of the Council were nodding their head in silent agreement.

"Prosecutor, please restrict your opinions," stated the judge.

"Please forgive me, your Honor," she said softly pausing for a moment as if the silence was exonerating her from her well-planned error. "Warrior Dax, how old were you the first time Commander Vying put you in harm's way?"

"I was nine. We were on a secret mission to the Shadow Planet Binery," he replied.

The audience burst out in protest. Sorrl pulled his sword and banged the hilt on the arm of his chair. He got up and looked at the audience. "I will not tolerate another outburst in my tribunal. If it occurs again, I will be forced to clear this chamber. Remember that!"

The lynch mob quickly quieted, but I could feel a growing sense of hatred directed toward me. I silently prayed to the Almighty to help me through this ordeal.

"Dax, would you please describe the planet Binery."

"Binery hides in the shadow of Mercus. It's freezing cold with lots of snow."

"More specifically, who lives on Binery?"

"Hoons."

"For the benefit of some, what is a Hoon?"

"It is a gorilla who has had a brain transplant with that of a convicted criminal."

"Have you ever seen a Hoon?"

"Yes, many times."

"Are they strong?"

"Extremely."

"Could a man defeat a Hoon in hand-to-hand combat?"

"Not easily. They are feared by most men."

"That's a very unfriendly place to take a young boy. Were you ever in any danger while on Binery?"

"All the time."

"Be specific."

"At one point we were surrounded by twenty Hoons, but I brought a cocoon containing zipdappers. When I released them the Hoons ran off and we escaped."

The prosecutor shook her head. "Was there another incident on Binery?"

Dax looked down and didn't answer.

"Let me rephrase the question. Was there another incident on Binery when your life was put in danger"

Dax answered in a low tone of voice as if apologizing. "When we were making our escape, they were firing photon blitzers at us. We had to fly beneath the huge trunk of a falling tree."

"How close did the tree come to you?"

"The smaller branches hit our wings and knocked us off course as the tree crashed behind us."

"Dax, was there another mission you went on to free someone else?"

Dax glanced at me and didn't answer.

"Warrior Dax, you are bound to answer the question!" she angrily demanded in a hostile tone of voice.

"Yes, ma'am"

"Please tell us about that mission."

"Sera had been captured by the forces of Za-Kar. Vying and King Wolks went to rescue her."

"You mean Queen Sera?"

"She wasn't queen at the time."

"How was she captured?"

"We were on a training mission with the new scintillas and we came upon a Za-Kar patrol of shuttle craft."

"Warrior Dax, what is a scintilla?"

"A small attack ship that flies at speeds greater than the speed of light."

"Please continue, how did she get captured?"

"She expended her fuel cells firing on enemy ships. We had just spotted the mother ship, a large battle carrier and we made a run at it."

Ariel waited as if thinking what to say next and then when the chamber was extremely quiet and all eyes focused on her she quietly asked, "Who was in charge of the patrol?"

"Vying."

Murmuring exploded from the audience. Sorrl banged the hilt of his sword on the arm of his chair silencing the chamber.

"And where was Sera's scintilla?"

"She was told to fly a holding pattern in the quadrant while we attacked the battle carrier."

"A battle carrier!" she repeated incredulously. "Is a scintilla capable of destroying a battle carrier?"

"I don't think so."

"Then why would Commander Vying attack it?"

"I don't know. You'll have to ask him."

"Oh, I will," she said. "At the expense of our future queen, Commander Vying chose to put her in harm's way."

"Objection your Eminence! We were at war!" Monka declared with resounding fervor.

"Overruled, you may continue, prosecutor," the judge declared.

"Dax, on the last training mission when Knight Cappy died, did you feel that the training was excessive?"

"No ma'am."

"In a statement recorded earlier you have testified that the two of you were racing to the top of the hill. Where were the rest of the knights?"

"They were far behind us."

"Were they also racing up the hill?"

"Yes, ma'am, but they were too far behind."

"Where was Commander Vying?"

How could this have happened, I wondered? Hadn't the Almighty sent me on this mission? I prayed hoping to feel His anointing, His presence, but nothing. Had I misunderstood His leading?

"No, ma'am. The Commander had other business to attend to."

"When did he leave?"

"Early in the morning, he said he'd be back the next day."

"Did he come back in the morning?"

"I don't know ma'am. After Cappy collapsed and we couldn't revive him, we quickly broke camp and headed for New Vardo."

"Do you think Cappy was pushed beyond what his body could take?"

"Of course. We were training. To build endurance you must push your body beyond its limits. Those were our orders."

"Who issued the orders?"

Dax couldn't look at me. "Commander Vying. He said it's the only way to get into shape."

"Pushed beyond what their bodies could take," the prosecutor said. "What more do we need to judge this matter?"

The prosecutor shook her head and looked at the Council of Peers. "You have heard that Commander Vying ordered mere boys, to push themselves beyond what their bodies could take. You have heard how he abandoned his post during the training exercise and you've heard how he takes daring risks with other people's lives.

"Yes, I will admit that he was involved in the Great War and perhaps even a hero, but that war is over! During wartime I can accept risk taking. We're not at war anymore and these young men are the future of New Vardo. Now one of them, perhaps the brightest is dead. Why? Because of poor judgment on the part of his commanding officer. I cannot exonerate this man before you for the death of one of his charges. We live by the code; 'A life for a life, no exceptions.' In spite of his glorious war record, I must call out for the death penalty!"

"Life for a life!" someone shouted from the crowd.

"Kill him," another called. "He deserves to die!"

"Murderer!" Cappy's mother shouted.

Chapter Seven

"Order! Order in my tribunal!" President Sorrl demanded loudly, "Or I will clear this Council session."

He slammed the handle of his huge sword on the arm of his chair and looked directly at Cappy's mother. "Hold your tongue, woman, or I'll have you removed!"

Cappy's mother paused until all eyes were on her and then opened her mouth to speak, but quickly took hold of her mouth. She slowly pointed at Vying and then fell back into her seat overwhelmed by her own grief. It was a noteworthy performance.

"Prosecutor Ariel have you made your summation? Do you have any more witnesses?" Sorrl asked.

"Please forgive me your Eminence. I was caught up in the moment. I wish to call Admiral Monka."

She was calling my Procouncil! I couldn't believe how she was slicing through all of my support.

After swearing him in, Ariel began. "Is it normal for an officer to leave his troops in the hands of a subordinate?"

"Of course, the Commanding Officer has many other duties," the tired Admiral replied, as if the questioning was obvious to anyone.

"How would communication take place between the Commanding Officer and his next-in-charge?"

"Normally, a communicator would be given to the subordinate."

"According to the statement given by Warrior Dax, communication was attempted, but no response was received. In his words and I quote, 'I tried to call Vying several times, but there was no reply.' Why do you suppose that was?"

"I don't know. I wasn't there. Sometimes reception is bad."

"Could it be that his communicator was turned off?"

"I don't know. I wasn't there."

"Can a communicator pick up transmission from anywhere?"

"Just about," Monka answered.

"According to his deposition, Warrior Dax tried no less than five times to communicate with Commander Vying and at no time was there any response. Do you find it odd that Vying never answered?"

"I find it odd that we are prosecuting a hero of the Realm, a Crown Champion; someone whose loyalty to the Realm is unquestioned! He has risked his life many times over in defending our planet."

"Your Eminence, please advise the witness to restrict his answer to the questions."

"Admiral Monka, as an official of the court, you should know better. Please confine your answers to the questions and save your comments for your closing remarks."

"Forgive me your Eminence, but I was just stating the truth."

A sick feeling came over as me I watched her carve up my Proconsul in front of the Council of Peers. I hoped Admiral Monka could deliver a good rebuttal.

The trial continued throughout the morning until Prosecutor Ariel finally called me to the stand.

"Commander Vying, why did you leave your troops?"

"I went on a mission."

"What was the mission?"

"To retrieve a book from the hull of the Crusader."

"A book," she mused puzzled. "Who authorized this mission?"

I knew where this was headed. "The Almighty instructed me."

"Do you expect this Council to believe that the God who created this universe gave you special instructions to leave your post?"

"I don't know what they will believe, but the Almighty sent me on a special mission."

"Did He talk to you in an audible tone?"

"No ma'am."

"Can you explain how He communicated His mission to you, but Dax tried several times to communicate, but he couldn't?"

"Thoughts kept coming into my mind that I should retrieve the Book. I knew they weren't mine."

"Whose were they?"

"The last thing I wanted to do was dive the Crusader. That's how I knew the thoughts weren't mine and came from the Almighty."

"And you expect me to believe that the Creator of this Universe speaks to you in thoughts and gives you instructions."

"Whether you believe it or not, ma'am, I do not know, but I'm telling the truth."

"I'm sure you think you are...By chance does He speak to everyone?"

"He does. Have you ever tried listening?"

Ariel's face turned beet red. "How dare you ask me a question! What impertinence. You shall answer my questions."

"Commander Vying, do not add your own comments. Just answer the prosecutor's questions," Sorrl interjected before the crowd got involved.

"Yes, your Eminence, I thought I was," I replied and uttered a short prayer for His help.

"Humor me. What exactly was your mission?"

"I was to dive the wreck of Crusader and retrieve the Almighty's Book."

"And were you successful?"

"I don't know."

"You have risked the lives of the knights for a Book and you don't know if you were successful."

"That is correct, ma'am."

The Prosecutor just shook her head. "What's the point of this Book? Don't we have enough books already?"

"The Almighty's Book encourages us to live above the law."

"Oh, oh, this just gets better and better. You violated protocol. You left your post, and now you claim to live above the law. Who do you think you are!"

"Objection your Eminence. The Prosecutor is badgering the witness!" Monka yelled above the resounding approval of the audience.

Sorrl slammed his sword down again, but didn't look to the crowd. "Objection overruled!" he stated as if declaring Vying guilty.

Ariel slowly shook her head and then looked at Vying as a mother would her child after catching him doing something terribly wrong. "I have no further questions for this witness. In light of his disclosure, I do not consider his reasoning sane. He freely admits that he hears voices in his head. In the past, we were at war and he embarked on missions that were openly questionable. I believe he has not stopped doing things that will endanger the lives of others. I have no other choice, but to demand that this tribunal find him guilty and sentence him to death. A life for a life!"

"Objection," Monka shouted, but he was overwhelmed by a cascading roar of voices.

As if on cue, they began throwing rotten fruit at me. An overripe koda fruit splattered against my face, but I took no offense. I knew the people were being manipulated. Thankfully the guards quickly entered the chamber and escorted me out as more putrid fruit splattered against my body.

Figure 7: Vying Standing Trial

"Enough! Clear the Council chamber," ordered Sorrl, but most of the spectators were leaving anyway.

In the afternoon, the crowd reconvened at the Seat of Judgment.

"This chamber will be permanently closed if anything else is thrown at the defendant!" Sorrl said slowly making eye contact with the crowd. "Admiral Monka, call your first witness."

Monka called warrior after warrior who had served with me. All testified of my bravery and loyalty to the Realm, but he couldn't nullify the effect of abandoning the knights to recover the Almighty's Book. I sat listening, wondering when the Almighty would come to my rescue with a great miracle, but He never did.

At the end of the day, guards led me away amidst a mocking frenzy that shouted hateful words at me. I remembered a few years ago how this city had turned out in mass to welcome my triumphant return from Mercus after defeating Megog in the Battle Circle. I was Micron's first Galactic Champion. Why had they turned against me? Why did they

PETER H. ZINDLER

want to repay my deeds of service with the death penalty? It didn't make sense.

The guards threw me into my cell. Exhausted, I prayed to the Almighty, but never felt so far from Him. Usually I could feel His presence, but now He seemed so distant. I'd been tried for murder because I did what the Almighty instructed. I wondered what would happen next. Would I die because of my obedience to Him? Is that what He wanted? Why?

Maybe the prosecutor was right. Maybe I was going crazy. I thought my relationship with the Almighty was special, but if it was, why would He allow me to go through this trial? I wasn't permitted any visitors. Who could I talk to who would understand? Emotionally and mentally, I was drained and I wondered if I'd ever see Tia and Tor again. Had they come to my trial? Where was Zelestar? I remembered her warmth and beauty and how we had spent an intimate moment sitting together on the wall in the City Beneath the Sea. How I wished I could go back in time and hold her in my arms. Would I ever see her again?

Chapter Eight

I lay on the floor, hoping to sleep, hoping to flee this bizarre reality, but tormenting thoughts tumbled through my mind and the elixir of sleep eluded me. The floor became hard. Soon I got up and began to pace in my cell. I ripped off my warrior's tunic and hurled it against the wall as hard as I could. Then I thought about the Hoon I'd seen in the forest. Something very strange was going on here, but I was powerless to investigate.

Were Og and Megog somehow alive? Had the Hoons raided the camp while I was gone? None of this added up to anything I could understand.

Finally I stretched out on the makeshift bunk in the cell.

How long I lay there, I couldn't tell. There was no one else in my windowless cellblock. The lights were soft and dim. Chilled air made me shiver. I grabbed my torn tunic and wrapped it tightly around my body. I didn't know what time it was or how long I'd been in the cell.

Again, my thoughts turned to the Almighty. Deep in my heart I knew with certainty the verdict wouldn't be favorable. Perhaps they would grant me grace in light of my war record and my life would be spared.

"What time is it?" I yelled, but there was no response. My stomach growled. "Are you going to feed me?"

Not a sound came from outside my cell. Maybe they were gone and I could escape. I grabbed the steel bars and pulled with all my might, but nothing moved.

A sinister voice echoed down the hallway. "Save your strength. The tribunal is recalling the officer's of the court. It will soon be over."

"Can't I have something to eat?" I yelled.

"We don't feed convicted criminals. If the death penalty is given we have found that whatever is in the body sometimes escapes, creating an unhealthy mess. It's much easier this way," the guard said over the speaker. "By the way, if you are wondering about the verdict, when the Council is gone for a short period of time, it's not a favorable decision. Justice is swift around here and executions follow quickly. So if I were you, I'd relax and enjoy the last few moments of your life, if you can."

Again I tried to sleep, but it was impossible. Raging thoughts assaulted my mind that somehow I'd missed the leading of the Almighty. I longed to speak to someone, anyone. Silent walls, like stoic sentries on guard duty, surrounded me with no sympathy. They'd heard innocent's cry many times before. Locked in my cramped cell, I longed to stretch my legs and run on the beach, a tonic that always invigorated my body and cleared my mind.

Like cadence echoing on a parade ground, the sound of boots hammered the floor as a squad of two warriors and four knights marched toward my cell.

"Commander Vying, your presence is required at the Seat of Judgment. The Council of Peers is ready to deliver its verdict," a warrior, announced as the cell door was opened.

"I told you it would be quick. You're guilty," the prison guard sneered as he watched me exit.

"Silence!" the warrior with two golden rings surrounding a silver one on each shoulder commanded.

"Thank you, friend," I said as I tried to straighten my tunic by rubbing my hands up and down my chest. I wished I could wash up before facing my accusers.

Stepping out of my cell, I looked at the warriors who had replaced the prison guards. I didn't like the subtle message of guilt the tribunal had sent and wondered who authorized it. I looked at one of them with whom I had fought alongside in the Great War, but he curtly avoided my eyes. I thought of breaking free, making a run for it, but where would I go? How could I escape this planet? Who would dare to help me?

Walking to the Council chamber reminded me of the impossible odds that I had faced many times in the past. With the help of the Almighty, I had been delivered many times. I hoped that it wasn't too late and somehow He would deliver me this terrible day. When we arrived at the chamber, I looked up at the anxious crowd that had gathered. Scanning them, I looked for Tor and Tia, but they were nowhere to be seen. Desperately, I looked for Zelestar, but only saw Dax. I looked up to him and nodded slightly. Then I saw the sad despair on King Wolks' and Queen Sera's faces. Instantly I knew!

"All rise for the magistrate," a warrior announced as Judge Sorrl strode out and took his seat.

"Commander Vying, please face the Council of Peers. I shall read the verdict. We, the Council of Peers, established during the reign of King Vardo have found Commander Vying guilty on all counts of negligence in the death of Knight Cappy. You are hereby stripped of all command."

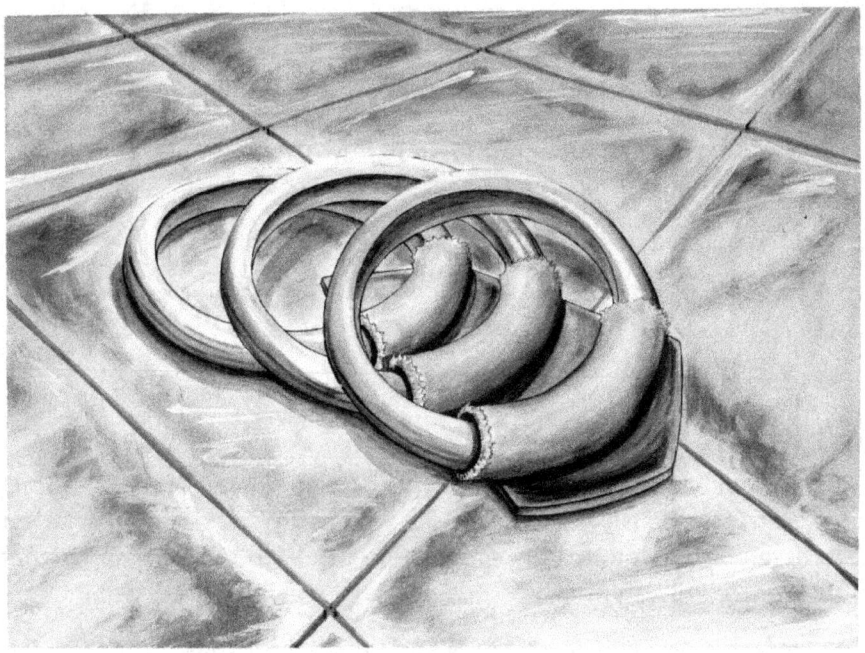

Figure 8: Rings Designating Command

I didn't want to hear the rest. I knew what was coming.

"Additionally, you know the new law; a life for a life! You will suffer the same fate as Cappy. Warrior Vying, the Council of Peers has ordered the death sentence. With this judgment, I sentence you to death!"

A hush filled the Council chamber.

"Execution will be carried out before the blue moon is full again."

A mixed cacophony of emotions swept through the chamber. Some applauded, others scorned, some wept.

"Mercy! Mercy for Vying!" someone called out.

"Mercy? Was there mercy for my Cappy? Justice is being done!" his mother screamed.

My head fell to my chest. I never felt more devastated in my life. All that I had done for the Realm meant nothing. I would be led to the gallows and hung as a common criminal, yet I knew I had done nothing wrong. Where was the Almighty? I began to lose hope.

Queen Sera arose and lifted her arm calling for the right to speak. The magistrate banged his sword handle on the arm of his chair. "Silence!" he called out to the chamber.

"As Queen of Micron, I am executing my royal right and commuting the death sentence for Warrior Vying."

"No! No!" screamed Cappy's mother. "That's not justice!"

Pandemonium erupted in the council chambers. The audience howled in protest.

"The verdict has been rendered and you can't change that," Sorrl declared.

"I cannot change the verdict, but must I remind you of the Warrior's Code, Sorrl? Based on his loyal service to the Realm as a fellow warrior and Queen of the Realm, I declare that he be exiled to the prison planet Zartex for the rest of his life."

"She can't do that. He killed my Cappy! A life for a life."

"Do you realize the extent of what you're doing?" Sorrl questioned. "If you commute his sentence you must abdicate your throne."

"No, Sera! Don't do this. I'm not worth it."

"You are more than worth it, Vying. You risked your life for me and now I will repay honor for honor. I willingly abdicate the throne. The royal lineage no longer passes through me. Do what you must, Warrior Sorrl," Sera proclaimed, reminding Sorrl that he too must abide by the Warrior's Code.

"I know the Code. As a warrior on the Council of Peers, I am overruling the death sentence and sentencing Vying to life on the prison planet Zartex. Take him from the chamber and send him to Zartex on the next available shuttle. This Council will reconvene to determine how we will elect a new King and Queen," Sorrl said banging his sword upon his chair as he rose to leave the chamber.

"No justice! Unfair." Cappy's mother screamed. "My son lies dead because of him!"

"Grace to the Almighty," shouted one of the older warriors.

Roughly I was escorted to my cell, no longer a hero of the Realm. It hurt that so many had turned against me.

"Justice wasn't served," one of the guards said as I walked by to my cell. They opened the cell and pushed me in. I heard hurried footsteps racing down the cellblock.

I turned around as the door to my cell opened. Two warriors came followed by King Wolks and Queen Sera.

"Sera, are you crazy? Do you realize what you've done?"

"Vying, something is very wrong. Your trial came too hastily and Admiral Monka was denied the right to investigate the scene of the alleged crime. I only did what you would have done for me. Your life is more valuable than a throne. Besides, Wolks has been getting fat from all the royal banquets."

"But you and Wolks are running the planet. Isn't that more important?"

"Normally, I might agree with you, but there's been a shift in power. The Council of Peers has voted themselves as the ruling body. My vote no longer counts."

"When did this happen?"

"Vying, you've been away for three years. When you returned, you wanted to train with the warriors and knights. I tried to get you to run for the Council, but you refused. Now, Wolks and I are powerless to stop their rulings."

I looked at my best friends and shook my head. Then we embraced.

"Now that I am free from royal duties, I'll be able to investigate the scene," Wolks said. "I miss being out in the open with a sword in my hand."

"Wolks, be careful. I thought I saw a Hoon observing us from the woods.

"What are you talking about? We saw the ground swallowed the Hoons."

"There are some very unusual things in the outback. During the night, I was attacked by a strange winged mechanical beast. I don't know how, but I believe the Hoons are responsible for Cappy's death."

"Why did you leave? What was so important that you would leave the training?"

"I know you might think I'm crazy, but I believe I've recovered the Almighty's Book."

"Vying, what are you talking about?"

"I know, it sounds crazy Wolks, but on Earth the Almighty's Book, the Bible, was written that contained wisdom and spiritual truth for this life and eternity."

"Time is up, Your Highness. The flight to Zartex is boarding," the prison commander called out.

"Do you see this crown on my head?" Sera demanded with a pointed look on her face as she stared unwavering into the man's eyes. Unconsciously, he backed away.

"Yes, Your Highness."

"Then render the respect the crown deserves. Until I take it off, I'm still Queen of Micron. When my business here is finished, I'll let you know. In the meantime, I order the shuttle's immediate departure. Vying will be taking the next transport to Zartex. Is that understood?"

"Yes, Your Highness."

"Very well. You are dismissed!"

"Yes, Your Highness," he said as he departed.

I waited until his footsteps faded. "Thanks, Sera. Have Tor or Tia shown up?"

"They're due in a couple of days. That's why I ordered the flight to leave. I know you want to see them."

"I do. Were you able to contact Zelestar?"

"I have left communications with her, but have received no response. You know how Zelestar lives. She may be the Queen of Milo, but she loves leaving the palace in one of her disguises to personally investigate."

"If I don't see her, please tell her I love her."

"You know I will," Sera replied.

"Vying, this isn't over. I'm still going to investigate Cappy's death. Hopefully I can turn up some clues to set you free, now that I've got plenty of time on my hands," the king said.

"Thanks, Wolks."

Hurried footsteps echoed down the cell block. Moments later Judge Sorrl burst into my cell.

"Sera you had no right to delay Vying's departure. He was to be on that shuttle to Zartex today!"

"Really, am I the only one who realizes that I'm still Queen here on Micron?"

"But you gave up the throne."

"Indeed I did, but have you forgotten that a Queen does not release her authority until the Blue Moon is full. Have you forgotten that clause?"

"I've never heard of that."

"Then Judge, I suggest you search your own records. I will abdicate the throne at that time as I have promised."

"But, but I... commuted the sentence with the understanding that Vying would be on the next flight."

"And he shall. As Queen, I needed to talk to my subject to make sure that justice was rendered to him."

"And was it?"

"Sorrl, you know it wasn't. The Council of Peers has changed since the days of my father, King Vardo."

"It has," Sorrl said reflecting on the former King of Micron. He nodded and took a deep breath.

"My father formed the Council of Peers with men of honor. I'm sure he'd be most pleased with you."

Sorrl stood taller. "Your father was a great man, Therefore I shall proudly bear the heat of your last ruling for Vying in respect for him and to you, though the Council will not be pleased." "Promise me you won't do anything else in regard to Vying."

"Sorrl, I'm still Queen, but I give you my word that Vying will be on the next flight to Zartex."

"I will honor your word, my Queen," Sorrl said bowing slightly before leaving the cell.

"Sera, could you please arrange for Dax to see me," I asked.

"I don't think that should be a problem. I think the jailor is just a little bit afraid of me."

"As he should, Sera, at least for another four days. Thank you, again for my life. I wish it could be another way."

"Who knows? Vying, did you ever think that maybe this is all part of the Almighty's plan?" Sera asked.

I looked at her and took a deep breath. How could a life of exile on a prison planet serve His plan?

Chapter Nine

Scorching anger seared the inner depths of my soul as I stared at the unforgiving walls of my cell. In spite of myself, I could not quiet the growing tempest within my mind. What was really going on? I heard a faint scratching noise in the passageway outside my cell getting closer and closer. I closed my eyes and listened again. What was it?

Scratch. Scratch.

A pitiful old woman dressed in black, with wrinkles on sagging weathered flesh pushed her broom through the walkway. Time hadn't been kind to her. The hump on her back shackled her forever in a bent over position. Her ugliness repulsed me as she slowly swept the cement floor. I wondered which back alley produced this hag? As if reading my condescending thoughts, she turned and looked directly at me. A huge gap separated her blackened upper teeth. Her long nose, accented by a darkened mole at the tip, was gruesome to look at. In revulsion, I turned away. Faintly I heard the "shhhing" of a whisper and turned toward her, but thankfully she had passed.

The old witch was probably one of the mockers let out of the courtroom condemning me even further, demanding my execution. But who cared about some old hag spending her last days sweeping a prison floor? My thoughts returned to the Almighty. Why had He allowed this to happen? I couldn't understand how a loving God could allow this injustice, especially if I was following His will.

The scratching noise again approached my cell. Irritated, I got up and walked to the door. The cold steel bars had a slit in the bottom where food was slid into the cell. Twin cameras mounted high in the corners observed the cells at all times.

Repugnant body odor assaulted me as the old woman passed by again. Slowly and methodically she swept the floor. Her witless motions were steady and redundant which drew my fascination. She must have lost her mind. I wondered if someday I'd be like her, unable to use my brain and body to its fullest. Maybe in this new prison I'd age quicker than I imagined.

Resting against her broom and looking both ways, she stretched her withered limbs. "Your enemies are closer than you think," she whispered, never looking at me. "They want you dead before you get on the next shuttle. There will be nothing the queen can do to help you this time."

Was this old shrew out of her mind? She looked every bit of crazy.

Turning she spotted something on the ground. She bent over to pick it up and then put it in her mouth, but I couldn't see anything.

"Don't eat your food tonight," she whispered as I looked at her while she swept.

I wondered about her words as I looked again at my white-washed tomb. I lay back down on my bunk. I was hungry and was looking forward to the break in the monotony of my own vexing thoughts. What were they serving for dinner? Anything would taste great after the Council ordeal. I hadn't eaten in two days and I wondered when Dax would visit me.

Figure 9: Evening Meal

Finally, I heard food trays being slid under the other cell doors. Mine was the last in the row and my appetite peaked. I heard the sounds of the other prisoners grunting as they ate.

"This steak sure has improved now that we have a celebrity in lockdown," one of them laughed as he shouted to another.

"Celebrity, my foot! He's just like one of us. Gonna spend the rest of his life caged like a wild animal."

"If he's lucky," another added.

The enticing aroma of roasted steak watered my mouth. My stomach growled in expectation. Finally my tray, skidded under the cell door, coming to a halt against the cement wall. Heat wafted up from the large portion of beef surrounded by plenty of vegetables.

Long and hard I looked at the meal, wanting to devour it, but the old woman's words echoed in my mind, *"Don't eat the food tonight."*

Wrestling with her warning, I turned my back to the tray and stared at the wall. I noticed how smooth it was. There were no jagged edges on the texture, but there were cracks where the foundation had settled. I followed one of the cracks as it climbed toward the ceiling, remembering a time when I was free to fly a scintilla into the stratosphere. My stomach growled again and I battled hunger pains and begin to meditate on the past, since the future held little promise.

I remembered the many conflicts I'd been in, and how Wolks and I had rescued Sera from Megog's battle carrier. I was so surprised when we freed her and she ran into Wolks waiting arms, kissing him deeply. To this day, it still hurt. I'd thought she was in love with me, but once again I had misjudged the emotions of a woman.

I rolled back over and stared at the plate of food. How could that hag know that the food was poisoned? It didn't make sense. In a few days, I was headed to the prison planet, Zartex, never to return. Why would anyone want to kill me now? Behind bars, I was a threat to no one.

I got off the rack and approached the food. The desire to eat was overwhelming. It looked delicious and the more I contemplated eating it, the more my stomach begged me to ignore the words of the old woman.

A thought suddenly popped into my mind. When we rescued Sera, we met Princess Zelestar, a double agent for the Realm. One of her disguises was that of an old woman. A breeze lifted the steak's aroma to my nose and I quickly dismissed the warning words from my mind. I reached for the food with my hand, but then quickly withdrew it. Wait a minute! There was something familiar about that old woman.

Could she be Queen Zelestar? Was the food really poisoned? I listened to the other prisoners smacking their lips as they finished their meals and heard nothing unusual. Maybe the food wasn't tainted.

Deep in my heart I knew the Almighty was telling me not to eat. Before I could change my mind I placed the tray back on the floor and slid it under my door towards the middle of the cellblock where I couldn't reach it in case I changed my mind.

"Hey man, what you doing? Ain't you hungry?" the prisoner asked across from me as he saw the uneaten tray in the middle of the hallway. "That was good chow. If you don't want it, next time give it a good push toward me and I'll eat it."

But I couldn't do that. What if it was poisoned? I didn't want to be responsible for another's death.

"Hey, what's wrong with you. You're going to need your strength if you want to survive in the yard."

I didn't look forward to going into general population when they allowed us out of our cells. I went back to my bunk and lay down. Somehow sleep overtook me.

During the night a strong evil presence came over me in my dream. Hoons were chasing me, but my escape path led to an even greater evil – a huge dragon perched on a cliff. Fire spewed from its mouth burning all that was around it. Many ran from the dragon to the safety of a cave. Awakening in a deep sweat, I called to the Almighty. The presence of an evil spirit was so strong, that I was afraid to open my eyes. I prayed to the Almighty's Son and after a while I drifted off to sleep.

A few hours later I awoke again, this time with a sense of peace. The lights came on in our cell block and I opened my eyes. I got up and walked to the door of my cell. There, in the center of the passageway, a large lifeless rat lay on top of the vegetables. His tongue was swollen, his eyes wide open, his leg stretched out, and hanging from his mouth was a large piece of meat.

Chapter Ten

"What's this?" the guard demanded looking down at the lifeless rat as he arrived with my next meal.

I watched him, trying to detect a note of guilt, as he looked down at the food, but he was totally bewildered. He shoved another plate of food under my cell door, but the desire to eat had left me.

The banging of metal trays echoed throughout the cellblock as the others finished eating. I renewed my emotional wrestling match, angry at the Almighty, wondering why I was here. It was futile. Grappling with the Almighty was a losing proposition.

I wondered when or if Dax would come to visit. I wanted to give him the disks to see if they could be transferred onto something viewable. I remembered something Tor had quoted from the Almighty's Book, *'He who dwells in the secret place of the Most High, will abide in the shadow of the Almighty. I will say to the Lord, My refuge and my fortress, my God in whom I trust.'*

I wanted to dwell in the secret place of the Most High and closed my eyes fixing them on the Son of the Almighty - Jesus. I desperately wanted answers to what had happened to me and why. Having not eaten for the last couple of days helped me focus on Jesus sitting on His throne. I remembered when Megog rammed his sword into me, ending my life. Immediately I had been transported into the third heaven. I saw His glory and people around the throne crying out, "Holy, holy, holy. Holy is the Lamb."

I found myself crying out, "Holy, holy, holy." How desperately I wanted an encounter with Jesus – the Lamb – losing all track of time. I lifted up my arms in submission worshipping Him. I felt a warm pulsation through the palms of my uplifted hands. I knew that I was in His glory and kept focusing on His Son. Slowly the holy fire began to spread down my arms and as I sat back against the wall of my cell, my whole body enveloped in His hot anointing.

Then I felt myself rising up, into the third heaven. Whether I was in my body or not, I couldn't tell, but I found myself lying face down on a street paved with gold.

The Almighty began to speak to me in a loud voice, like the roar of many waters and I was terrified. "You must be sent away so that you can return to Micron and through me conquer the forces of evil. Darkness grows stronger since the end of the war and the children of the Light have been pursuing worldly things since peace has arrived. The principalities of evil remain, but you must take up the Sword of the Spirit to fight them. My Word is written on the disks you are carrying. Give them to Dax and tell him to take them to Tor. Tell him to produce many holographic messages for my followers."

Figure 10: Before the Throne of Glory

"But why am I being sent away? Can't I do that here?" I asked the Almighty's Son still afraid to look up.

I heard nothing, but a thought came into my mind. *"Yes you could, but I am sending you on a mission, a tough mission that must be won at all costs."*

"What is it?"

"When the time is right, I will reveal the rest of your mission to you."

I slowly lifted my head and looked up. Seven golden lampstands surrounded the Son of Man who was clothed with a long robe and with a golden sash around His chest. The hairs of His head were white like wool, as white as snow. His eyes were like flames of fire, his feet, like burnished bronze, refined in a furnace. In his right hand he held seven stars, from his mouth came a sharp two-edged sword, and his face was like the sun shining in full strength.

All around the throne, on each side were four living creatures, full of eyes in front and behind: the first living creature was like a lion, and the second living creature like an ox, the third living creature had the face of a man, and fourth living creature was like an eagle in flight. And the four living creatures, each of them with six wings, full of eyes all around and within, and day and night they said, "Holy, holy, holy is the Lord God Almighty, who was and is and is to come."

And when the living creatures gave glory and honor and thanks to Him who is seated on the throne, the twenty-four elders fell down before Him. They cast their golden crowns before Him, saying: "Worthy are you, our Lord and God, to receive glory and honor and power, for you created all things, and by your will they existed and were created."

Suddenly I felt myself plummeting back down to Micron. In my cell, I kept my eyes closed continuing to soak in His loving presence, feeling very special that He allowed me entrance to His throne room, but more than that was that He loved me very much and I could feel His love, it was so thick that I could almost touch it. I hungered for greater intimacy with Him.

Six hours later another meal arrived. I was surprised that I had been in the spirit for what seemed seconds and yet time had rocketed by. I wondered if I should eat it and recalled another time Tor had told me about the Almighty's Book. I remembered him saying that if we go out and proclaim the Kingdom of the Most High that even if the enemy served us poison, it would not harm us.

Springing from the cot, I grabbed the tray, asked the Almighty to bless the food and began to eat. Each morsel exploded in flavor, even the greens, which were usually dull in taste. When I finished, my stomach began to feel intensely warm. Maybe the food was poisoned. I remembered the warning the old lady had given me and the lifeless rat lying on the last tray of food. I got up and slid the empty tray under the cell door and lay down. A soothing fire warmed my belly and made me drowsy. I lay there half asleep, when I heard whispers in the shadows outside my cell.

"Is he moving?"

"I don't think so."

"He should be dead by now."

"Let's go see."

"There's no need. If he's dead we'll know by morning. Word will spread throughout the Realm."

"I have the key right here. No one will know."

"Og will somehow find out. He always does."

I jerked at the mention of Og.

"I could run my sword through him, just in case."

"That's not the master's plan. Let's get out of here. We'll report that the food was eaten and the prisoner is dead."

The faint brushing footsteps signaled that the two men had departed. I knew without a shadow of a doubt that my food had been poisoned, but I hadn't felt any side effects. The warm glow in my belly slowly vanished and for the first time since the trial, I felt confident and optimistic about my future, whatever it held. I knew I was in my Master's will and fell asleep.

Banging steel against the bars of my cell door jarred me from my sleep.

"Wake up in there. You have a visitor."

I arose and felt my face. A three-day growth of stubble covered my skin and I caught a whiff of a ripe aroma that was me.

"You have ten minutes," the guard called out.

I hoped it would it would be Tor or Tia, daring not to think of Zelestar. Dax walked in and my face betrayed my disappointment at seeing him, not Zelestar.

"I know it's not right, Vying, and I'm sorry my testimony couldn't have been more positive, but I answered truthfully."

"I know you did, Dax. Don't worry about it."

"Don't worry about it! This may be the last time I ever see you, Vying."

"Everything will be okay."

"How can you say that? No one has ever returned from Zartex! You were framed."

"It's the Almighty's plan."

"Was it the Almighty's plan that Cappy would die?"

"That I don't know, Dax, but the Almighty works all things to the good for those who love Him and are called according to His purpose."

"Yeah right! Cappy's dead and you're going to be walking around Zartex as good as dead. This isn't fair."

"Nobody said this life would be fair. How many times did the Almighty get us out of tight jams?"

"Plenty, but this seems so different. At least we knew who our enemies were."

"Dax, the Almighty is still on His throne and in control. You've got to believe that brother," I said giving him a hug with one arm as he embraced me. With my other hand I slipped the disks into the folds of his tunic.

"Don't say a word," I whispered.

"Let's go!" the guard demanded. "Your time's up."

With a bewildered look on his face Dax clutched the discs hidden from view.

"Yes, I love you too, Dax. But I have more love for Tor and Tia. When you see them, give them all my love. They are treasures," I said as I put my hand to my chest.

I could see the comprehension brighten Dax's face. He knew what to do.

"If you ever see Zelestar again, please give her all my love. Tell her she is constantly in my thoughts."

"I will, Vying."

"Oh, and Dax, I'll be back."

Another puzzled look quickly crossed his face, but he quickly recovered. "Of course you will. Of course you will."

"That's it. Let's go," the guard stated unsympathetically.

After Dax departed, I went back to my cot. It wasn't long before my cell door opened again.

"Let's go, Vying. Your shuttle to Zartex awaits you."

Guards attached manacles and chains to my feet and hands and escorted me down the long hallway through some heavy doors. After walking through the first door, we stopped and waited to go outside into the prison yard. Out of the corner of my eye I could see two men looking intently at me from a side room. For some reason, the acoustics were amplified and I could hear their conversation.

"I thought you gave him the poison."

"I did. He ate his food. He should be dead."

"Megog isn't going to be happy."

I couldn't believe my ears. Megog alive too! How had he and Og survived the last battle?

Chapter Eleven

Hobbled by leg bracelets, I shuffled aboard the shuttlecraft. The other criminals already were boxed in by red lasers. The guards removed my wrist and ankle chains, making the seating a little more comfortable. We could move a little, but the lasers defined our perimeters. I could feel their heat which warned of burning if I accidentally got too close.

Most of the prisoners stole furtive glances at each other, checking to see who looked the toughest. All were rough hewed with scars and tattoos on various parts of their bodies. One of them looked familiar. Where had I seen him before? Sensing my thoughts, he quickly turned away. Another prisoner rocked back and forth slamming his head backwards into the bulkhead.

I closed my eyes and began to focus on the Almighty. I felt his power pulsating in my hands. Trying not to draw attention to myself, I began to pray to Him. I don't know how long I prayed, but finally the big ship began to accelerate from the spaceport and the men let out a battle cry.

"What do you know about Zartex?" the big rugged man sitting next to me asked. His face had pock marks and a scar running across the middle of his forehead. His corded forearms flexed as he opened the box of flavorless nutrients provided for the trip.

Figure 11: Nafuka

"Not much. All I know is that nobody leaves alive."

"That depends on who you talk to."

"What do you mean?" I asked.

"This will be my second stint on Zartex."

"What? How did you get off?"

"I defeated the others when competing in Zartex's Crucible. After I won, a nobleman from Coralia purchased my freedom."

Hope suddenly surged within me. "I've never heard that. Were you his slave?"

"Not exactly. They hold a competition each year and all the

prisoners compete to see who is the best runner and fighter."

"What kind of contest is it?" I asked as the shuttle dipped and slid violently starboard hitting a pocket of turbulence. Some of the nutrients the man was eating spilled out of the box. They were fried to a crisp by the lasers as they dropped to the deck. The smell of burnt rubber filled the air.

"It's the kind you might do well in," he replied with a knowing look.

I'd never seen this man before and wondered what he was talking about. Something about him made me feel very uncomfortable. He wasn't the kind of person I'd spend time with.

He laughed, sensing my discomfort, but his face betrayed the forced humor.

"What are you talking about?"

"I was there on Mercus the night you defeated Megog in the battle ring, a match few will ever forget. How you got up after he hammered you was amazing."

"It was the Almighty. He empowered me."

"Yeah, well this contest is no different. The noblemen will want someone like you. Just remember, you'll have to go through me and a host of others. Maybe we can form an alliance."

"If I have to go through you, why would you want an alliance with me?"

"Life on Zartex is brutal. It's good to have friends. If we form an alliance, we won't have to face each other until the final match. That's about the only rule they have on Zartex."

I didn't know what to say to his offer. I knew little about the prison planet and hadn't heard anything like this. But then I'd never heard of anyone leaving Zartex either. Here was a formidable man going back for a second term, if he was telling the truth. I didn't want to commit myself. "What's your name?"

"Nafuka," he replied, his shiny ebony face offsetting the intensity of his coal-black eyes as he looked me up and down.

"Let me think about it."

He laughed again. "Oh you'll have plenty of time to think about it, if you survive. Having a friend can make the difference between life and death."

"Thanks," I replied half heartily as I lay my head back and closed my eyes. Time seemed to stand still as the ship rocketed through space. I dozed off, but something bumped me out of my sleep. A strange looking man with a skull tattooed on his bald head and a full unkempt grey beard stood up. His tight black leather vest prominently displayed the muscle tone of his arms from pumping iron.

What was going on? How could he get up without the lasers burning his body? Then he freely walked forward.

"You see him?" Nafuka whispered out of the corner of his mouth. "The competition has begun."

"Why did the guards allow him up?"

"Why isn't the point. The point is he has connections and now he is flaunting them, challenging all of us. He's already formed an alliance. His Crucible is financed by others. I've seen this before and it's nothing but trouble."

"What do you mean?"

"You'll see in a moment. With his power he can get food. An alliance with him will provide you food to keep you healthy and help you train more effectively, but there are things he must do. Nothing is free on Zartex."

"I'll survive without help."

"What? You're a marked man, Vying. We all know who you are and that we must defeat you. I didn't offer my alliance lightly and I've been there once. There's not much on Zartex, so you have to be wise with whom you deal."

Nafuka appeared to have closed his eyes as the freed man, a wild look in his eyes, turned around with a steel bar in his hand. Where did he get it? He started coming toward the back of the shuttle. He stopped and looked straight at me. Instantly the lasers around me disappeared.

"Get up!" Nafuka yelled startling me.

I jumped to my feet and dodged to the right as the heavy pipe came crashing into the bulkhead where I had been sitting. Had Nafuka not warned me, I would have been killed.

The ship erupted in a surly cheer as I faced the man. I'd have to fight with all my might to defeat him. On Micron I'd trained with the knights and kept in great shape, but it had been years since I had fought in the battle ring. Years of training instantly returned. Instinctively my hands flew up and I went into a defensive crouch.

Tossing his weapon from hand to hand, he arrogantly smiled at me knowing he had the advantage. I kept my eyes focused on his. Movement in the shuttle was limited and I knew that I wouldn't get a second chance if he hit me. He advanced toward me. I backed up, waiting for an opening. Instinctively, I timed his steps and as he shifted his weight from one foot to the other I launched a sidekick striking him in the left thigh. I'd scored heavily, but it didn't seem to matter. I noticed his dilated eyes. He'd been drugged or was on steroids. That blow should have felled him. I'd fought a man like this in the war and unless you killed them they wouldn't stop. They were oblivious to pain and injury!

With his right hand he swung the bar down just as I shifted my weight back. The bar grazed my thigh.

Committed to the blow, his body followed his swing and exposed his side. I hammered a powerful upper cut to his exposed kidney.

Pain contorted his face. His knees buckled. I knew I had scored, but it wasn't over. Sucking in his breath, he retreated. Out of the corner of my eye I saw the guard watching, but he made no effort to stop the fight. I guessed we were the in-flight entertainment on our ride to Zartex.

Physically my opponent was overmatched, but there was no fear in his eyes. He waited for me to make my move, but I stood fast.

"Finish him," one of the inmates shouted.

"Use the bar," another encouraged as the other prisoners chimed in a cacophony of electrified voices.

He charged forward, swinging the bar at my head with reckless abandon.

I seized the opening, dropping to the deck. I ducked his blow and quickly shot up, driving my head into his solar plexus. I grabbed behind both his knees and pulled him off the deck. Lunging forward, I crushed his back to the steel deck. He swung the pipe again, but with little power or speed. Still, the hard steel hurt when it landed against my ear. In desperation, he tried to hit me again with the pipe. I grabbed his wrist and slammed it to the deck. The pipe rolled away, but I was off balance. He twisted his wrist away from my thumb and jumped to his feet immediately launching a knee kick to my stomach.

Pain riveted my body. Trying to catch a breath of air, I rolled backwards and scrambled to my feet. Without his weapon, I owned him and quickly moved in landing a flurry of punches. Just when I had the upper hand, a guard stepped between us, ending the fight.

The prisoners booed. They wanted blood! Two guards grabbed him and threw him into his seat. Instantly the lasers came on.

The other guard pointed to me and then to my seat. I sat down and the lasers surrounding me lit up.

"Nicely done. You passed your first test," Nafuka whispered. "There will be many more. Consider my alliance. Now that I think about it, maybe I shouldn't have made the offer, the way you attract attention."

"That's up to you," I said.

"Clearly, you don't understand. That was a deathtrap. The guards gave him the bar and his mission was to kill you. Watch and see if he stays on Zartex. He might not even be a prisoner."

"What do you mean?"

"Things aren't what they seem."

Chapter Twelve

I closed my eyes after noticing how many prisoners were staring at me. I didn't want the attention. From some of the looks they gave me, I knew that they were trying to intimidate me. So I returned their glares with my own. I was thankful that Nafuka had warned me, but I still was hesitant to strike up a friendship with anyone. *'Where was the Almighty in all this?'* I knew that God used people, but why Nafuka?

Although he was big and tough, I wasn't in any mood to make new acquaintances. My best friends, Wolks and Sera, had given up their throne to save my life, for which I was very grateful, but unworthy. Besides, sending me to Zartex was a one-way trip to an inescapable hellhole. I would do my best to stay alive on this desolate planet in the Solar System Ulana. If this was living, I must have missed it. And whatever happened to Zelestar?

Being in the presence of the Almighty in the third heaven had changed my life forever. His embracing love was warm and deep, so deep that it touched the very core of my being, changing me forever. I had no desire to enter the violent fight scene again. I wondered what He meant when He told me to fight with the Sword of the Spirit. Whatever that meant, I knew the Almighty was showing me a better way to live. A way of kindness and helping others, yet I knew that if I were to survive on Zartex, I would have to fight for my life.

"That's just the beginning," Nafuka said. "It'll get worse on Zartex when they let the monkeys out."

I wished he'd shut his mouth. I wanted to be alone with my thoughts.

The rest of the trip on the shuttle through the dimension of plasma energy was uneventful. For the next two days, with my eyes closed, I stoically awaited our arrival on Zartex. Finally the ship's speed decreased as it shuddered slighty and cracked into dimensional space.

"You can open your eyes now, Vying," Nafuka said knowing that I had avoided him for days. "We're almost there."

I turned my head and peered out the porthole. The planet was a sea of grey – devoid of vegetation, no lakes of any size, not even a puddle.

Having traveled to many planets, the cold dead rock of Zartex held little promise that it could sustain life. The shuttle's engines began to throb as it throttled down and pierced the atmosphere surrounding the planet. I looked again, hoping vainly to see some foliage.

"Nothing but rock," my self-appointed tour guide said sarcastically.

The shuttle finally touched down. Time dragged on as the ship's manifest was carefully checked and rechecked. More guards came aboard. These muscular men were quite healthy. I wondered how that could be on a planet so sparse, but I'd seen supplies being loaded before we left Micron. They fitted all the prisoners with ankle bracelets and handcuffs.

"On your feet," one of them commanded as the lasers separating us disappeared.

"When are you going to feed us?" one of the prisoners called out.

"I'm thirsty," another complained.

"Shut your mouths you worthless gutter scum and listen up. Each of you will leave the shuttle chained. You'll receive rations once off the ship, but if there's any problem you'll be thrown into an isolation hut where you will bake in the hot sun for a day or two. It doesn't matter to us."

Nor me either, I thought.

As we walked to the front of the shuttle, Nafuka leaned forward and whispered, "When the time comes, don't forget our alliance."

Yeah, right, I thought. *That's the last thing I want.*

Walking slowly, I followed behind Nafuka to the head of the shuttle. Light poured through the hatch and I was anxious for a first hand look at Zartex. I looked out one of the portholes as I passed by and couldn't believe my eyes! Several palm trees were swaying in the wind and there was green grass everywhere. How strange. I hadn't seen that flying in. I thought Zartex was nothing but a rock pile.

Walking out, the humidity slapped me in the face, clinging to me like a wet blanket. Immediately I began sweating. The musty, pungent smell of a tropical jungle reached my nose. I walked past the shuttle and had a panoramic view of a lush paradise set among several small pools of water. I began to take hope that maybe this wasn't going to be so bad.

"Don't let this complex fool you. This is just for the guards and their families. We won't live here. We'll live outside those walls unless they round us up and put us to work," Nafuka said, interrupting my thoughts.

Figure 12: Tuskers

Gazing in the direction of Nafuka's line of sight, I saw the tall thick stone fortress walls with guards patrolling along the top. Caged four-legged animals, with sharp tusks curled forward on the sides of their mouths, paced back and forth. They were stationed on the ground next to an imposing wooden gate. In the distance, I thought I heard the sound of children laughing, screaming, and shouting. I turned my head to see.

"Keep moving," a guard ordered as he hit me on the head and shoved me toward a building near the wall. My second attempt to look again in the direction of their voices earned me another blow to the head. I stumbled forward.

"Take a good look. You won't see this again until the competition," Nafuka called out from ahead.

It seemed as though none of the prisoners were too eager to go into the building near the wall as if they knew this was a one-way trip. The guards pushed them, exerting their power and control over the new arrivals.

We entered the gray stone building and were seated on hard cement benches. Again, I could see men looking in my direction and for the first time noticed two women were in our group. They looked rough, but the unkempt one with the high cheekbones and long black hair could have been a fashion model if she cleaned up. I wondered what crimes they'd committed.

A tall thin man with a long narrow nose walked into the room dressed in judicial robes. I'd never seen a nose that long and I checked myself from staring at it. He was flanked by two guards whose uniforms were spotless. The other guards in the room looked at him and nodded their heads, as if it were their duty to do so. The man didn't pay any attention to their obeisance. He waited until all the prisoners had settled down as he looked at us, commanding our undivided attention. When one man didn't give it, he continued to stare at him with a pained expression on his face.

Pulling out a small rectangular box from under his robe, he aimed it at us and pushed a small button. Pain shot up our legs from the ankle bracelets. He laughed and waited for us to focus on him while he continued to hold his finger on the button. Finally, he released it and the pain ceased. He raised the box again and the room instantly became silent! He looked around studying each of us.

"All of you have committed serious crimes on various planets and have either been sentenced to death or life without parole. Your stay here on Zartex will be difficult at best. What you saw as you left the shuttle is a mirage for all practical purposes. This complex was built to house my guards and to keep you out. As you can see, we have significantly improved our environment. In the future, some of you may want to work here. Some of you may want to get as far away from this complex as possible. I really don't care where you go, because each of you has been fitted with an electronic bracelet to monitor your whereabouts, and to let me know if you're still alive."

"You will face many challenges outside these walls, perhaps even death," he said in a whisper and then began to slowly examine each of us. "Survival and the Crucible should be your only goals. If you win the Crucible I, your master, will grant you freedom!" he said with a wide-eyed look on his face and his thumb resting on the button.

"I, and I alone have the power to commute your sentence, but you must work hard. I have made arrangements with the nobles from Coralia. They need battle tested men, but only the very best. On this rock-hell you are entertainment for my guards. I, the Warder, am providing you an opportunity to win the Crucible and the privilege of leaving Zartex. To do that you must finish an endurance race through the most desolate part of the planet and defeat all contestants in the battle ring. You will need to be in great physical condition. It's a rare opportunity for someone to leave this planet other than in a box," he said and then laughed at his own joke.

His smiling face beamed bright red and he laughed some more. He looked around and stopped speaking for a moment.

"I see a familiar face sitting amongst us. We should be proud to have him with us, for he truly is a hero."

I knew at once he was talking about me, mocking me. My head was down, but I felt his glaze riveted on me. I refused to look up. I wanted to be left alone. The warder had been here way too long. He was beyond crazy.

"Stand to your feet," the warder demanded.

But I didn't move. I refused. I would rather take a beating and be thrown outside the wall than stand for this maniac.

To my surprise, Nafuka rose to his feet.

"Nafuka, Nafuka, you bad, bad man. Couldn't you stay out of trouble? Was life too pleasant in the real world?"

I looked up at Nafuka who was beaming proudly at the recognition afforded him by the warder.

"Nafuka is the only one among you who has won the Crucible, left Zartex and has now returned. Is that correct?"

"Yes boss," he replied obsequiously.

"I would have thought you learned your lesson, but the Milo wine is shall we say, tempting?"

"Yes boss."

"Well you don't have to worry, Nafuka. Beyond the wall there is no Milo wine, so you can't get into trouble. I can't ever recall anyone winning the Crucible twice. How fortunate for you. You, a criminal, have an opportunity to write history. I can see it now, Nafuka the two-time Crucible champion," he said smiling truly delighted as if his prodigal son had returned.

"Here on Zartex, I will allow you to form alliances. You may wonder why. I have seen that in order to train fighters they need sparring partners and it helps in surviving the danger outside the compound walls. Also, I have a larger pool of prisoners to choose from in the battle ring and I like that for the competition."

"Nafuka, you may sit down."

"Yes boss," he said quietly. Nafuka turned toward me and nodded. I wondered why he did it and didn't return his gesture. I'd trained in harsh climates before and knew how to survive. I didn't need his help.

"As you walk out this room, be sure to take a water bottle with you. Drink it slowly. Once its gone, you will have to find another source. Once the gate is opened and you are released into the oceans of rock, the gate to the complex will only reopen when the competition begins. That will be in four cycles of our moons. This will give you plenty of time to train. You're not allowed inside the walls until then. If you are caught, my tuskers will tear you to pieces. That is their job and they do it well. If you find life too tough outside the walls you may petition the guard to see me. At that time I might accept you as my slave. No guarantees."

"Slaves! Who does he think he is?" one of the prisoners whispered.

"Who said that? Did I give permission to speak, Nafuka?"

"No Boss."

"Who said something?" the Warder exclaimed as his eyes opened wide, not blinking as he slowly looked around the room at each person, holding up the small black box with his finger on the button looking for the person who spoke. Red rage ignited his as he smashed the button with his palm.

The prisoners screamed from the intense pain being inflicted.

He released the button and looked at Nafuka. "Was I hearing voices or did you hear someone talk?"

"Yes, boss, I heard someone say something."

"Who was it?"

"I don't know, boss. The last time I was here, my right eardrum was shattered in the battle ring."

The Warder laughed hysterically. "Oh, good answer. Wonderful. I've never heard that one before."

The Warder went on about Nafuka and forgot about the person who had whispered the remark.

"The last bit of advice I can give you is stay alert. Inside these walls is safety, but outside I have heard there are many strange things happening, evil things. Things that frighten the normal person, but then, none of you are normal or you wouldn't be here," he said and started laughing again as he walked out of the room tossing the black box to a guard as if it were a game. The hungry tuskers pulling on their leashes stood poised, ready to attack as the guards removed the shackles and chains, but not the electronic ankle bracelets.

Chapter Thirteen

Figure 13-1: Guard Compound on Zartex

The guards handed us water bottles as we were herded out of the room like cattle to the slaughterhouse. We were led to the open gates and thrust out of the secure walls to brave the elements of the outback. A sudden gust of wind snapped at my skin, penetrating my flesh with lethal fangs of bone chilling cold. I looked to the darkened sky and saw reflectors beaming the sun's light into the compound. Mirrored reflectors orbited the sky, constantly keeping the compound warm and bright during the night.

The further away from the compound I walked, the deeper I stepped into the frigid darkness. Thoughts of the Almighty flooded my mind and a warm touch suddenly enveloped me. Hungering for His presence, I continued thinking of the Almighty, distancing myself from the others. God had a reason for bringing me here, but I couldn't understand it. I needed time in His presence, away from the others. Looking down, I scanned the rugged terrain for any trip hazards.

"Do you feel the presence of evil?" Nafuka yelled in a loud voice jarring me from my thoughts and scaring me half to death. I whirled around. His profile stood like a mighty tree against the compound's lights. "There are many strange things out here and few men know about them. That's why an alliance is so important."

"What part of I don't need you or an alliance, don't you understand? I've got to settle things in my mind as to why I'm here."

Nafuka laughed. "I understand. I thought like that too. All prisoners think that they're innocent. Your innocence isn't an issue here – your survival is."

"I'm not questioning my innocence. I'm questioning why the Almighty has sent me here in the first place."

"The Almighty didn't send you here. Your sins have paved your way," Nafuka said laughing. "If you change you mind, I'll be around. Just one last piece of advice. Don't go near the light and drink your water sparingly."

"What are you talking about?"

"At night, the guards let out one or two tuskers that haven't eaten for days. They patrol the compound perimeter hidden in the darkness seeking whom they can devour. Desperate souls who have drank their water too quickly and think the warder will have mercy on them and refill their bottles are instantly shredded."

"Thanks, I'll remember that," I said walking away from him.

An eerie howl erupted! Immediately I searched for Nafuka, but he was gone. A tusker trumpeted again sounding his hunting cry. I walked on feeling very alone. Perhaps, I shouldn't have been so hard on Nafuka. Maybe he was right. Maybe an alliance was the only way to survive, but I wanted to seek the Almighty alone. The guards had given us glow lights to use in the night, but I didn't want to attract any attention. I continued walking along often stumbling over the loose rock and sipping my water judiciously.

Finally, my night vision became crisp. I could see dim outlines and headed for an outcropping of rocks. I saw a stand of dead trees and immediately headed away from them. I knew the others would be inclined to find shelter amongst them, so I headed in the opposite direction into the vast wasteland. I desired companionship, but not with just anyone. I climbed the first incline and sat down on the cold rock surface. I remembered the view from the shuttle that most of the planet was gray. Everywhere I looked there were fields and hills of rocks and more rocks. I slipped down a shale incline and continued walking. When I reached the next incline, I turned around and was surprised that the compound was far away.

The further I journeyed into the blackened wasteland the greater I sensed the veil of evil shrouding the outback. Suddenly, my spirit jumped within me. My fists shot up instantly, ready to defend myself. Standing motionless, I strained to hear the faintest sound. Then I smelled something so foul and rotten, it made me gag. Mentally I bore down demanding my body to be still. Slowly, I turned my head around. I couldn't see anything, but the rancid smell of death and decay was overpowering.

I knew that if I made a noise, I'd have to fight. My nose itched. I wanted to scratch it, but I didn't move a muscle. I waited for what seemed like eternity, sequestered in silence. Then I heard the sound of rocks hitting each other as they rolled down the incline. Soon the foul fumes dissipated and I inhaled a huge gulp of fresh air. Looking back to the compound I saw the furry outline of a four-legged animal crawl out of the darkness and up the hill I'd just been on. Lifting its nose, it looked all around. It wasn't a tusker. It was much bigger. As it slowly walked away from me, I wondered what it was.

Quietly I moved into the darkness away from the creature. After walking for some time, I found a natural alcove tucked into a hill. I looked inside and waited to see if someone lived in it. Cupping my ears with my hands, I strained to hear any noise at all. I heard none and moved deeper into the rocks. It was pitch black and I couldn't see a thing. Wearily I sat down and leaned against a smooth rock, moving around until I could get somewhat comfortable. For the first time since I'd been incarcerated on Micron, I relaxed. I hugged my chest to keep warm. The frigid stone alcove wasn't the least bit comfortable, but soon I felt my eyes closing and my chin dropping to my chest. I fought to stay awake and prayed to the Almighty, but only a few words escaped my lips before I slipped into sleep's dark grotto.

A blood-curdling scream shattered the night's silence. Instantly I leapt to my feet and reached for my sword, but I had none. Another desperate cry erupted and I crawled up the hill and looked toward the compound. All was suddenly silent and I wondered which of my fellow prisoners had become the evening entrée for a hungry tusker.

Streaks of light burst from the mountains behind the compound illuminating the clouds. Dawn was rapidly approaching. Hunger claimed its throne in my stomach and I wondered when I would eat again. I knew from my many trips on different planets that no matter how rugged the outback, food and water were always available. The ponds in the compound indicated springs of water. With dry lips I returned to the rock cave, and slowly drained the last of my water from the bottle, savoring every drop.

Scanning the rocks above with my glow light, I saw that they were bone dry, covered in dust. Sudden movement in the back of the cave caught my attention and I quietly slid over the boulders to see what it was. Lifting my arm, the lamp revealed more rock overhead. A cool breeze blew through the cave sliding over my skin. That was strange.

I looked at the hillside outside the cave as dawn was in full bloom. Zartex's blue sun was making its warm presence known. Quickly I scanned the slope hoping to see something, but there was nothing but dry stone everywhere. In the distance was a mountain and I wondered if there was water on the other side.

Dejected I sat down and cried out. "Almighty Father why have you brought me here?"

Sitting down quietly, I hoped His thoughts would come into my mind and enlighten me, but I heard nothing. The soothing breeze gently blew by me again as if it were calling me.

Curious, I walked into the dim cavity and couldn't believe what I heard. Was my mind playing tricks on me? Faint drops of water hitting stone echoed from within the alcove. My glow light was running low so I shut it off. I stilled my breath and strained my ears, trying to discern the direction of the dripping. Using my hands and slowly moving my feet, I realized that there was a jagged crevice in the rock and I began to slip between the two huge stones to move deeper into the cave. In the darkness, I groped with my hands and slid further between the stones pushing off with my feet. Sweat began to form on my brow as I continued to push farther into the cave.

Unexpectedly, I slipped into a smooth fissure and couldn't move. Panic gripped me! I twisted and turned, but the rock wouldn't release its grip. I couldn't go any further. How could this have happened? Claustrophobia engulfed me. The last time this happened, Zelestar was with me. She guided me through a tight spot in an underground tunnel. This time I was alone. Frozen.

Sweating profusely, I had to fight to overcome my fears. "Almighty, please help me," I prayed desperately. I had to get free.

I didn't feel anything and decided that if He was real, I had to trust Him and move forward believing that He would help me. With that stubborn thought, I inched forward and the claustrophobic fear dissipated. Encouraged, I continued sliding between the rocks and knew I was getting closer.

Plink! Plink! Splish! I could hear water! I was getting closer and closer.

But then the fissure dead-ended. The resonance of dripping water intensified, but my way was blocked. What was happening? My tongue stuck to the roof of my mouth as I emptied the last of my water bottle. I could smell the liquid, but all around me was rock. How could the Almighty have taken me this far through this winding slender crevice only to lead me to a dead end? Yet the sound of water was closer. I became angry and dropped to the cave floor.

Something didn't add up. Water was near, but I couldn't get to it. A cool breeze descended from above and I snapped the glow light on and looked up! Directly above me was a shaft that looked like the barrel of a laser cannon. I pondered how I would climb up when a sudden calmness descended upon me. I could feel a warm presence around my head and knew the Almighty was right there with me. Standing, I lifted my head, closed my eyes and took a deep breath. The water was so close I could taste it.

Another breeze came down from above and refreshed me with its coolness. It was as if the Almighty was calling me up to Him, telling me to follow His leading. I put the glow light between my teeth so I could see where to place my feet. Lifting my right foot, I jammed the toe of my boot into a small crack. As I raised my other foot, I pushed against the rock chimney with my back and inched my way off the ground.

Using my hands as guides I placed my palms above me and pulled up. Slowly I ascended, working my way up.

Figure 13-2: Vying Searching for Water

Mark Rubne '8

Light sweat slid down my face and dampened my shirt. My back began to throb from the pressure of pushing against the smooth rock wall. I had no clue how far I had climbed, but I knew I had to keep going. Suddenly my foot slipped and I lost my grip slipping down the shaft and scraping my hands and feet. I gritted my teeth as I stopped my fall pushing harder against the wall.

My glow light fell out of my mouth and tumbled down into the abyss below. I watched it drop and realized I had climbed to such a height that if I fallen to the bottom, I would have been seriously hurt or dead.

An evil presence entered the shaft. I could feel its cold loneliness all around me, telling me that I wouldn't make it, telling me that I was fool and I going to die.

Plink, plink, plink, came the sound of the water from above. With newfound strength, I pressed against the shaft and pushed upward. The sound of dripping water got louder and louder. I climbed up further. Reaching up with my right hand, I grabbed a ledge. Using all the strength left to me, I pulled my body up and over a ledge and found myself in a subterranean cavern.

"Thank you, Lord," I said as I sat there out of breath. The room was dimly lit by phosphorescent stalactites and in the center was a pool of water. I got up, rushed over, and skidded to a halt. I wasn't alone!

Chapter Fourteen

The acrid smell of sulfur slammed my nostrils. Yellow bile erupted like an organic volcano from my stomach rushing toward my mouth. The stench was overpowering in this closed off area. My stomach evacuated everything I had eaten.

Recovering, I looked to the far end of the pool of water and saw three sets of violet eyes charging toward me in a single file. Sharp white teeth gleamed in the dim light. I searched the cave, but there was nothing on the cavern floor that I could use as a weapon.

They were four leeds away and moving quickly. The first one suddenly launched into the air claws fully extended. The second one was right behind the first and attacked low. Using an over-under lateral drop, I slammed the first beast into the wall. I pivoted, throwing a blind round sidekick that found its mark in the nose of the second beast.

The third beast raked my exposed side with its claws. I countered with a powerful elbow striking him squarely in the chest. Stunned, I followed with a pulverizing push kick to his belly toppling him. Rolling to its feet, the creature wobbled away from me.

Even though staggering like wine bibbers from Milo, the beasts couldn't be taken lightly. On a planet with very little food, I knew I was fresh meat.

Repulsed in their first attempt, the hairy creatures regrouped, but this time moved cautiously, as a unit. They were keenly intelligent with the instinctive ability to communicate and attack as one.

I faked going right and they tracked me, but remained in formation.

I considered jumping over them and into the pool, but didn't know how deep it was. It might even be to their advantage if I did so. I needed to stay mobile and on my feet.

Looking toward heaven in dire need, I prayed. Halfway through my prayer, I spotted colorful stalactites hanging from the ceiling, but out of my reach.

Picking up some rocks, I threw them with all my might, but the mineral formations held firm.

I spied a larger rock, but it was right behind the middle beast. To get to it, I would have to attack which would play right into their formation. By the time I would hit the first beast to get the rock, the other two would be attacking my sides.

Leaping into the air, I tucked myself into a ball and landed feet first on the middle beast's head, sending it to the rock floor. The creature let out a shrieking howl as it staggered off into the shadows. I grabbed the rock and with careful aim I hurled it at the closest stalactite's base. Down it came. I snatched it in midair before it smashed itself against the floor.

The other two beasts turned around and attacked. I drove the stalactite into the neck of the first one. Swiftly I withdrew it and impaled the mineral deposit into the skull of the other. Immediately it fell to the ground. Both lay motionless.

Utterly exhausted, I went to the pool to get a drink of water. The water tasted stale, but then I remembered my prison cell and how I'd eaten the poisoned meat and prayed to the Almighty to protect me.

In quick gulps, I drank the cool water with cupped hands. Suddenly, I was slammed head first into the water. The beast I'd knocked to the ground was back with a vengeance and bit my leg. I dove into the water. The pool was deeper than expected and I swam to the bottom twisting and turning, but the beast still had a firm grip on my leg. I knew I could hold my breath for a long time and felt for the jagged side of the rock cavern. I turned and repeatedly smashed the animal into the rocks. Finally he'd had enough and swam off into an underwater tunnel.

Gasping for air, I shot to the surface and pulled myself from the water. I looked for the other two creatures, but they were gone. Bloody streaks marked the direction they had been dragged. I filled my water bottle and looked for a way out. The stalactite I'd used as a weapon was nowhere to be seen. I drank as much water as I could and quickly climbed the rock wall. I felt the cool fresh air on my skin and looked up to see a small speck of light at the top. When I reached the surface I lay on the ground for a long time out of breath, bloody, tired and hungry. I relaxed in the cool of the morning and dozed off.

Some hours later cascading rocks from the next mound awakened me and I saw Nafuka walking toward me. He looked tired, as if he'd been up all night.

"Hey, Vying. Can you spare any water?"

"Sure," I said tossing him my bottle.

"You fool! Do you know how precious this is around here?"

"Sure," I said.

"Wait a minute. You've got a full bottle."

Nafuka laughed, unscrewed the cap and took a long drink. "You found a spring, didn't you? And by the looks of your wounds, you must have fought some tuskers to get to it."

"I don't think they were tuskers. These creatures wobbled around and had the foulest odor I'd ever inhaled. They're mean little beasties."

"You ran into some sniffers."

"Sniffers? They did more than sniff."

"I'll say. They fight in packs. Most people either retreat from their spring or die trying to get water. It looks like you were lucky. How many were there?"

"I fought three, but I think there were more."

"You think?" Nafuka laughed again, that deep hearty laugh that I now welcomed. "Usually they guard their pools in packs of ten or more. People don't survive, unless they have some sort of weapon. Did you find an intact stalactite?"

"How did you know that?"

"I've been in the caves before. Did you keep it?"

"No, I lost it."

"Too bad. They make good weapons. Listen you've survived your first night out here, but I'm headed to a mountain training camp. I know you're not keen about forming an alliance, but I'm sure you heard the screaming last night."

"Yeah, I suppose somebody bought it."

"That's right and it could've been you."

"True enough. Alright Nafuka, I'll form an alliance, but only to get to the mountain camp. It's not you. I just needed to be alone for a while."

"I understand. You need your space, but it will be a lot easier if we guard each other's backs. There's plenty of danger out here."

"You realize that we may have to fight each other to get off this planet. Don't think that I will cut you any slack in the battle ring. I want off this planet and if it's by fighting, I'll do it, but I won't let a friendship get in my way. I never was buddy-buddy with my opponents."

"Look at it this way, Vying. If we train against each other, we'll have the best chance of one of us winning and leaving this place."

"Nafuka, how could you have gone through all this hardship, win the right to leave and then end up back here? Didn't you learn anything?" This question had been in the back of my mind since he told me he'd won his freedom from Zartex once before.

"Wine, women, and dumb luck can put a good man down. Let's get going. We've got to get out of this area before nightfall. I didn't get much sleep last night and tonight the tuskers will be going out further and further. They picked off an easy one last night."

I followed Nafuka's lead as we headed towards the mountains, but deep inside I still didn't trust him. He seemed tough enough. Why would he need this alliance?

Chapter Fifteen

Nafuka and I journeyed for several hours making steady progress towards the foothills despite the relentless beating of the blazing afternoon sun. We put bandanas over our mouths to filter the dirt impregnated air, but our throats were chalky, robbed of moisture by the dusty winds. By the time we began our ascent, our water containers were near empty. Gradually, I could feel the temperature begin to drop ever so slightly. In the distance a lone tree stood, a defiant survivor on this harsh planet. We made our way up to it and sat under its shade. With our last drops of precious water we washed the dust from our throats and cemented our resolve to make it to the top.

"Why does the Warder hold this tournament?"

"He gets what he wants from the nobles. The winner of the Crucible is allowed off the planet to make 'The Run' for the highest bidding nobleman. If he succeeds the Warder is well compensated."

"What does the Warder get?"

"He gets a share of the forbidden fruit. Since I've seen him last he's really gotten strange. He seemed very nervous and kept looking around the room."

"Strange is putting it mildly. I think he's way over the edge. So what does the winner of the tournament have to do?"

"To completely regain your freedom you must complete the Crucible here on Zartex and win the battle ring tournament. The winner goes to the highest bidder. The noblemen also bet on the tournament bouts. You'll see them as we begin the early matches. They check out all the fighters. Sometimes, the tournament winner isn't chosen by the nobleman who makes the highest bid. You can't just be good in the battle ring, you've got to be in great shape."

"What's 'The Run' all about?"

"Once the winner is acquired from the Warder, the prisoner becomes slave to the nobleman and goes to Coralia and makes 'The Run.' If he comes back with the fruit and he's a free man."

"Where do you make the run to?"

"There is a river on Coralia that surrounds the floating city. At night, you can look across the river to the mainland. Trees on the mainland grow multi-colored fruit. On a moonless night, the colorful fruit can be seen. The fruit's lure is so seductive people cross the river to get them."

"Sounds simple enough."

"It may sound simple, but it's not. To begin with you have to cross the river undetected. Then, you must stealthily climb a steep cliff. Finally, you make the run into the Beast's cave to retrieve the mature fruit."

"The Beast? What's that?"

"A deadly creature that guards the fruit in his cave."

"Why don't you pick the fruit off the trees and return?"

"They're not ripe or ready. The Beast carefully guards each of the trees and harvests the fruit only when tbey're ready. He stores the ripened fruit in his cave."

"What's so great about the fruit?" I asked.

"I've heard when you make the run and taste the fruit, it sends you into the greatest state of happiness a man can imagine," he said reverently.

"Sounds like a drug to me."

"Oh it is! The best drug known to man."

"Have you tasted of this fruit?"

Catching himself Nafuka stammered. "No, no, what are you talking about?"

From the fierce, faraway hunger in his eyes I knew he'd tasted the forbidden fruit. I looked at him, but didn't say a word.

"Why are you staring at me?"

"You're lying. You've eaten the fruit."

Nafuka looked at me for a moment sizing me up and then shook his head. His face became quite serious. "We need to get moving. We can't stay out here in the open especially under this tree. The sniffers or tuskers will come this way."

A high flying black carnivore with a long, teeth lined beak and an incredible wingspan, floated by buffeted by the mountain updrafts, eyeing us as if we were his next meal. I shuddered as the large bird flew lower, wondering what lay ahead.

"Then go on without me, I'm not moving."

"What? Are you crazy? Didn't you see that bird? Don't you realize that he's just waiting for us to die?"

"I need to know. Did you eat some of the fruit?"

The big ebony man quickly turned his head away from me.

"If we're to form an alliance, we have to trust one another. Someday, I may need you and I've got to know that you've got my back. Relationships without trust are easily broken."

A darkened scowl clouded his ebony face. I could see that he'd never been in this situation before. He'd always been in control and now he had to relinquish it. If we were to continue as a team, he had to trust me. I watched him wrestle with this test.

Finally he spoke. "Alright, alright. I've tasted the fruit. It's addictive. It's destructive. It's why I'm back here. I want to win the Crucible to get back to Coralia and make the run again."

"What? I thought you said you have to turn in the fruit to the nobleman. How did you manage to make the run and keep some of it for yourself?"

"Normally, you take as much as you can carry, but before I crossed the river with the fruit, I stashed some on the river bank."

"And what about the Beast? Did you encounter him?"

"Yes. I encountered him. But I listened to the stories and learned something. I took with me a long spear dipped in poison. I climbed the embankment and hid deep in the jungle for several days, away from the forbidden fruit. I ate what I could scrounge and slept in the leaves so that I'd smell like the jungle. After the week was up, I hid out near his cave and observed him for several days."

"You waited him out."

"Yeah, pretty clever huh? Most of the runners want to rush into the cave, grab the fruit and cross back over the river. But that's not smart."

"So you switched tactics. You became the hunter."

"Exactly," Nafuka said smiling with pride.

"Very clever, how did you attack the beast?"

"After a few days, giving the Beast no inkling of my presence in the jungle and allowing the animals to grow acquainted with me, I rushed the Beast and drove my poisoned spear deep into his heart when he came out of his cave in the mid-afternoon.

"The expression on the Beast's face was priceless. He couldn't believe what had happened. The poison quickly debilitated him and I made two runs into the cave, gathering all the forbidden fruit I could carry to the edge of the cliffs. I climbed down the hillside and buried the first load on the riverbank. I brought the second load to my boat. I quickly paddled across the river and gave the nobleman the load of fruit. "

"What happened to the other load?"

"The next night, without anyone knowing, I crossed the river again and retrieved the second load."

"What about the Beast? Did he die?"

"No, but his howls were so great the next night that everyone was afraid to leave their homes. It was perfect for me. The people in the floating village were very afraid and thought he would cross the river to destroy them. After I told my story in one of the hovels, a local overheard me and made the run that night. He crossed the river, climbed the bank, but never returned."

"What does the Beast look like?"

"His skin is shiny and smooth. He runs on four legs, but can stand on two. He has a long tail and his red tongue flickers from his mouth grabbing his prey. He has sharp teeth and his body is strong and muscular."

"I know someone more powerful than the Beast and more fulfilling than the forbidden fruit."

Nafuka's gave me his full attention. "Who?"

"The Almighty."

"Save that talk for someone else. Now let's get going before it gets dark. The training ground is up in the mountains. You'll like it there," Nafuka said as he began the climb.

The trail was steeper as we journeyed up the mountainside. The sun was closing the gap on the horizon and I didn't think we'd make it up the hill before dark. Nafuka was relentless in his climb looking above as if expecting something. He got well ahead of me.

Suddenly he called out. "Vying! Boulders... Look out!"

I looked up and saw giant rocks bouncing off the hillside coming toward us! I was completely exposed with nowhere to hide! The careening rocks were gathering momentum and would soon be upon me. Vainly, I looked all around. The thundering rockslide was headed straight for me. I chanced a quick glance upward, but Nafuka had disappeared!

Figure 15: A Rockslide

Chapter Sixteen

A huge boulder was barreling straight for me. "Almighty, shield me!" I frantically prayed tightly pressing myself against the mountainside. There was nothing I could do, nowhere to hide. Rapidly the boulder closed without course deviation. Images of Zelestar, Tor and Tia, Wolks, Sera, and Dax, quickly flooded my mind. I would never see any of them again. I'd failed. Helplessly I looked up as the rock took one more bounce and headed straight for me.

Suddenly a powerful hand reached out from above and pulled me up and into darkness as the rock pulverized the stone ledge where I'd been standing. *The hand of the Almighty*, I thought to myself, but then through a cloud of dust, I saw a grin on Nafuka's face as the deafening roar of rocks cascaded by.

Grey soot washed the alcove and covered us from head to toe. I smiled as I looked at Nafuka. He'd changed from a black to gray. He laughed deeply.

"The Che-Wa's like to test their candidates. Those that come to the mountains must survive the rockslide. They check their ability to move under pressure and if it weren't for me, you'd be dead."

"Live or die, my trust is in the Almighty. But thanks for saving me. Why did you do it? You were supposed to kill me."

"What are you talking about? I asked to form an alliance with you. Why would I want to kill you?"

"Don't kid me. My guard's been up the moment I stepped on that shuttle. Something told me not to take my eyes off you. That's why I wouldn't form an alliance with you. Whatever you're about, I don't want any part of it."

Nafuka looked at me long and hard and I knew the truth would finally come.

"You're right. I've been assigned to assassinate you at just the right moment here on Zartex. You're never to leave here. I've had a couple of opportunities, but for some reason I couldn't do it. I engineered this rock slide with the Che-Wa's, but at the last moment, I couldn't let you die. I don't know why, but there's something about you. For all the bad

I've done in my life, I couldn't add your death to that list."

"So who hired you?"

Nafuka again looked at me long and hard. "I was recruited by Megog."

"What!" I exclaimed. "I thought he was dead."

"Oh, he's very much alive and very active on Micron."

"What about Og?"

"I saw the emperor too. He's in charge. I met Megog at the floating fishing village on Coralia where I was selling the rest of the forbidden fruit."

I stood there stunned. My spirit had been restless for quite some time and now I knew why. Og and Megog were still alive and their relentless pursuit for control of the Blue Ring Galaxy hadn't diminished. Now it all made sense. Somehow they'd killed Cappy and blamed his death on me.

"Where's Og's base of operation?"

"Somewhere on Micron. They drugged me and then I was brought to him. I suppose my life will be worthless now that I've allowed you to live."

"Not at all. Your life may have just started. The Almighty's Son can change anything, if you truly want him to."

"Do I have a choice?"

"Sure. You can die and go to the Lake of Fire for all eternity or you can choose life and follow Him."

"But I've done so many terrible things. I've killed people, during the war and after. Why would He want a man like me?"

"The Almighty created you. He knows you better than yourself and He loves you. He is a God of forgiveness, if you truly repent."

Nafuka hesitated, not ready for this life changing decision. "We'd better get going. We still have a long climb to the top and night will be here soon. I don't want to be out here any longer than I must. Besides there's safety and comfort when we get to the training camp."

"Nafuka, you can run from the Almighty, but you can't hide! He's everywhere."

"Look, you don't understand. I'm way past forgiveness from anyone. I killed a man to have his wife. We can talk about this later."

"You don't know what's going to happen here on Zartex. Now is the defining moment in your life. Choose the Almighty and your life will have great meaning."

"My life has been nothing but death and destruction. I've never liked myself even when things were going good. I've had my fill of wine and women, and come up empty. I've met some great ladies. I don't know what it is. They're attracted to me, but I always want something better. That's what gets me into trouble and in the end, I've got nothing. Can the Almighty fill my emptiness?"

"He filled my emptiness. He will yours too."

"Can He take away the lust for the forbidden fruit. My mind and body craves another taste. Every waking thought is to get back to Coralia, to the fruit. It's destroying me. If it wasn't so hard to get, I'd be eating it right now."

"The Almighty can remove that taste from you, if you ask Him."

"Then where is He? I want to ask Him."

"You've already taken the first step. You've acknowledged that you are lost without Him. Now you've got to ask Him into your life and promise to serve Him all the days of your life."

"Vying, you don't understand. I'm going to fail if I make that promise."

"Nafuka, that's the best part of the Almighty. He knows that you'll fail. I've failed Him many, many times and yet He still loves me and stays with me all the days of my life. Without His Son, I wouldn't be standing here right now and yet I've done bad things too."

"I don't believe that. Not the great Vying. You defeated Megog in the battle ring on Mercus."

"Here's a news flash, I didn't defeat Megog. The Almighty did. I know the Almighty gave me His power to defeat Megog and now I must enter the battle ring again to win a championship so I can get off this wasteland of a planet. I've got to go back to Micron and fight my enemies, Og and Megog. That's the last thing I want, but I've got to follow the Almighty's lead for my life and rely on Him to help me."

The big man stood there and shook his head. "I've got to tell you something. I've always respected you. There's something inside you that I can't defeat."

"What? What are you talking about?"

"Vying, there's something strong in you. Something I didn't want to challenge and now I want that."

"It's the presence of the Almighty's Son, Jesus. Do you want Him to be Lord of your life?"

"Yes, I do."

"Then let's pray," I said as I led Nafuka in prayer to receive the Almighty's Son as his Lord and Savior."

"Thanks, Vying. I want to form an alliance with you."

I looked at Nafuka in wonderment and then I understood.

"Since the time Og gave me the assignment to kill you, I've had this thought in my mind to form an alliance with you instead. I know it doesn't make any sense."

"You're right, it doesn't, but the Almighty's ways are foolishness to the wise. Alright, I'll form the alliance with you."

Nafuka smiled and I could see joy rising up within him and a twinkle in his eye.

We continued up the mountainside as the sun set. A full moon arose and brightened the sky. It provided more than enough light for us to make it to the top of the mountain. Reaching the summit, we sat down. The cold mountain air whistled through the tall trees and cooled us. I looked at the evergreens and couldn't believe there was something living on the planet. We gathered enough bark and sticks to build a blazing fire. The heat soaked through our clothes warming us. Each of us gathered leaves and made beds to lie in. From across the fire Nafuka said, "Sleep well, my friend. Tomorrow we train for the ring."

I looked at him and wondered how the Almighty had brought us together. How could we get off this planet? Only one man could leave the planet to make the run earning his freedom. I needed to win the Crucible now more than ever. Looking back at the death of Cappy and my trial, I realized what had happened on Micron. The Micronites were oblivious to the great danger, rising up amongst them. I had to get back to oppose Og and Megog, before it was too late! But would I have to defeat Nafuka here on Zartex to do that?

Exhaustion overtook me as I wrestled with those thoughts. My eyelids became heavy and closed.

I had just drifted off to sleep, when something pointed, poked me in the side. Instantly I came awake. The fire was out, but I could see Nafuka. Spears were poised all around us, ready to be thrust into our bodies if we moved a muscle. All I could see were the whites of their eyes framed by their dark hoods.

Chapter Seventeen

Figure 17-1: Che-Wa Warriors

Cold sharp steel bit my skin again. I didn't move. "Nafuka, I thought you said the Che-Wa's were friendly. Didn't they train you?"

"I thought they were too. I don't know why they've attacked. I've never done anything to them."

Suddenly the circle of spears opened and a Che-Wa warrior prominently stepped forward.

"Na sa jo ma nafeely, hama lo jee, Nafuka. So jo suso drata un sna fuu dith jo?"

"Sa, fo esrock ton, Darcel. Na ham raven grinb yna mrah jee jo roe s Che-Wa," Nafuka answered in Che-Wa without missing a beat.

I should've known he would be able to speak their language, but I was quite surprised at how well he spoke it. Just then the Che-Wa that held his spear to my side reached into his cloak, took out a round object with a metal clip and threw it to me.

"Put the ear piece in your right ear and attach the clip to the left side of your mouth with the larger end facing out," Nafuka said to me while continuing to stare at the Che-Wa in front of him.

"Why?" I asked.

"If you want to communicate with the Che-Wa, you'll need it to speak and understand their language."

Again the spear poked my side. I inserted the round object into my ear and clipped on the mouthpiece.

"Can you understand me, Vying?" Nafuka asked.

"Of course I can. You're speaking my language."

"Guess again. You're understanding me, but I'm speaking Che-Wa. The earpiece translates the Che-Wa language into our language and the mouthpiece takes your words as you speak them and translates them into Che-Wa. Now just relax and let me handle this. I know these people and they'll listen to me."

"Reeeally..." a voice said as another Che-Wa slowly strolled up to Nafuka and threw back their hooded cloak. Long fiery auburn tresses cascaded down an olive face with large, round dark eyes. With lightning speed her hand lashed out and slapped Nafuka across the face.

I rolled my eyes. We were definitely in trouble again.

"It's good to see you too, Darcel," Nafuka said laughing deeply. He didn't seem the least bit upset that he had just been struck.

"That's for leaving me on this dump of a planet. You said you'd come back for me as soon as you finished the run. The Warder even wondered why you never returned. He gave you special permission to do so."

"But I have returned! Here I am."

"Yes, a couple of years late. I've heard of your exploits. Word travels even to this hellhole."

"I had every intention of returning and here I am."

"The Warder informed me that you were coming from the prison manifest. He was most surprised you didn't return as a free man. You forgot about me."

"Darcel, how could you say that? I have returned. I said I would and I have," Nafuka announced as he got to his feet.

She slapped him again, but then floated into his arms and kissed him long and deep. She pulled back again, anger returning to her face.

Figure 17-2: Nafuka and Darcel Mark Rudge 12/24/08

"You worthless dog of a man. Let his friend stand," Darcel said to the hooded men.

The spears were pulled back and I arose.

"Give him the package from Zelestar," Darcel said. One of the Che-Wa's handed me something bound in animal skins.

"Zelestar?" I said astonished.

"She said to open it when you're alone. Oh, she also said to say hello. She misses her walks with you."

"How do you know her?" I asked taking the package.

"Queen Zelestar and I have fought many battles together. She just left here."

"What? Zelestar here - on Zartex? When?"

"She waited for you, but this clod of a rock took his time bringing you up the mountainside. She said you would need the package to fight the Beast on Coralia."

"I wish I could have seen her."

"You know Queen Zelestar has many duties and responsibilities," Darcel said. She quickly turned to Nafuka. "What's wrong with you? What took you so long?"

"I couldn't find him. I lost track of him once we left the prison compound and entered the wasteland. I looked for him, but he'd gone underground."

Darcel turned toward me. Through the dim light, I could see her high cheek bones accenting delicate black eyebrows, making her quite beautiful. I did a double-take.

"What's going on here? Who are you?" I demanded.

Darcel laughed. "I wondered what you would say when you saw me."

If I hadn't seen her auburn hair, I would have thought I was looking at Zelestar.

"I wonder what she sees in you, Vying. You're such a puny man."

"Don't let Vying fool you, Darcel," Nafuka said, defending me. "He defeated Megog in the battle ring for the Crown Championship."

"Nafuka, darling. You are such a baffoon? I know about Vying. Zelestar told me all about the championship fight and how she is forever grateful to him for saving her from Megog. She has also instructed me to train you well. He is desperately needed back on Micron before it's too late."

"Will she be back?" I asked.

"I don't know. I can't keep track of my sister."

"What? I thought she was an only child."

"Did she tell you that?"

"Yes."

"She's always protecting me."

"What do you mean?"

"You know how Zelestar operates. She doesn't want anyone to know of me or they might use me against her."

"No, that's not it," Nafuka said and then laughed deeply.

Fire exploded from Darcel's eyes. She turned and glared at him. His attitude immediately sobered.

"Let's go, time is precious."

"And so are you, Darcel," Nafuka said warmly. He walked beside Darcel as I followed behind.

"I want you to know that I'm a changed man," Nafuka said.

"Oh please. You return as a convict and you claim you've changed. Yeah right."

"No really, Darcel. I've accepted the Almighty's Son as my Savior."

Immediately Darcel stopped in her tracks. "Don't play with me. It's enough that I have to listen to my sister, now you," she said with a hardened gaze upon her face.

"No really, I'm not kidding. Ask Vying."

Sensing hostility, all the Che-Wa halted and trained their spears on us. She turned and looked at me with piercing eyes. "Vying, is it true?"

"Yes, Nafuka is a believer."

"Now, I can die and go to heaven. I've heard everything there is under the sun," she said turning around and marching off.

I looked at Nafuka. He was smiling from ear to ear and began to laugh uncontrollably.

Darcel whirled around. In one motion, she grabbed a spear from a Che-Was and hurled it at him. The blade struck between his feet with such force that the shaft quivered side-to-side right beside his face. His laughter immediately ceased. He pulled the spear from the ground.

"Don't be stupid," she said walking off.

We continued our climb up a mountain trail. The sky was getting lighter and we made a speedy ascent up the mountainside. We journeyed onto a dry rocky plateau and I began to wonder where the training camp might be. Surely we wouldn't be training out here in the open.

Approaching a wall of rock, the Che-Wa walked beside it for a long time. Finally they stopped and looked around in all directions. Darcel pulled out a cloaking device and de-energized the hologram protecting the entrance to the camp. Single-file we walked through a narrow crevice in the rock as Darcel waited for all of us to pass. I watched as she looked all around and stepped through.

"What were you looking for?" I asked.

"Did you encounter any of the sniffers?"

"Yes, I found some water and was attacked by three of them. I killed two and the other got away."

"I thought I sensed their pursuit. That's why we sent the boulders over the side. The sniffers were following, but I think they were slowed and are now approaching our training ground cautiously."

"I'm sorry, but it was them or me."

"I understand, but we'll have to fight them again. They have your scent and won't stop until they have vindicated their loss. You said you killed two of them?"

"That's right."

"If it was just one, we wouldn't have much to worry about, but now the entire pack will be after us. We must be ready. Wait till I see Zelestar again!" she said angrily.

Chapter Eighteen

We walked through narrow rock canyons, switchbacks, steep inclines and declines, finally coming to a lush valley covered with majestic towering trees surrounding a lake glistening in the sunlight. We descended to the floor of the valley and were greeted by many Che-Wa wearing long hooded cloaks. In the light I could barely see the features that distinguished the men from the women. One unhooded little Che-Wa with long blonde hair raced across the lush green meadow to greet the returning warriors. We continued walking through the sunlight until we were under the canopy of trees. Immediately The Che-Wa squad broke up and slipped into their homes. The entrances were hard to spot hidden in the lush foliage and no dwelling had any visible definition.

I stood there wondering what would happen next. Nafuka walked over to me.

"This is the best part of the training."

"What do you mean?"

"You'll see."

Darcel came up to us accompanied by another hooded Che-Wa. "This is Peen, she will be your trainer as long as you remain with us. You are to obey her in all tribal protocols. At night she will partner with you to keep you warm."

"Wait a minute. I don't need a trainer and there's only one woman for me."

"Vying, don't be so hasty. The Che-Wa women are known for their beauty and warm hearts. You shouldn't turn down their hospitality. It will be considered hostile," Nafuka quickly interjected.

"I should take advice from the king of hostilities?"

"He's right. Very few from the outside ever get here, let alone live here. You must not turn down our most generous offer, but I think I understand. Follow Peen anyway. She will show you where you will live while you are with us," Darcel added.

"She can show me where I will sleep, but I won't be living with her."

127

"Vying, you're a bright man. You must understand why I have to assign someone to you," Darcel said looking intently at me.

"You don't trust me," I replied.

"Can you blame me? I know the sniffers are going to attack. They will find a way through the mountains even if they have to climb all the way up there to get to you," Darcel said pointing to the top of the snow capped mountains overlooking the valley.

"Just go with it, Vying. It'll be the experience of a lifetime," Nafuka added.

"I'm sure it could be, but my heart is already committed."

"Speaking of Zelestar, she said for you to study hard. You will need the spiritual knowledge for your fight against the evil spirits on Coralia and Micron. Now go with Peen," Darcel ordered.

Peen was already walking away and I was tired, so I turned and followed her. I walked behind her for a long way through a path in the abundant foliage beneath the humid canopy of the hidden mountain jungle. Snow capped spires overshadowed lush vegetation on an otherwise desolate planet. I wondered how I'd missed seeing this when I arrived on the prison shuttle.

"How much farther?" I asked.

Peen never broke stride and I knew my refusal offended her. Finally she stopped and pulled back some huge green leaves and we both stepped up into a round stone structure. The floors were up off the ground and there was a fire smoldering with an iron pot hanging over the flames. Off to the left was another room separated by a bamboo screen.

Figure 18: Peen

"If you're tired and don't want my company, go in there and sleep." Turning her back to me, she took off her long flowing cloak and hung it on a hook and turned around.

Nafuka was right! Honey blond tresses framed Peen's slanted jet-black eyebrows. High cheekbones set off crystal blue eyes and I couldn't help but notice the muscle tone in her arms and legs. She was an extraordinary woman.

"If you change your mind or you get cold, let me know."

"Peen, I mean you no disrespect. It's just that my heart's been broken once before. I---."

"I was there with Darcel, in case you missed that."

"I'm sorry, Peen. I have one request."

"I am here to serve your every desire."

I was stunned by her answer. "Could you please let me have some time alone here in your home?"

"What? First you reject me. Then you throw me out of my own home. I don't know who you think you are!" she said grabbing her cloak and marching toward the door. Turning her shoulder, she looked back. "Don't take too long. Your training will start soon. I'll be back later, if that's okay with you?"

Peen slammed the door in my face. I dropped to my knees. "Almighty Father, I need all the help I can get here on Zartex. Help me to get off this planet and return to Micron. I ask you in the name of Your Son, Lord Jesus, to help me with the battles ahead."

I laid down on the floor with my head down and began to focus on the Almighty. I didn't feel anything at first, but I knew that I wanted to be in His holy presence and to do that I focused on His throne and the One who sat on it. I got down on my knees and began to pray for my parents, Tor and Tia, for Zelestar, for Dax, and for Wolks and Sera, for Nafuka and Micron. For a long time I prayed kneeling, bent over with my head touching the wooden deck.

Getting up I stretched my hands toward the heaven and began praising the Almighty Father, His Son, and the Holy Spirit. I kept disciplining my mind as it would drift off and I would begin thinking of other things. Thoughts of Zelestar entered my mind, but I refocused on the Almighty. I got back down on my knees and turned my palms to heaven and waited. I don't know how long I waited, but I began to soak in His presence. I felt a warm sensation, like oil flowing from my head and going down my body. I knew He was here with me and I didn't move a muscle. Thoughts came into my mind about Micron and how I would have to fight a great spiritual battle. I stayed in that position for as long as I felt His presence, not understanding everything, but not wanting His presence to leave. I wondered what I should do next and then saw the package that Zelestar had left for me.

I ripped open the box and pulled out a circular device. I wondered what it was. As I ran my hand along the edge, a cylinder of light appeared and in the midst a hologram of Dax popped up. I was astounded and disappointed. I was hoping it would be an image of Zelestar.

"Vying, Zelestar and I have worked on transferring the Almighty's Book into something you can use. You must get off Zartex immediately and return to Micron. There are so many bad things happening here. Wolks and Sera are now in jail. They tried to recruit the old knights and lead a rebellion, but someone betrayed them. A heavy darkness is enveloping Micron. We need you to lead us. You're not going to believe this, but there have been some sightings of Hoons near the capital city. I've gone out into the outback with a photo imager to confirm that rumor, but I haven't seen any. Something is very wrong here. We desperately need you!"

The image of a shaken Dax faded out replaced by the lovely Zelestar. She was more beautiful than I had remembered, but lines of concern etched her face.

"I've put the Almighty's Book in audio and visual form, so you can listen and read it anytime you want. Vying, my dear friend, please study it. The Beast on Coralia is getting more and more powerful. You will need this knowledge to defeat him and return to Micron."

Brushing my hand against the screen, I froze the hologram. I gazed at Zelestar's image for a long time. It was the third time I'd seen her since the final battle on Mercus. Her flowing black hair, exquisite brown eyes, and shapely figure made her every bit as beautiful as I remembered. Her soft voice melted the core of my inner being. I couldn't believe that I'd missed seeing her here. I'd have to thank Nafuka for that later.

After gazing at her for a long time, reluctantly I moved my hand over the screen again and she began speaking again.

"I'm sorry to tell you this, but Tor and Tia have been captured. People who are in disagreement with the Council of Peers disappear at night. No one seems to know anything about it. The Almighty has his hand on your life or you wouldn't have survived the jail poisoning on Micron."

I stopped the hologram. How could she have known that, unless she was that old hag that swept the floor near my cell?

"The Blue Ring Galaxy is in great danger. I believe Og and Megog are alive and controlling the Council. You must get back and help me fight this evil!"

I stopped the hologram again and thought for a moment. Micron was in danger and the people I loved, my family, were in jail. I had to get off this planet in a hurry. I heard a knock on the door.

"Please come in, Peen," I said, but Nafuka entered in her place.

"So where is she?"

"I guess on Micron."

"No, fool. I'm talking about Peen. I know she's here somewhere."

"I sent her away, so I could view this hologram."

"You what? Darcel is going to be furious. Look, I was thinking, let's not be in a hurry to train. I might want to stay here for a while."

"Nafuka, I must get off this planet. Micron is in big trouble!"

"And why should that concern you? Didn't they try you at the Seat of Judgment and find you guilty of murder? And you want to do what?"

"Things have gotten much worse. They've captured my parents and some of the older warriors, those whom I fought with. I've got to get back there as soon as possible."

"A man who couldn't get used to these surroundings."

"Nafuka, you've had your chance at freedom and blew it. Whether they falsely charged me or not, I must return. Someone must lead the resistance against the evil."

There was a gentle knock at the door.

"Come in," I called out.

Peen walked in.

Nafuka laughed deeply. "I knew she'd be lovely. I'd better leave and let you get acquainted. Darcel awaits me, but tomorrow morning we start training."

He left and I turned to Peen. "I want to start training today."

"Fine, follow me," she said taking off her cloak and running out the door. Her flowing blond hair bounced against her back. She reached back and pulled it into a ponytail and continued jogging uphill. I looked ahead and saw the steep incline and knew this would be tough, but Peen continued on without breaking stride. I wasn't ready for hills, but I pushed myself. She looked back from time to time and I thought there was a smile on her face as she saw me struggle.

I wanted to throw up, but I hadn't eaten anything since leaving the compound. The pain was intense and my lungs and legs wanted to stop, but I refused. We continued up the hill as sweat blinded my eyes. I wondered if she would run until I dropped. Mercifully the trail came to an end and there she was waiting.

"That was a nice little run," I said.

"Really," she said smiling with a knowing look. "It's a start and you're right, it was a little run. You're going to need to be in better shape if you want to beat Nafuka and win the all-around championship."

"Don't worry, I can train my body. Are you ready to go back down?"

"Vying, don't move," Peen whispered very firmly.

Chapter Nineteen

Figure 19: Vying Battling a Tusker

I sensed something behind me. Peen's eyes opened wide. Using my body as a shield, Peen slowly bent down and picked up a large rock.

"Duck!" she yelled hurling the rock straight at me. It bounced off something as I hit the ground, rolling. Without looking, I threw a hard sidekick as I got up. My foot struck the tusker's forward leg and his head hit the ground. With all my might, I drop kicked him right under the chin. With a loud crack his neck snapped. The tusker went limp.

"Tuskers! I better get back and warn Darcel," Peen cried out.

"Wait! We have to look around for others."

"We've just gotten here. This one might be a forward scout for the main attack body."

"Then backtrack our path and wipe it clean. This one discovered a crack in your defenses and we better block it off. It'll be hard to fight the tuskers if they come through the rocks to your camp."

"Vying, I need to alert Darcel. She'll be furious if I don't!"

"You're right. Go back and get Darcel and Nafuka. Tell them to bring some weapons."

"Nafuka? We don't need him. I don't think you realize how tough the Che-Wa warriors are. I was watching you. You were breathing hard when we made it up here. If you had been in better shape, you would have seen the tusker before you rested. But your body demanded rest and, if I wasn't with you, it would have cost you your life."

"Peen, you're wasting precious time. Get the other warriors and bring some weapons. I'll stand guard up here just in case any others come this way. Now go!"

Peen flew down the trail using long strides, literally bouncing off the mountain trail and gliding down the hill. I turned my attention to the tusker. I wanted to burn it, but the smoke would alert the others. I grabbed it by the legs and pulled it under the trees and away from the path. Gathering fallen branches from the trees, I covered the animal's body.

Walking toward the area where I had killed him, I looked for his spoor, but found nothing. The rocks didn't provide any clues. I searched for a path through them. That's when I saw a column of tuskers slowly hiking up the mountain trail. There must have been twenty of them making steady progress through a protective stone canyon up the mountain. The Che-Wa watchers couldn't possibly have seen them as the crevice they walked in provided cover from above.

We didn't have much time before the attack. The tuskers were moving at a steady pace and I hoped that Nafuka and Darcel would arrive soon. This was a perfect time for a sudden surprise strike. Where were they? What was taking them so long? Didn't they realize the danger?

Someone touched me lightly on the shoulder. I pivoted ready to land a hammer strike with my elbow. At the last moment, I pulled my punch as I saw Darcel ready to defend herself.

"I never heard you. Next time make a little noise. I almost punched you," I said very quietly looking at Darcel.

She shook her head. "Never before have we had tuskers up here."

"Where is Nafuka? Where are the others?" I curtly demanded as I whispered.

"Calm down. They're coming with their weapons."

"I hope they hurry up. We have a perfect window of opportunity to strike a blow to their advance. How good are your people with their spears?"

"My warriors' lives depend on their ability to fight with them."

"Darcel, how accurate are they with throwing them long distances?"

"Throw them? Are you crazy? A warrior never gives up his spear!"

"Well, let's hope your warriors can throw. If they launch them all at once, we might be able to defuse their attack before they ever get here."

"We'll roll rocks and boulders down the side to defend ourselves from their attack. We're very accurate or have you forgotten?" she asked with a confident smile on her face.

She was making me angry. "You don't get it! They're coming up a path your sentries missed. If you roll the boulders at them, they'll duck into the canyon. Remember, they know your tactics and aren't afraid of you. If you throw your precious spears you might be able to kill enough of them to make the others turn back."

"Who put you in charge? We've defended ourselves long before you showed up."

"Look Darcel, I've been in numerous battles and I know how to fight. You've got to use strategy. They know you're going to roll boulders down, so you've got to do something different. Something unexpected."

"Like throwing spears at them."

"Yes, you can pick up your precious spears after the battle. But if we don't stop them now, you'll have bigger worries. Here they come," I said as the tuskers got closer. Nafuka arrived with the Che-Wa.

"Quiet," I whispered.

Nafuka held his hand up and everyone stopped.

"If you make noise, we'll lose the element of surprise. Now line up here along the ridge and get down. Nafuka, come over here."

The Che-Wa lined up and ducked below the rock ledge so they couldn't be seen. With spears in hand, they got ready.

"Now very carefully, look and select a target. Don't blindly throw your spears. You won't hit anything. Take careful aim, and wait for my signal."

They turned and looked at Darcel. She nodded her head. They eased above the rocks, took a quick look and quickly dropped down. There was murmuring along the Che-Wa line and I could sense they didn't want to throw their precious spears.

"Quiet!" Darcel hissed. "Focus on your targets. Follow Vying's lead and we can strike a powerful blow to their column."

I waited until all eyes looked at me. "Alright, I'll count to three and then stand up and throw your weapons at the advancing tuskers."

I waited hearing them getting closer. Counting softly using my fingers, I mouthed the words. With my hand signal the Che-Wa rose up as one and hurled their spears at the approaching column.

Screams of pain echoed through the canyon as many of the weapons hit their marks. The heavy losses momentarily stalled the tusker advance.

The Che-Wa looked over the edge of the mountain and were excited. We stopped the tusker attack and now they were retreating. Leaning against a boulder, I relaxed and said a silent prayer thanking the Almighty. To my right the Che-Wa warriors were laughing and drinking water. They had placed their remaining spears against the rock wall. I walked over to one of the spears and picked it up. It was so well balanced I wanted to throw it. I walked to the edge of the cliff and looked to see if I could inflict anymore punishment on the tuskers.

"Nafuka, get over here! We've got real problems! Look who's coming up the mountainside."

Chapter Twenty

"Look at them! Do you see the size of their muscles! They're enormous. What are they?" Darcel asked.

"Og's experiment. Initially, he took apes and surgically implanted brains from criminals into their skulls, but they're hard to control. He took the next step and injected human brain cells into ape embryos. He raised them like pets and trained them. They're the ultimate fighting machines."

"Why would Hoons be here on Zartex?"

"They've come for me. You'd better evacuate the Che-Wa. If we don't stop the Hoons, they'll slaughter everyone."

"I remember Zelestar talking about them. They're vicious fighters," Darcel said with a troubled look on her face.

I looked back down the hill. Fighting Hoons was never easy, especially with few weapons. I looked over at Nafuka and wondered if he was up for the fight of his life.

"Darcel, do you have any other weapons besides spears?"

"No, that's all we have, but now we don't have them to defend ourselves. All we've ever needed is rocks and spears."

"We're going to need something more powerful. We need weapons that will give us an advantage."

"Vying, there are ten of them and two of us. We can handle this," Nafuka said with false confidence.

"Nafuka, you're tough, but Hoons are relentless. They won't stop until you kill them all. Darcel, how have you defended yourself in the past?"

"We've never been attacked up here, but if we could lure them over to this ridge, my warriors and I could throw large rocks down on them."

"That might work, but I'd like something more formative than rocks before they get here. Maybe we could pick off a few of them."

With heads barely above the rocks, the column of Hoons kept a slow and steady advance up the mountain trail.

"Vying, whatever you're planning to do, you better hurry up! They're getting closer."

"Wait. I have an idea. Peen, I need you to get me some rope or vines."

The Hoons continued their trek up the mountainside, making their way slowly through the canyon as one stood stationary looking up the mountainside while the others moved forward. They weren't going to be surprised by any spears being launched at them.

Peen quickly returned with more spears and rope.

"Follow me up on the ledge. We've got work to do," I said as we moved quickly to set some traps. The Hoons were eighty leeds away and almost to the top when we finished. I snapped all but two spears in half.

"The Che-Wa will stay with you. We will not abandon a fight."

"No, Darcel. There's no guarantee that we'll defeat the Hoons. Take your people and hide further up the mountain pass. If they get past us, your warriors will have to defend your people. Leave us, now!"

"You don't give orders here and that's not our way to turn and run from a fight."

"Darcel, please listen to Vying. He knows what he's doing," Nafuka pleaded.

"You're wasting precious time. Go! This isn't going to be easy."

Reluctantly, they left. I knew we were no match against ten Hoons with just ten spears. Then I noticed the lead Hoon had scars on his face. I remembered him from Mercus. He was fearless and I realized the relentless desire Emperor Og had to kill me.

The hairy creatures neared the top and Nafuka and I stood on the ridge. All was ready.

"Nafuka, we need to pray and ask the Almighty for His power." I looked to heaven. "Almighty Father, please grant us wisdom and courage to fight and destroy these Hoons, in Jesus name we ask."

Just as I finished Nafuka picked up a Che-Wa lance and with all his might hurled it at Scarface. The muscular Hoon laughed as he easily ducked, but the Hoon behind him had just made it to the top and never saw the incoming spear. It penetrated his chest, knocking him down the mountainside.

"Great throw, but why on earth did you do that after I told you they would be wise to another attack with spears."

"Something inside me told me just to pick up a spear and throw it, so I did. It wasn't logical. I knew Scarface would duck, but I just did it."

"That was the leading of the Holy Spirit," I said marveling at Nafuka's obedience.

Scarface looked up and roared. As a precise unit, the Hoons picked up their pace with a vengeance and stormed the mountainside. They stood at the top unafraid of our weapons. Quickly, we slipped down the path toward the village. Waiting till they caught a glimpse of me, I ran down the path to the sapling and triggered the bigger branch. Thirty spears launched into the air toward the middle of the path. A mighty roar sounded from the Hoons and I knew the Che-Wa lances had found their marks again. I'd know the outcome in a little while by how many rounded the trail. With just spears, I knew we had little chance of defeating them. We took up position in the saddle of the tight mountain pass that led to the village. It was a strategic chokehold. I climbed up one side of the embankment and watched as the Hoons moved forward.

Cautiously, the first two Hoons made their way down the trail. With every step they took, they looked around. They had their swords out ready for use. Scarface wasn't one of them. Maybe he was dead. He always led from the front. For the first time I thought we stood a chance.

"It's just two of them, Nafuka. The ambush worked," I said as he raised his spear.

"Stay on the ledge and I'll run out against the first one and divert their attention."

As they approached, Nafuka bravely charged forward and battled the first Hoon. If I had any doubt about his loyalty, it was instantly dispelled as he furiously fought parrying against the Hoon's sword and thrusting his spear when he had the chance.

The other Hoon rushed me. I dashed down the embankment and straight at him. Timing my jump I did a mid-air somersault and forcefully drove my spear into his back. The Hoon hit the dirt face first. He tried to roll over, but couldn't. I picked up his sword and chopped his head off.

"Do you want him to die, Vying?"

I looked up. Scarface had his sword pressed against Nafuka's neck. Instantly I realized I had been outflanked.

"It's been awhile, Vying. The emperor will be pleased when I bring him both of you, dead or alive. It doesn't matter to me," Scarface growled. "Drop your sword!"

"Vying, don't worry about me. My life is meaningless," Nafuka pleaded.

Nafuka's life had great meaning, but I wouldn't go down without a fight. It was the warrior's way in me.

"Have you ever fought in the Battle Ring, Scarface?"

"You know Hoons aren't allowed in the ring. They keep us out because they know we would win."

"You think you're tough. I challenge you here and now."

"Good. I've always wanted to defeat you in battle," Scarface said as he walked out to meet me with a raised sword, ready for use.

In my heart, I prayed a silent prayer that the Almighty would give me the strength and skill to kill this Hoon. I didn't know how that would be possible especially since the other Hoon held his blade to Nafuka's neck. If I killed Scarface, the other Hoon would slit Nafuka's throat. I didn't know how this would play out, but I trusted in the Almighty. I needed His divine intervention or we'd be dead.

"One last chance, if you drop your sword, you and your friend live. Then we take a trip to the emperor. Use your brain, Vying. Choose life!"

I couldn't believe what I was hearing from this merchant of death. Choose life? Who was he kidding? There would only be death if I dropped my sword. Og had sent his destroyers after me and now these killing man-beasts were here. Did Scarface really think that I would give up?

"I come against you in the name of the Lord Jesus!" I shouted out as I ran toward him with my sword extended and fire in my eyes.

Scarface laughed. "You fool! Emperor Og is the god of this universe. Take the other prisoner back to him while I finish this one."

Suddenly, Scarface took his eyes off me and looked up. I seized the opening and attacked. A look of utter fear transformed his face as he dropped his sword arm. Was this a trick to draw me in? I slowed my charge. His eyes widened and he released his weapon. It clanged off a rock. Before I could strike a blow, he turned and ran. I'd never seen a Hoon run from a fight. Scarface was fearless. He'd rather die than run.

Figure 20: Vying and an Angel

Trembling, the two others dropped their swords and backed away from Nafuka and ran after Scarface. Nafuka too was mesmerized, his mouth open wide, awe filling his face. I wondered what he was looking at. Slowly I turned around and saw a mighty angel robed in a bright cloud. Lightning flashed from the cloud. A rainbow crested above his head.

His face was like the sun and his legs were fiery pillars. In one hand he held a spear and the other a flaming sword. The angel looked to be forty leeds tall and he hovered in the air above the crevice that led to the village. I looked at him for a while, but he never took his eyes off the escaping Hoons. Slowly I walked over to Nafuka and said, "Come on, let's go back to the village."

"What are we going to tell the others when we get there?"

"The truth. The Almighty's angel turned back the Hoons."

Chapter Twenty-One

I returned to Peen's home and went into the back room. I began listening to the voice of Zelestar as she read from the Almighty's Book. The hologram showed the words and I could scroll down each page with my finger. Later in the night, I got weary and left the room. Peen was asleep in the outer room on the floor. I covered her up with a blanket and took a walk outside. With the moon full and light slipping through the forest canopy, I walked up the hill to see if the angel was still there.

I got to the embankment where we had fought the Hoons and looked all around, but there was nothing and the body of the fallen Hoon was gone as well. I wondered if Nafuka had come back and buried it.

Falling to my knees, I thanked the Almighty Father for His warrior angel. As I turned around, Peen was standing there back lit by the moon's soft light. She was more beautiful than I realized. If I hadn't promised my heart to Zelestar, I could have easily been smitten by her gentle nature, her comeliness and her humble spirit.

"Are you alright?" she asked.

I was at a loss for words, but finally spoke up, "I was thanking the Almighty Father for His help in defeating the Hoons today."

"You're very brave. I didn't think you and Nafuka would make it."

"The Almighty delivered us from the Hoons. I think we'll be able to train in peace and get ready for the competition."

"Good, because you haven't much time. We received word that the Warder is calling for the contest to be on the eve of the next full moon," she said pointing to the half-moon that ruled the night.

Golden light danced across her delicate features making her long tresses shine brightly. Although I wanted to gaze at her to take in her loveliness, I quickly turned away knowing that to look upon her beauty would only pull my heart in a direction I didn't want it to go.

"Do you find me attractive, Vying?" she asked softly in a sweet tone of voice.

"Very much so."

"Then why do you turn away from me as if looking at me is painful?"

"I'm sorry, Peen, but the very opposite is true."

She put her hand on my arm and turned me around. I didn't resist, but I kept my eyes fixed to a rock on the ground. I didn't want to look at her. I didn't know if I could take it. Part of me wanted to run, but my feet were like immovable objects. I had to make a choice between a woman who I'd loved for a long time, but rarely saw and a beauty who was here and offering warm companionship.

Turning my face toward the village I took one step when I felt her lips brush my cheek ever so lightly, ever so quickly. I wasn't even sure if it had really happened. I sprinted toward her abode and ducked into the inner room closing the curtain, hoping she wouldn't follow.

I heard her enter, but she didn't come near me. Relieved I closed my eyes, laid down, and pulled the cover over my body and fell asleep.

*   *   *

"Get up, Vying!" Nafuka yelled from outside the small house.

"What is it now?" I asked throwing off the covers and getting up. I left the inner room and noticed that Peen wasn't there. I went outside.

"Darcel is furious and wants to see you."

"What have I done now?"

"How should I know? Do you think I understand women? I have no idea what makes them tick. All I know is that she's very angry. Hurry up."

We walked down to the main corral where the village livestock were kept. I looked for Peen, but she was nowhere to be seen. Darcel was barking orders at the Che-Wa. I wondered if there were any men. I'd only seen two with their cloaks pulled back.

"Why have you done this?"

"What are you talking about? Why are you angry?"

"First the tuskers threaten our village, then the Hoons and now Peen is gone. She left me a note saying she no longer wants to train you. You insulted her, Vying!"

"I think you Che-Wa have a misconception of what a fighter needs,"

146

I said turning around and leaving Darcel with a look of frustration on her face. I returned to Peen's home and took out the hologram. I began to study the Almighty's Book.

I closed my eyes and listened as the hologram recited these words: "We fight not against flesh and blood, but against rulers, against the authorities, against principalities of this dark world, against spiritual forces of evil in heavenly places."

Figure 21: Hologram of the Almighty's Word

I stopped the hologram and thought about that for a long time. I remembered the mist monsters on the energy collectors who were conquered when I used the name of Jesus. In the battle ring for the Crown Championship against Megog, I was knocked out, defeated. But that night a supernatural strength came over me and I was able to recover, defeat him and claim the Crown Championship. The thought entered my mind that all of the battles I'd fought were really against spiritual forces operating through someone or something. I shook my head and marveled at this. My whole life I had been pitted against Og and his nephew Megog, but maybe they weren't the real enemy. Maybe my enemies were driven by unseen evil spirits. I wondered how to do battle against them and win.

I started the hologram again and the machine stopped in the book of Ephesians that spoke about the armor of God and praying in the spirit.

What was this, I wondered. I'd never heard about praying in the spirit, so I told the hologram to tell me all about the Spirit.

The hologram took me to a place in the book of Acts where Jesus was speaking to the disciples saying, *"It is not for you to know times or seasons that the Father has fixed by His own authority, but you will receive power when the Holy Spirit has come upon you, and you will be my witnesses in Jerusalem and in all Judea and Samaria, and to the end of the earth."*

I knew that I needed to be a witness for Jesus in the Blue Ring Galaxy, and that I needed the Holy Spirit's power to defeat these forces of evil. After many hours of praying, I fell asleep.

"Hey Vying! We've got to train and get ready for the fights. The Warder will be calling us soon and we've got to be ready at a moment's notice," Nafuka shouted from outside the door.

Jarring me from my sleep, I knew he was right. But I also knew that the battle in the spiritual dimension was real and I had to study the Almighty's Book to be ready.

"Not now, Nafuka. I'm busy."

"Busy? You better get busy and come out here or I'm coming in and dragging you out!" Nafuka shouted.

"You've got it all wrong! I stayed up late last night studying the Almighty's Book and I need to study more to prepare myself for the spiritual battle on Coralia."

"I'll bring you some water," Nafuka snarled, walking away.

I had found the source of living water that was much more refreshing. I continued to study the Almighty's Book the rest of the day. I needed to know all that I could about the power of the Holy Spirit. There was so much that Tor and Tia had taught me about Jesus, but they hadn't taught about the Holy Spirit and His power. I wanted to know more. I began listening to the book of Acts and came to a passage explaining the event that happened at the Feast of Pentecost. Peter and the other disciples were praying when a sound like a mighty rushing wind came from heaven and filled the entire house where they were staying. Suddenly there appeared over their heads tongues of fire. At that moment, they were all filled with the Holy Spirit and power. They began to speak in different languages as they were guided by the Spirit.

After reading that passage, I knew the only way the Beast would be defeated was if the Almighty's power was working through me. I knew the great battle wouldn't be in the battle ring here on Zartex, but on Coralia against the Beast.

I continued to study the Almighty's Book and began to write the words on the tablets of my heart. I knew that when I made the run on Coralia I might not be able to use the hologram. So I prayed, "Almighty Father; I want the Holy Spirit, the authority and your power. I can't do this alone. I ask, if it is your will, please fill me with your Spirit. Amen."

Nothing happened at first, but I just waited on the Almighty. I was so hungry for more of Him. Without warning, a warm heavy feeling, like hot honey, came pouring over my head. Instantly, I knew the presence of the Lord was with me, but I didn't know what to do. I began speaking words that sounded like Che-Wa, but I couldn't understand what I was saying. I knew that God had given me a gift and I was overwhelmed. I got down on my knees and put my head to the matted floor and continued praying in the strange language that I didn't understand for a long time. Darkness seeped into the room, but I didn't care. I didn't know why, but something told me to keep praying in this new language.

Hunger issued its protest, my stomach rumbled, but I continued praying. I tried to pray all night, but as the line between falling asleep and staying awake began to blur, my mind slipped into a dream...

A tusker growled fiercely! The snarling guttural bark deeply frightened me. I sensed a heavy demonic presence hovering over me. It was overwhelming. I was afraid. I had no weapons. The tusker inched forward, snapping his jaws and growling louder. Fiery unwavering red eyes, eyes that wanted to kill me, came closer and closer. I backed up. But I was trapped against a wall. I could smell the decaying flesh in his teeth from a prior kill. I hoped there weren't more. The tusker dropped low into a crouch and got ready to launch. I could feel his warm breath against my face, when suddenly he jumped straight at me! I couldn't move. My legs and arms were frozen. A thought flashed through my mind. *Fight him with the power of God! The Sword of the Spirit.*

I raised my hand and commanded with authority, "In the name of Jesus be gone!"

Nothing happened. The tusker's front paws were around my neck, choking me as he growled louder.

"Jesus," I cried before I lost consciousness.

Immediately, it disappeared.

I awoke breathing heavily and sweating as if I had just run the desert course. I was afraid to move. Slowly I opened my eyes and looked around, but saw nothing. I listened for any sound, but the only sound I heard was my own breathing. Quietly I moved toward the door and stepped out into the night. Nafuka had left a water jug at my door and I reached down and drained it.

All was quiet in the village. I walked up the hill where Peen and I had been two nights before, where we had battled the tuskers and the Hoons. I was alone. An idea came tumbling into my mind that a great war was being waged in the supernatural and I was in the midst of it. I knew then that I had to study the Almighty's Book as much as possible because my very life depended on it.

Chapter Twenty-Two

I returned to Peen's home and lay down to sleep before the sun rose. This time my sleep was pleasant.

"Vying, wake up!" Nafuka said as he shook my shoulder.

I tried to focus, wiping the lack of sleep from my tired eyes.

"Let's get going. We've got to start training."

"I know. I know, but I've got more important things to do."

"Vying, are you out of your mind? You have to be ready to run and then fight to get off this planet. Have you gone soft on me?"

I thought about that for a moment. I wondered if I could win in the battle ring again. It had been seven years since I'd competed. The war had interrupted the matches and I hadn't paid any attention to the new winner. I didn't even know who currently reigned as Crown Champion.

"No, Nafuka, I haven't gone soft on you, but other things are much more important."

"Are you kidding me? Do you want to spend the rest of your life on this hellhole? Sure, the Che-Wa are good people, but you're isolated, away from your family and friends."

"Remember what I told you about the Almighty?"

"Sure, why?"

"Well, the hologram has the Almighty's Book on it, and I think its words are more important than physical training."

"Really! Let me tell you, Vying, getting off Zartex should be first. Win the competition and you go to Coralia. If you return from 'the run,' then you can go to Micron and study the Almighty's Book to your heart's content. But to do that, you have to win! Unless you train intensely, you're going to lose. The run is through the desert and up the mountains. It's no easy task. You've got to begin training or you won't stand a chance."

"Okay, okay. I hear you, Nafuka."

"Oh, I almost forgot. Darcel is waiting for you."

"Is she mad at me?"

"I don't know. Don't keep her waiting."

I got up and washed my face and left Peen's home. I wondered where she had gone. We walked up to Darcel's home. She was standing outside of her small hut with Peen by her side. Neither woman looked very happy. I walked up to them slowly hoping I could interject some reason into why I wanted to sleep alone.

"Where have you been?" Darcel demanded glaring at me. "I don't like to be kept waiting."

"Sorry, I was in the hut listening to the hologram you gave me."

"And what about Peen. Don't you find her attractive?"

"She's very beautiful and I'm grateful for staying in her home, but that's as far as its going to go. Look, I don't think you understand. I love someone else. I've told the Almighty if I can't have her, I don't want another. Its nothing against you, Peen, but my heart belongs to someone else. I don't know if I'll ever see her again, but I will always be faithful to her."

"As I have been to you, Vying," Zelestar said as she pushed aside the curtain of Darcel's hut and rushed into my arms, crushing me with a warm embrace.

Figure 22: The Lovely Zelestar

Nafuka laughed deeply.

"Zelestar!" I cried out from a depth in my heart I'd never known. Tears rolled down my cheeks as I tightly held her against my chest smelling her jasmine perfume, not wanting the moment to end.

"Oh, Vying, I've thought of you so often."

"How did you get here?" I asked, blinking back more tears.

"Come, let's sit in my sister's hut like we did in the City beneath the Sea."

Warm intimate thoughts flooded my mind remembering that day during the war that we found refuge in each others' arms. Peen caught my eye and nodded her head approving of my faithfulness. I went into Darcel's home. It was sparsely furnished with two chairs by a warm fire.

"Zelestar, why did you come?"

"I'm not sure, but the Almighty told me to do so. I know that being obedient to Him is more important than any sacrifice. I must say, it was sweet to hear your declaration of love, but I've wondered why you never visited me."

"What? Every time I tried to set up a trip to Milo to see you, I'd check with your administrators and they said you were on official travel."

"Oh, Vying, they're told to say that. Did you ever leave your name and contact information?"

"Sure, but I never heard from you."

"That's strange. I never received any information about you."

"Really? Why didn't you visit me while I was in prison? I had Dax contact your palace on Milo."

"That doesn't make sense. The only message I ever received about you was from Sorrl."

"Sorrl?" I asked in disbelief. "That only means one thing. You have a betrayer in your inner group."

"Hmm,' she mused. "I've felt that for some time. I travel undercover often. I've been afraid to leave Milo in my capacity as the Queen."

"Why?"

"I believe Og and Megog are still alive."

"They are. In fact they've tried to kill me several times."

"When I was on Micron, I heard how the people talked about you."

"What? You were on Micron and you didn't try and see me!"

Zelestar laughed and smiled mischievously. "I wondered if I fooled you."

"What are you talking about?"

"I visited you on Micron."

"Let me get this right. The woman I truly love visited me and I missed her."

"Do you remember when you were in prison and an old woman was sweeping the floor near your cell?"

"No. No way."

"Way."

"I can't believe it. That was you? Why didn't you say something to me?"

"Og has spies everywhere. I knew he might be watching through the cameras. I couldn't take a chance of speaking to you without him knowing. He's still upset that I escaped the night you beat Megog for the Crown Championship."

"Every time someone came to my cell, I was hoping it was you."

"Yes, I know."

"How could you?"

"Dax told me. He came to your cell the last time and you barely looked at him, but he understood. Have you been studying the hologram?"

"For the last two days, I've done nothing else. It's a very powerful document."

"It's much more than a document. It's a mighty weapon against the forces of evil, but I agree with Nafuka, you've got to start physical training. Micron desperately needs you."

"Really? They convicted and sentenced me to life in prison and you say they need me. I got the distinct impression they didn't want me on Micron."

"Public opinion isn't very high about you right now, but Sera and Wolks are also in prison for sparing your life."

"What's going on there?"

"Something strange is happening on Micron. People aren't interested in what's right. They're concentrating on the pleasures of peace and to some extent, I can understand that. During the Great War everything was taken from them, and now they have a chance to rebuild, but most of them have taken their eyes off the Almighty and put them on material possessions. Many are in the pursuit of worldly things and I see the pureness we once had as a people slowly fading."

"Why do you want me to come back?"

"Someone's got to stand up and tell them the truth!"

"Why me? They wouldn't believe me in the trial."

"If you came back from the prison planet, things would change. Many people believe you were set up and are innocent in spite of how the Council of Peers voted."

"But why should I do that? Why should I risk my life again for those people?"

"The old warriors know you're innocent and so do I."

"Lot of good that does me. They incarcerated me here on Zartex."

"Vying! Snap out of it! The Almighty sent His Son and He was innocent, yet crucified on a cross so that we might live."

"Zelestar, I'm not Jesus!"

"Nobody said you were, but there is another great war coming. I don't think the last one extinguished Og. My intel informs me that he's building his army again and has a hybrid weapon."

"I think I already fought it. It was easy to defeat."

"That's not what I've been hearing. Many of the warriors who fought along side you are either dead or in prison. Micron will be defenseless unless you come back."

"This isn't going to be easy."

"Now I know why the Almighty wanted me to come, Vying."

I looked at Zelestar and the kindness of her face touched my heart deeply. Her external beauty was magnified by the pureness of her heart, but it was her inner virtue that made me want to rise up and fight for what was right. I shook my head and laughed quietly.

"If anyone else had come to tell me all these things, I wouldn't have believed them. Only you could do this to me," I said.

"That's why the Almighty sent me," she said reflectively.

"Sometimes I don't understand His plan for me."

"Nafuka's waiting for you and you have a lot of training to do, so get going, Commander!"

I didn't want to leave her. I wanted to hold her in my arms to feel her warmth tightly pressed against my chest basking in her love. Why couldn't we be together? It was unfair. What more did the Almighty want from me?

"Will you be here when I return from training?"

"Perhaps, but I will follow the leading of the Almighty Father. If His Spirit tells me to stay, I will. If not, I won't be here when you return."

"There's something else. Have you ever been in prayer and the Holy Spirit allows you to speak in another language?" I asked.

Her face lit up and she smiled so beautifully. "I wanted to talk to you about that."

"Great, I heard the passage that says, 'You shall receive power when the Holy Spirit comes upon you.' So I prayed and asked the Almighty Father if He would give me the Holy Spirit."

"And what happened?"

"I felt a warm sensation, like a fire burning on my head. I began praying with words I'd never heard before. At first, I didn't notice it because I was so focused on praying. Then I realized that I was speaking in a different language."

"And how did you feel?"

"Fine. I just kept praying and felt a deep inner peace. I remember reading that we should pray in the spirit."

Zelestar laughed with glee as a young child discovering something brand new.

"What's so funny?"

"You. You have such an innocent trust of the Almighty. It's so good to hear you tell of your experience. Keep praying that the Almighty guide you during these times. When you're praying in your heavenly language, only the Holy Spirit knows what you are praying."

"Has the Almighty allowed you to pray in a different language?" I asked.

"Of course. I couldn't pray for hours if I didn't have the Holy Spirit in my life."

"Well that explains a lot of things to me."

"Vying, let's go!" Nafuka shouted from outside of the tent.

I got up to go and reached down and hugged her again. She smelled so good and I breathed in, deeply hoping to capture every essence of her. I walked out feeling strong and empowered. For the first time in a long time I felt totally invigorated, as if I could do anything.

"Do you want to go for a run to start the day out?" Nafuka asked me.

"Sure, let's do it. Where do you want to go?"

"Before we take off, here strap this water pack on and make sure the tube is near your chin."

"Got it," I said as I strapped the pack on my back. I looked down at my feet and knew my boots would be fine. I'd run in them many times before and they had some spring in them. "Which way do we need to go?"

"We need to head up the hill and then down into the desert. We've got to increase our wind."

"What are we waiting for, Nafuka?"

"Nothing, but I think somebody wants to say something to you."

Zelestar walked up to me and gave me a long and deep kiss then pulled away quickly. She'd never done that before and I wondered when I'd see her again.

Chapter Twenty-Three

Figure 23: Endurance Training

I took off running up the sharp incline that led to the mountain pass. At the top of the hill, I changed gears, widening my strides becoming slightly airborne as I flew downhill. As I approached the bottom of the hill, there was a rolling incline I had to go up. I tightened my strides using short choppy steps as I attacked the incline. Halfway up, stitches of pain laid siege to my side, but I didn't care. No amount of pain could slow me down. I got to the top and waited for Nafuka.

"What took you so long?" I asked.

"Man! You look like you were shot out of a laser cannon. You better save some energy for the desert heat and the return up this mountain."

"Which path do we take?"

"Let's go down the canyon where the tuskers and Hoons came up."

"Lead the way," I said and we took off.

I lengthened my strides and floated down the hill. Nafuka, being taller, stayed ahead of me with longer strides and covered more ground as we went down. He pulled up when he got to the bottom.

"You see those rocks at the base of that far mountain?"

"That's quite a long way."

"Good thing it's cool this morning, but I'm sure it will heat up on the return. Conserve your strength. The desert has a way of draining you. Running back up this mountain to the Che-Wa village won't be easy."

We started out and Nafuka took the lead. I felt strong, invincible. With every step, I sensed myself getting stronger and stronger. I didn't know if it was the Almighty's power or the fact that I'd finally seen Zelestar or both. Either way, it didn't matter. I was training again and my body felt great as if it had awakened from a long slumber. Every step was invigorating and I pushed harder and harder. A cool breeze blanketed my face, refreshing me. Even though the trail had small inclines and declines, it felt easy. I took a pull of water from the camelback.

The gap between us widened and pretty soon I couldn't hear Nafuka's breathing or his steps. I began to open my stride. I felt a burst of indestructible power flow through me. Usually when I ran I maintained a good pace, but this time I was pushing it.

My steps were light and I moved briskly. None of the stones or obstacles bothered me. I glided over them smoothly.

Halfway across the desert, the pain in my sides erupted as the sweat dripped down my forehead and stung my eyes. I wiped the perspiration from my head and eyes, took a long drink of water and continued to run. The pain gradually grew stronger, making me wonder where all the power I had earlier had gone. Maybe Nafuka was right. I should have saved some energy, but having trained for many years I knew that the real battle was between my ears.

"Dear Almighty, help me to overcome this," I prayed, but nothing happened. I knew the Almighty heard my prayer, but there was no relief.

I laughed to myself. The Almighty was always with me. I knew the seriousness of this training, so I pushed the pain from my mind. As I continued, I felt like I'd never get relief and then as I powered up and over a moderately steep incline, I opened my stride and felt a sudden surge of strength as my second wind kicked in. I wondered how Nafuka was doing and turned my head slightly, but I couldn't see him. I began to worry about him, but remembered he'd done this before and his pace was probably measured, unlike mine.

I continued the fast pace holding nothing in reserve. Finally, I reached the base of the other mountain range we'd seen earlier. The temperature cooled as I ran up the foothill and circled the rocks that Nafuka had pointed out three hours ago. The cool air renewed my strength as I headed back along the path, through the open desert. The hot sand radiated heat waves. I saw Nafuka lumbering towards me on the path.

"Good running, keep it up!" he shouted as we passed each other going in opposite directions.

The desert's temperature exacted its toll, draining me. Piercing pain besieged my sides and my body screamed in protest to stop, but I refused to bow to the acute agony. I knew better. All I had to do was stop and the pain would instantly go away. It was at this point in the run that I was really pushing myself and building endurance. Developing greater lung capacity exacted its price.

The racking torture continued as I refused to slow down. I remembered words from the Almighty's Book, *"But those who hope in the Lord will renew their strength. They will soar on wings like eagles. They will run and not grow weary."*

My mind felt invigorated. I knew this wasn't a test of physical endurance, but a test to see if I would trust in the Almighty. I kept repeating the words from the Almighty's Book, *"I will run and not grow weary… I will run by faith and not by sight."*

No matter the pain, I drove forward. Somehow, the words from the Almighty's Book renewed my strength. I took a pull of water and increased my pace. Maybe I was crazy. The desert heat was climbing and the searing pain in my sides hadn't diminished. It was illogical that I should increase the pace, but doggedly I kept it up. Either the Almighty's Word worked or it didn't. I knew that if I was doing something foolish, He'd let me know. Whether I obeyed or not, that was the real question.

Pushing myself for what seemed to be an eternity, I suddenly realized that I was halfway across the desert on the return. I hadn't bothered looking back. I glanced at the distant mountains for a moment and a verse from the Almighty's Book flowed into my mind, *I lift my eyes to the hills, where does my help come from? My help comes from the Lord, the Maker of heaven and earth.*

Sweat streamed down my face stinging my eyes, I smiled. I straightened up and surged forward. *"It's not by strength or power, but by My Spirit,"* came to mind. Suddenly my strength was renewed as I approached the foothills anticipating the hill climb. I knew that I'd need everything I had to make it to the top. Doggedly, I refused to stop. The top to me was the finish line. I pushed hard up the incline again taking short choppy steps. Loose stones suddenly shot out from under my feet as I tumbled forward. My hands hit first on the rocky surface, but in a burst of energy I pushed back up never stopping. Somehow I continued running uphill.

About half-way to the top, my legs were in full-blown rebellion. My thighs and calves raged in agonizing fire. My mind begged me to stop, but I pushed harder. I kept my head down and got angry with the pain. I'd completed ninety percent of the course and wasn't about to stop. I'd surpassed all of my expectations, but that didn't matter to my legs. The agony in them played tricks on my mind and a thought came to me. *It would be okay to stop for a while. Nafuka was nowhere in sight. He'd never know, but I would.*

I knew that wasn't the Almighty's thought or mine, so I knew it came from the evil one.

"You can do it, Vying!" a familiar female voice yelled encouraging me from the stones above. Zelestar was still here! I was completely reenergized and I surged upward. I'd prepared my mind that she would be gone by the time I returned. I hadn't expected to see her again.

"Come on, Vying. I'll finish this with you," she said.

Rounding a bend in the trail, I was shocked. It wasn't Zelestar, but Peen! A crushing weight pulverized my hope. The top of the mountain was impossible! Pain, seizing its moment, racked my legs. I shook my head at the confusion, but knew I had be an overcomer of my emotions.

I took another drink of water and decided to attack. This wasn't about Zelestar. There were far greater obstacles in play. This was just one more test. Stubbornly, I refused to quit and focused on the next step.

"Come on, Vying! You've almost made it!" Peen yelled.

I looked to the summit. It was just a short distance away. Determined to succeed, I kept pushing and finally crested the top of the mountain. But, I still didn't stop. I took long strides downhill toward the village, stumbling a few times, but never falling.

"That was incredible," Peen said trying to catch me. "No one has ever run faster than you did today."

"May the Almighty be praised!" I said completely out of breath. "Where's Zelestar?"

"She had to go back. Her window of opportunity to return to Milo undetected was closing quickly. She gave me this note."

I shoved it under my belt.

"Don't you want to read it?" Peen asked puzzled.

I did, but not here, not with Peen. I was hurt and disappointed, but it wasn't Peen's fault. I'd already upset her and I had no reason to take my emotions out on her. "Yes, but not now. I've to go back and help Nafuka up the mountainside. Come on!"

Peen and I jogged to the hidden mountain village, turned around and headed back up the trail to the edge of the overview. I could see a tiny dot lumbering slowly in the desert below. I wanted to go down and run with him, but I was ready to collapse. I knew if I went down, I wouldn't make the climb back up.

Peen sensed my reluctance and with long strides flew down the mountain trail reaching the bottom quickly. I watched as she met the big man and together they climbed to the top.

Once they returned to where I sat, Nafuka said, "Vying, I don't know what you've been doing for the last few days, but whatever it is, keep it up."

"Thanks, Nafuka, it's the Almighty's power surging through me."

"I believe it. Now let's go get some rest so that we can train this evening."

"Tomorrow. Tonight I've got to study the Almighty's Book."

"I won't argue. I'm exhausted," the big man said as he lumbered toward Darcel's hut.

That night, I studied the hologram listening to the words, writing some down. I'd saved Zelestar's letter and just before I was about to go to sleep I opened it.

My dearest Vying,

I couldn't believe it when I heard your declaration of love for me. I don't know if I can return such passion. There are many things that are happening in the Blue Ring Galaxy. Few are aware of the growing evil. You must get off Zartex and oppose the Beast on Coralia. The Beast is a fearsome demon. Nafuka has made the run before, but I'm sure the tricks that he used against the Beast won't work a second time. He is crafty and very cunning and has been around a long, long time. I will be praying for you, as always.

Once you're free, you must return to Micron and raise up the warriors. The evil is growing. Until all is settled, we stay apart. The enemy will use anything he can to destroy you and me and if he knows of your love for me, it puts me in great danger, as before, but this time I think it's even worse.

Warmly,

Zelestar

I reread the letter and was deeply saddened. I wanted to spend more time with her, a lot more time, but that wasn't possible. I knew she was right in all that she had written. Even though I should have burned the letter, I couldn't. I wondered if this would come back to hurt me, but I didn't care. If I couldn't have Zelestar, I would keep her letter on the inside of my tunic close to my heart. Exhaustion overcame me and I fell asleep.

Chapter Twenty-Four

"Vying, get up! How could you have been Crown Champion of the Blue Ring Galaxy with such lazy training habits?" Nafuka shouted outside of Peen's abode.

I struggled to open my eyes. It was no use to explain to him that I had been studying the Almighty's Book most of the night. I didn't know how I'd make it through the day without sleep, but I got up anyway. I knew from the battles during the Great War, that I could go two days without rest. My training needed to be both spiritual and physical. Once I got into the bright sunshine, I shook off the stupor and was ready to train.

Peen served a breakfast of fruits and vegetables. I ate a lot. I was very hungry, but I wasn't sure if it was my body or my spirit. I consumed the words of the Almighty's Book. I didn't try to figure it out and ate. I knew I shouldn't overeat or it would all be coming back up once we pushed our bodies way beyond the limits that our minds thought we could handle.

Nafuka stretched slowly. This gave my stomach time to digest the food. With torches in hand, we trekked into a cave that had been carved out of the mountain. There were scattered stones of various sizes and shapes lying on the floor of the cave.

"Let's begin," Nafuka ordered as he lifted the largest stone first. "Lift it above your head ten times and then move to the next smallest."

I thought it would be easy, but the sweat began rolling down my forehead even though the air was cool. I watched as four Che-Wa came together with large dried bamboo shoots. They banged them together a few times and then stopped.

"What are they for?" I asked.

"Oh you'll see soon. Pick up the last stone."

I hesitated, my arms completely wasted.

"Above your head."

I picked it up and forced my body to finish up the exercise.

"Very good, Vying. Now let's move on."

The Che-Wa started banging the poles together again.

"Alright, now jump between the bamboo and keep jumping before they swing them together."

I got in between the poles and before I was ready, they slammed the two hard pieces of bamboo together, catching my ankles.

"Yeoow!" I yelled. "That hurt."

"Don't worry, that was soft. They knew you weren't ready, but next time they'll go full speed."

"Great," I murmured.

At first it seemed quite easy, but then the sweat started rolling off my body again. The Che-Wa picked up the pace. The first time they hit me at full speed, they laughed. They enjoyed it when they caught either of us. To them it was a great game, but I saw the pained expression on Nafuka's face. The last time they hit him ignited his temper, but he held it in check. Finally, we were through with that discipline. I grabbed a towel and wiped the sweat off.

"Vying, pick up a heavier stone and slowly twist your body all the way to one side and hold it for a moment. Then turn the other way and hold it. We've got to warm-up our stomachs and backs before we go to the battle ring."

I could tell by Nafuka's endurance and his knowledge of training that he'd been here before and knew exactly what to do. That was fine with me as I concentrated on fulfilling his training regime.

"Are you warmed up?" he asked.

"Yeah, but I didn't really care for the bamboo exercise."

Nafuka laughed. "The Che-Was love that drill. They taught it to me the first time I came here. It really speeds up your footwork."

"I don't see any battle ring. Where is it?"

"Deeper in the cave. They laid out mats as cushion from the rocks underneath us. Use one-third of your strength or one of us could get hurt."

I wondered if it would be me. Did Nafuka want to hurt me up here because he didn't want to face me in the battle ring? I thought again and remembered when he saved me from the falling rock. No, Nafuka, and I had an alliance. I believed he would stick to it.

The rest of the morning, we practiced different body throws and lateral drops from our feet. In the afternoon, we practiced elbow strikes, jabs and punches with gloves then mixed it up with leg and knee kicks again, still not using our full strength.

There were two vines hanging from the tall ceiling of the cave.

"Nafuka, I'll race you to the top!"

"Sure! Why not?" he replied jumping, grabbing the vine and climbing up. He caught me flat-footed, but I quickly recovered. He made it to the top then fast roped down beating me by several leeds.

"You've got to be quicker than that, Vying, if you're going to get off this planet."

"You cheated. You started before me."

"What's your point? Do you think they will fight fair in the battle ring? It's an all out war. Winning the match is the only thing that counts. You better remember that when we go down the mountain to the competition. It's every man for himself, unless you have an alliance."

"I'll remember that," I said as I jumped up the vine and climbed to the top. I had a huge lead on Nafuka this time, but I noticed that he hadn't even started. I quickly came down.

"What's up? I thought we were training."

Nafuka laughed that deep laugh. "We were, but we're finished. We always finish with a vine climb."

"Maybe we should step it up. Two climbs are better than one."

"I'll remember that next time."

We left the cave as the sun slowly kissed the horizon. We hadn't stopped for lunch and my stomach growled. I left Nafuka as he went to

Darcel's hut and I went to Peen's. She was cooking something in the stone fire ring in the center of the hut.

"Smells awesome, Peen. I didn't know you could cook."

"There's a lot of things you don't know about me. I've collected water in a catch-all hanging in the back. Let it trickle down to wash up before dinner."

I left Peen and went in the back room and saw the makeshift water barrel overhead. It had a spout and a lever. I stripped down and pulled the lever slightly and a gated valve lifted. The sun-warmed water spilled out. It was incredibly refreshing and I felt great. I released the handle and saw a small cloth and soap hanging on a hook. I used them to lather my body. I could feel the tension leaving the muscles in my legs. They were very sore from the previous day's long run. If I hadn't trained with the knights in the outback, walking would have been extremely difficult.

I pulled on the valve and washed off. Stepping out, I noticed a change of clothes to the side door. This would be the first time I'd not worn my uniform in a long time.

Figure 24: Vying's Change of Clothes

The clothes felt soft to my body and I wondered where she had gotten them. I was amazed at the quiet kindness Peen expressed while serving me. I felt convicted. I had treated her roughly and yet she still had a servant's heart. I shook my head as I remembered the hologram, *"The greatest among you shall be a servant."* Peen was demonstrating the humble and loving character of the Almighty without saying a word.

I walked into the outer room and saw two steaming bowls were on a slightly raised table. Peen was sitting opposite me as I sat down.

She watched as I bowed my head and offered thanks to the Almighty Father.

The aroma of fresh herbs filled the room and I could see vegetables pushing through the thick gravy. I wanted to taste it, but before I ate, I had to clear something up.

"Peen, please forgive me, if I have offended you in any way."

"Vying, you don't need to explain. I saw your love for Zelestar."

"The Almighty's Book says that we should serve each other and you have exemplified that verse. I thank you. I appreciate all you do for me."

She smiled beautifully. Then a tear slid out of her eye and quickly ran down her cheek.

I looked down at my bowl and saw a piece of meat. "What is this?"

"It's clarion."

"What's a clarion?"

"A small antelope that lives in the mountains."

"Why aren't you eating any?"

"You need the protein, if you're going to grow strong for your training."

"Do you like clarion?"

"Yes, of course, we all do. It's a delicacy."

"Who caught it?"

173

"I did."

"Then you deserve some of the meat and don't argue with me."

"I won't argue with you, if you let me sleep in my home."

"You may. Do you want your bedroom?"

"No, you can have it."

"Thanks, I will be studying the hologram until late. Will it bother you?"

"No, in fact, I've enjoyed listening to it. Besides it's much better than your snoring," she said laughing easily. Her melodious laughter broke the tension between us.

"Don't think I was sleeping outside every night. You never heard me, but I slipped into the front room. I don't want the people of my village to think that I'm not caring for you."

"But you know about Zelestar?"

"Yes, of course, how could I not?"

"Then you know where my heart is."

"I understand, but the people of the village are expecting me to meet all of your needs."

"I see, but I'm saving myself until I get married."

"That's unusual."

"I know and it's not easy."

"So have you and Zelestar had, you know what I mean?"

"No Peen. I haven't been intimate with Zelestar. I'm waiting till I marry her."

The next day, Nafuka devised a creative variety of exercises using the stones to make us stronger. The following day, we ran in the desert again. This time, I didn't feel as powerful on the run, but I still made it out of the desert and back to the mountain far ahead of Nafuka.

Peen must have known that it was a tougher run for me and met me at the base of the mountain. Together we headed up the incline. Without her, I might not have made it.

That night, we ate with Darcel and Nafuka, and they drank some Milo wine. It was a warm evening, but the conversation between us was even warmer. That night I went back and continued to study the hologram of the Almighty's Book. I heard the words, *"Fight the good fight of faith."* I wondered how those words applied to my life because I knew that going to Coralia wasn't going to be easy. I trusted that if the Almighty had brought me this far, He had a plan. All I had to do was prepare for the moment when I'd need everything from His Holy Book to defeat the Beast.

Chapter Twenty-Five

The next morning Nafuka and I wrestled with each other using different holds and techniques to gain an advantage in the battle ring. He landed a round house kick catching me in the inner thigh, hitting a major nerve.

"OW!" I groaned dropping to the ground. "Nafuka, back off! That really hurt!"

"Sorry, but perfect practice makes you perfect. I'm just trying to keep it real."

I knew deep in my heart he was right. Once we returned to the prison compound, there would be no apologies, and I hoped I wouldn't have to fight Nafuka.

He was strong and skilled. He fought like Megog and a thought came to me, that without the Almighty's help I couldn't have defeated Megog. I wondered if I had trained sufficiently this time and if I had spent enough time studying the hologram of the Almighty's Holy Book. It seemed that the more I listened and read the words of His Book, the more I wanted to know Him. I sensed His presence and every time I sat before Him, I felt His joy well up in me. I loved it when He touched me with the warm anointing of His Spirit. My mind slipped off and I missed an elbow strike that hammered me to the ground.

"Nafuka! What are you doing?"

"Stay focused. Keep your mind off Zelestar. I saw that faraway look in your eyes!" he said laughing and helping me to my feet.

"I wasn't thinking of her."

"Oh, okay then, maybe it was the lovely Peen."

"Nafuka, I was thinking about the Almighty's Book and what it says."

"Right, and I'm Scarface."

My temper flared and I hammered him with an uppercut under the chin knocking him back. "That's how I've hit a Hoon."

"Now you did it," Nafuka said, lunging at me.

I dodged to the right and sent a forward kick to his solar plexus.

"Ohh!" he groaned deeply, his eyes tearing. "Let's go!" he yelled, recovering and coming at me with both arms extended.

This time instead of sidestepping his outstretched arms, I grabbed him in an over-under move and threw him to the ground. I jumped on top of him and executed a rear-naked choke hold. I cranked hard on the hold and a few seconds later he tapped the ground. I released him and quickly got up from my seated position on his back while maintaining my defensive posture.

Nafuka arose and massaged the back of his neck. "Good series. Full speed. I think I've completed my job."

"Your job? What are you talking about?"

He laughed. "I had to figure out a way to get you back in the game. I don't know where your head's been, so I cranked it up a notch. If we can get a few more desert runs in, then we'll be ready to face anyone. I must warn you, some of the fighters will take advantage of any situation and will use others to distract you. You need to stay focused. No more daydreaming."

"I hear you."

"So when are you going to teach me from the Almighty's Book?"

"Nafuka, you're full of surprises. Do you really want to listen to some of it?"

"Of course."

Just then our ankle bracelets began to tingle and light up.

"Perfect timing! It's the Warder's signal. He's calling the fighters. It'll take us a day to get to the prison compound, so we'll start out early in the morning. Usually, the prisoner's have a couple of days to get there. The course for the Crucible is laid out through the desert and the mountains. The Warder reviews it with us."

"Is it a different course from the one you ran?"

"It has to be. Some of the competitors hide weapons out there, hoping to take out some of the competition during the run. There are no rules, so if you can gain the advantage on your opponent while running the Crucible, you do it. Only the top twenty finishers are allowed into the second phase of the championship."

"How long does it take to run the Crucible?"

"All day and night. Tonight we must eat hardy and store up energy."

We sat around the fire as Darcel and Peen prepared an excellent meal. We filled our bellies knowing that we would need all our strength for the days ahead. Nafuka was very loving toward Darcel while Peen and I sat next to each other as friends. I'd come to like and appreciate her more and more, but I knew it wouldn't go any further than a warm friendship. She was a beautiful woman and in the soft moonlight her blond hair glistened and her face emitted an inner radiance that could only have come from a woman whose heart was pure. I knew that if I hadn't set my mind on Zelestar, I'd come back for Peen. I hoped someday that a fine young man would meet her and love her as she deserved.

Peen had somehow trapped another young clarion near our camp and for the second night in a row we ate a most succulent meal. There was enough meat for all of us and I was glad when I saw them eating instead of giving it all to us.

After dinner was over, Nafuka put his arm around Darcel and drew her close to him. In the glimpse of a moment, I saw the resemblance of Zelestar and immediately wished she was here.

The cool of the evening set in and we adjourned to our separate dwellings. I went into the bedroom and began studying the words of the Almighty's Book. I tried to memorize some of the verses. I repeated them over and over again, pounding them into my brain. This was one of those rare moments when I was glad I didn't have a photographic memory. As I memorized the verses, I had to think about each verse and truly understand the Almighty's Book in order to commit the verses to memory.

"Can I come and listen to the words from the Almighty's Book?" Peen called out from the other room.

Figure 25: Peen Studies the Almighty's Word with Vying

Who was I to deny her? "Of course."

She came in and sat on the edge of the bed. We began to listen together, but as weariness overcame me, I leaned back. Just for a moment, I closed my eyes listening to the Almighty's Book. It was more comfortable this way.

.   .   .

"Wake up, Vying. Where's Peen?" Nafuka whispered as he pushed back the curtain that separated the bedroom from the outer room.

"Well, well," he laughed. "I see you two finally got together,"

Peen got up and looked him square in the eye. "It's not what you think and if I ever hear a word, I will know that it was you. I'll come and hunt you down like a clarion."

The tough big man looked flustered. He hadn't expected that level of fire from Peen.

"She fell asleep while we were listening to the Almighty's Book. I'm sure I fell asleep first."

"Fine, fine by me. I didn't see a thing. Sorry Peen. It was only a joke," he said lifting his powerful arms in defense.

"Not to me!" Her eyes flared, piercing through Nafuka like hot daggers.

I turned off the hologram, put it under my belt and grabbed my other clothes.

"Don't change. Wait till we get to the prison compound. Is that alright with you, Peen?" Nafuka asked obsequiously.

Looking at Nafuka for a pregnant moment, she slowly replied. "Yes. Give me a moment with Vying."

"Of course," he said and quickly exited the hut.

She watched him as he left. "Vying, I've never met anyone like you. Most men take what they want from a woman."

"I'm sorry to hear that."

"I want you to remember me as a true friend, not merely an acquaintance," Peen stated.

"I shall, but I want to know you forever," Vying offered.

"What do you mean forever? When we die, we go back to the earth."

"No Peen. We either go to heaven or hell."

"Where are you going?" she asked.

"Heaven?"

"Why?" she asked curious.

"Because Jesus is my Lord and Savior. You heard the Almighty's Book talk about Him."

Peen considered what I said and suddenly blurted out, "I really want this Jesus!"

I led her in a prayer. "I will never forget your kindness, Peen. One day I will return."

"You better, I'm counting on it," she said sweetly and then gave me a warm embrace and a kiss on the cheek as she darted out the back.

Nafuka and I journeyed down the mountainside. The sun had not risen and the cool of the night felt good against my skin. We had to focus on the trail and didn't see the sniffer blocking our path until it was too late.

"It took them awhile, but they tracked you. We'll have to kill it to get by."

"The Almighty has given us dominion over these beasts of the fields and the fowl of the air. It's time to walk in faith."

"What are you talking about?"

"In the name of the Son of the Almighty, in the name of Jesus, I command this sniffer to keep his mouth closed and not to move."

"Great, I don't see him moving, but he's looking at us as if we are his next meal."

"We walk by faith, not by sight. Now come on, let's go past him."

"Yeah, right, Vying. Ah, why don't you go first?"

I looked at Nafuka and then to the sky and proceeded forward. The sniffer was much bigger than the ones in the cave, twice as big as Nafuka. I kept moving forward focused on the words of the Almighty's Book. *"We walk by faith, not by sight."*

It snorted and looked all around. Fear crept into my mind, but I took captive those thoughts and began to recite the Almighty's Book about faith being the evidence of things hoped for and the substance of things not seen. I went up to the sniffer. He still hadn't moved his head and I quickly slipped right past him all the time expecting his head to turn and bite me. His nose couldn't have been more than an arm's length away from me, but he never moved. I looked back at Nafuka and he was right behind me.

We walked quickly putting several leeds between us and the sniffer. We stopped and turned around. The hairy beast was still trying to catch our scent, sniffing all around going one way and then the other. He was very confused, and I knew the Almighty had worked another miracle in my life.

Sparingly, we drank water from our packs as the oven-hot desert sand began baking the moisture out of our bodies. There were few trees and only outcroppings of rock gave us shelter. It didn't seem as bad as the first day. I knew the training had been quite good. The day was long, but finally the prison loomed on the horizon just before the sun began to set. As we arrived, the huge prison gates opened and we entered. The big gates closed behind us as we walked into the sunlit compound.

"Go to the room with the others and wait," a guard yelled from his tower on the wall.

We walked into the room where the Warder had spoken to us and looked at the men sprawled out on the floor and against the walls, all trying to sleep. A couple of them hid under blankets.

"Do you want to take the first watch?"

"Sure," I said wondering what Nafuka meant as I stayed awake observing the others. The lights in the room dimmed and a few hours later the clandestine activity began.

Chapter Twenty-Six

Nafuka's prominent proboscis heartly joined the others in creating a riot of nasal noise. The unabridged symphony kept me awake all night. We shouldn't have taken our time getting to the compound, because we were pinned in a corner without an escape. At least we didn't have to cover our backs.

Dim moonlight, seeped through a cracked window and I noticed a quick flash from the palm of one of the prisoner's hands. It happened so quickly, I wasn't sure what I saw. Surreptitiously, I watched the little man. His slight of build was accented by furtive eyes, crunched up against his nose that intently searched the room, looking for something. When our eyes met, he quickly turned away.

I knew that if I had to fight him, he wouldn't be much of a match. I wondered how he expected to win against more formable opponents. Looking around, I scouted my opponents and saw a few men bigger than Nafuka. Feelings of inadequacy instantly filled my mind as if someone was reading my thoughts. I took captive those thoughts and pushed them from my mind. I began to repeat some of the sayings I'd heard from the hologram. I wished I could view it here, or go some place where I could have privacy, but I knew that wouldn't happen anytime soon.

In the midst of meditating on the verses from the Almighty's Book, I saw the slender man slink away while the others were resting. With his back to me, I saw him creep over to a very large man sleeping in the shadows. In the fading moonlight, I saw his arm shoot forward as if he was throwing a punch, but I heard no noise. Then he crept back to where he had been sitting as if nothing had happened. The other men in the room weren't disturbed and I wondered what had just happened. From watching him, I learned that he was extremely fast with his hands. I made a mental note that his attack would be pure speed.

When I felt sleepy, I nudged Nafuka. I noticed a few of the others had formed alliances and were also switching around.

"Anything unusual?" he asked in soft tone of voice, his eyes instantly alert.

"No, just that small man over there moved a little, nothing else."

"Which one?"

"That little guy over there."

"Vying, when are you going to learn?" he whispered shaking his head in disbelief.

"What are you talking about?"

"Where did he go?"

"Over to that big guy sleeping against the wall. I thought he was looking for a better place to sleep."

"Tomorrow morning, you watch," Nafuka said.

"What do you mean?"

"You'll see. Now get some rest."

I sat on the floor, leaned against the wall and fell asleep.

Figure 26: The Warder and a Starving Tusker

The next morning, as the sun rose, the Warder and two men appeared. Tuskers, pulling at their leashes, savagely growled with ferocious looks on their faces as if they hadn't been fed in a long time.

"Well, I see most of you have made it through your time in the outback. Soon we will begin the race. It will begin in the lower desert. My guards have set a course that will take you up into the foothills of the far mountain. There are three check points where you must pick up a yellow card from the guards as you run past. You are free to come back any way you choose, but you cannot enter the second part of the tournament without three yellow cards. So don't lose them," the Warder said as the tusker kept growling and looking at the big man who hadn't awakened.

An agitated tusker jumped forward pulling hard against his leash. The guard holding the leather gave him some slack. He went right over to the big man sleeping against the wall and began growling loudly, but the big man never moved. The tusker growled even louder and licked the man's face. Then he licked his tusks as if he were tasting his next meal.

"Oh my! What have we here?" the warder exclaimed with delight, smiling from ear to ear as he walked over to the fighter. He kicked him hard in the leg, but the man never moved.

"Quickly! Get the attendants!" the Warder shouted with greater excitement. One of the guards ran from the room returning with three others. They walked over to the tusker and roughly pushed it aside. It growled and I expected the tusker to lash out, but it was well-trained.

"He's dead," one of them said.

"You know what to do," the Warder said.

They carried the big man out as the tusker turned his head and carefully watched his meal depart, hungrily licking his lips.

The Warder laughed in a crazy delirious way, watching the scene unfold before him. His bizarre behavior was even more pronounced since we'd seen him before. "Unfortunately, we've lost one of the competitors."

His eyes searched the room as if looking for something or someone finally settling on the small man whose head was down. He stared at him. All eyes were directed toward him.

"Mousy, did you have something to do with the recent demise of that rather large fighter? You've been here for many years. Perhaps this year will be your year."

Mousy kept his eyes on the ground as if he hadn't heard the Warder.

"Look at me when I speak to you, Mousy, or has your guilt shamed you?" the Warder asked in delight at the events unfolding before him.

Still the little man refused to look up.

The Warder smiled looking at the discomfort he rained down. "Some of you may underestimate your opponents. I think Mousy has drawn first blood while the rest of you were sleeping and for that he is to be rewarded. Good Mousy, come here. You shall be first in line for the morning meal."

Mousy moved forward, turning his head at an usual angle looking to the Warder out of the corner of his eye.

"Mousy knows that the race is not to the swift, nor the battle to the strong. Only the top twenty-four finishers will be able to enter the battle ring. So run your best! You'll have a couple days to train here and then I will start the Crucible."

I couldn't believe my ears. How bizarre! How was it possible that this crazy man was quoting the Almighty's Book? How had the Warder learned the verses that I had just read? As I was thinking, I missed the last part of what he said.

"Let's get training, Vying. We have only two days," Nafuka said.

The men shuffled out and began working out, punching and kicking heavy bags, lifting stones, metal bars, climbing ropes and other types of equipment.

"What did he say?"

"You saw what just happened. Look over there!"

I looked to the other side of the compound. Two tuskers were ripping the flesh and bones from the body of the big man.

"He said that anyone who stops or drops out of the race will become food for his pets. Nothing here on Zartex is wasted."

"I'm not going to worry about that, but I know one thing, this is no ordinary competition."

"You've got that right, Vying, but you shouldn't have to worry. You'll be out in front."

"I don't know about that!"

"What do you mean? You run like the wind."

"You heard what the Warder said. The race is not to the swift. Besides, we have an alliance and I'm running with you, Nafuka."

"Don't worry about me. Look out for yourself and stay away from Mousy. He's already begun fighting. I wonder who will be next."

Chapter Twenty-Seven

I could hear the explosion of breath as men sparred against each other. Bodies slammed the mats. The unmistakable musty smell of stale sweat greeted us as we walked across the outdoor compound to the open training area.

"Were we the last to arrive?" I asked.

"It looks that way. The others must have stayed closer to the compound, but it won't matter. Training in the mountains gave us a huge advantage over the others in lung capacity and endurance."

I watched as a slender but agile competitor was sparring with a big man. He was wiry and elusive. He darted in and out, landing jabs and body punches without being touched. The big man was taking a pounding when he stepped forward with a punishing uppercut, landing a blow that snapped the man's head back. Drops of sweat burst off the man's face as he went sprawling across the ring.

"That's Bork. Watch out for him. I was glad I didn't have to fight him. He has the strength to knock a man out with one punch," Nafuka said.

When Wolks and I trained for the Crown Championship, there was a camaraderie bred from hard work with a great purpose that bound all the competitors together. Here on Zartex, the promise of freedom from a living hell bred a mercenary spirit. I thought about Wolks and what was happening on Micron. When we trained at "The Olde Gym" we were always greeted by pats on the back and words of encouragement. Veteran fighters would share their battle ring experiences laced with pearls of wisdom, but I knew that wouldn't happen here.

Heavy black bags hung from sturdy branches of the few trees in the compound. Three fighters were pounding away at them with their hands and feet. I watched as one of the fighters threw kick after kick. Each blow snapped the bag. Sweat rolled down their backs as the heavy bags exploded from their powerful leg kicks. Nafuka and I walked over to the trees and began stretching.

"Shouldn't we check in?" I asked.

"The Warder knows we're here. Have you forgotten the locator around your ankle?"

The warm sun felt good as I lay on the ground and stretching my quads and calves putting one leg over the other, while I twisted my upper body in the opposite direction. I watched as one of the guards walked up to us with a growling tusker pulling on the leash. The guard was big and quite muscular.

His bulbous nose was like the bow of a ship, slightly cocked to the right, set on a wide flat forehead. His upper body and legs were well defined with unusual bumps and scars criss-crossing both knees. I knew he'd been a fighter sometime in the past. When he walked up next to us, we could smell the tusker's rotten breath as he began sniffing us. I didn't move a muscle and let the animal do his job. When he was finished the guard pulled once on the leash and the tusker backed up sitting on his haunches. His eyes focused straight ahead.

Figure 27: A Prison Guard

"The competition begins at sunup. Gather by the main gate. The course is laid out with orange flags. Any questions?"

"I thought the Warder said a couple of days," I said.

"I'm in charge around here. I tell the Warder when the race begins," he replied turning around and walking off.

I waited until he was out of earshot. "What was that all about?"

"Some of the guards like to let you know that they're the boss."

"Are they?"

"Maybe. It's impossible to predict how the Warder thinks."

"We should have gotten here earlier."

"Are you crazy? Coming early is for fools. One thing's true, the competition has already begun. Sure, the food is good and there's plenty of water, but don't think for a moment that each one of the fighters hasn't studied the other and knows their moves."

"Are we going to train at all?"

"Of course Vying, but only on the heavy bags. Don't throw all your kicks. Just do a basic workout to break a sweat."

I didn't like this new training regime. When I trained for the Crown Championship, Wolks and I sparred up until the day before the competition. I wanted to get my timing down to feel more confident when I entered the ring.

"I know you're thinking that we should go through all of your techniques, but if you're not ready now, you'll never be. Besides with all the hours you've spent training, it's second nature to you, instinctive. Don't worry, after the first blow lands everything will come back to you. Besides, your body can use the rest."

"I hope you're right, Nafuka."

"For once, trust me. To train out in the open would be foolish. I had a perfect combination move with elbow strikes and a takedown. One of the older fighters picked up on it in practice and the first time I fought, he waited for the elbow strike, slipped it, and slammed his knee into my chin. He knocked me out. He never won another bout in the tournament, but I was finished that year."

We trained hard on the power bags for the next couple of hours and it felt good to get the blood flowing. Stopping long enough for a cool drink of water, I remembered my fight with the sniffer in the underground cavern. I knew these upcoming bouts would be just as fierce.

Out of the sky a shuttle suddenly appeared and slowly descended to the far end of the compound near some buildings surrounded by fences. I watched as the Warder and his entourage hurried over and graciously greeted several robed men disembarking the shuttle. Each had male and female attendants which the Warder ignored. I looked hard to see if any Hoons were arriving.

As if reading my thoughts, Nafuka said, "Don't worry, they're just noblemen. That's always a good sign."

"Why?"

"If the bidding gets high enough, more than one fighter is sold. You see that skinny brown fighter over there sweating heavily?"

"Yeah, why?"

"His name's Velongo. He comes from the swamps on Mercus. He's so fast, few can stop him. His feet and hands are deadly. I'm surprised he's still here. He made it to the final round of competition before I stopped him."

"Maybe he won his freedom and is now back like you."

Nafuka looked at me hard and finally answered, "Could be. His favorite move is a jab combination with a knee kick to the solar plexus. When you're trying to catch your breath, he throws punishing body blows to the kidneys. He's fast and effective."

"How do you stop him?"

"When I fought him, I attacked immediately and never let up. Watch him work the small bag."

We watched as Velongo peppered the speed bag with lightning quickness, as if a bolt had struck and empowered them. Sometimes he'd mix an elbow strike with his jabs without breaking the rhythm of his hands.

"I sure wouldn't want to be on the receiving end of those blows."

"You got that right. Here," Nafuka said handing me a water bottle. "Drink as much as you can today so you'll be hydrated for the run tomorrow."

We continued pounding the heavy bags until my arms were dead. I jogged around the compound and noticed that the children were no longer present. Tuskers hungrily eyed me as I ran by. Saliva drooled from their open mouths and I wondered when they'd last been fed. Their ravenous looks were eerie and I knew they considered us their next meal. As the sun began to set, I saw a few more fighters stagger through the gates. I finished jogging with a final burst of speed and slowed down. I strolled over to Nafuka, who was stretching his legs to keep them loose.

"Those tuskers really look hungry."

"No kidding. Do you know why?"

"I suppose they haven't been fed."

"That's right, but tomorrow they'll eat."

"How's that?"

"As an added incentive to the runners, anyone falling out of the race will become their dinner. The Warder likes to inspire the strong and weed out the weak."

Dinner was put on outdoor tables by the guards and the competitors ate with hearty appetites. Scraps were gathered, but they didn't go to the growling tuskers. We found a place to sleep in the middle of the barracks and I took the first watch of the night. Darkness settled over the room as my eyes adjusted to the fading light. Nafuka fell asleep quickly and began his evening concert of nasal notes. I felt confident that I would do well in the Crucible and began to map my strategy for the race when I noticed someone moving toward me in the shadows. Immediately my hands came up, ready to fight. The man stopped. I looked to see if he had a weapon in his hands. He waited. His face became more visible. I couldn't remember seeing him in the training compound. I rose up on the balls of my feet and got ready for his attack. I knew in tight quarters I'd have to strike hard and quick. My open hands came up and I got ready to attack. Confidently, he came closer.

"I come in peace, my friend," the small man whispered.

"Peace? Who are you?"

"I'm from planet Milo."

"Really? Who do you know on Milo?"

"Queen Zelestar. She sent me here because she learned that Og has set a trap for you on the run. You must be very careful."

"How do I know you're really from Milo?"

"The hologram that you carry illustrates the Almighty's Book. I studied many of the sayings as we programmed it."

"Tell me one of the sayings."

"*The Sword of the Spirit is the Word of God.*"

I couldn't remember that scripture because there were so many. "Why did you pick that verse?"

"I didn't. Queen Zelestar told me to tell you that."

"Do you understand the Almighty's Book?"

"I have learned much from it, but there is much more I need to study," said the slim stranger.

"Are you staying for the competition?"

"No, my mission is complete. I will be leaving soon."

"How will you get off Zartex?" I asked the man.

"For someone like me, there are many ways off this planet."

"What do you mean?"

"One moment I was walking away from Queen Zelestar and the next moment I was here. The Almighty translated me here, like in the Almighty's Book. Phillip was translated to meet the Ethiopian Eunuch

"No, my mission is complete. I will be leaving very soon."

"Take me with you."

He laughed quietly. "I wish it were that easy. I don't control where I go, besides you are a marked man. If you were to leave with me, you couldn't return to Micron, and Micron desperately needs your leadership. Wickedness and perversion are subtly claiming your planet."

"I know."

"Be vigilant on the run. Queen Zelestar was unable to discover what the trap was. Trust no one. Now I must go," he said turning to leave.

"Wait, what's your name?"

"Vying, I'm unimportant, but I pray the Almighty's divine protection on you."

With that, he took two steps and vanished. Nafuka woke up.

"Who were you talking to?"

"A friend."

"Really? Vying, I'm your only friend on Zartex."

I remembered the man's words, *"Trust no one."* I wondered if Nafuka was my enemy? Could I trust him?

"Get some sleep, Vying. I'll take the next watch."

I lay in the bunk, but sleep wouldn't come. I wondered what would happen next. I knew I needed to rest, so I prayed and asked the Almighty to have His angels watch over me. Slowly, I drifted off to an uneasy sleep.

Chapter Twenty-Eight

Light suddenly torched the overhead as the Warder barged into the barracks, flanked by two tuskers and four guards.

"I hope you've slept well. Tomorrow the competition begins," he said looking at all of us. Then for some reason his gaze rested on me. I returned his glare expecting something to be said to me, but the Warder broke out into a laugh that reminded me of a Hoon howling. He was a horror show straight from the lake of fire.

Focusing on me as if we were having a private conversation he continued, "Be careful on the run. I've watched this race from above and have seen some very unfortunate things happen to some of the competitors. The outback here on Zartex, as some of you already know, can be very inhospitable. You must stay alert at all times."

"You can say that again," mumbled Nafuka.

"What was that? Who said something? Ah ha, was that you Nafuka?" the Warder laughed, taking his eyes off me and quickly focusing on Nafuka.

"Yes, boss. I was just agreeing with you. The heat can be deadly out there."

"Oh yes, yes the heat," he said relaxing and enjoying the moment, continuing in a very mild and loving tone of voice. "How could I have forgotten about that? Of course you are right Nafuka to remember. You've been away, but the heat of the desert never leaves us. Part of me hopes you make it through the competition. Do you know why?"

"No boss, I don't."

"You're one of my pets, Nafuka, just like one of these tuskers," the Warder said laughing, his eyebrows arching, his mouth open wide. The growling war animals snapped the slack out of their leashes dragging their guards closer to Nafuka, threatening him in case he moved. The Warder laughed some more at his own joke while he watched the tuskers smelling Nafuka. Then one of the guards whispered something in his ear.

The Warder nodded his head. "Yes, yes, good. On the run you may bring anything you want. Be sure to take some water. I know some of you have fashioned weapons since you've been here," he said with a glint of evil escaping his eyes as he stared at Mousy.

"Take them with you. You may need to defend yourselves against the wild beasties that roam around out there. Be careful, I wouldn't want anything to happen to you. Remember I can't spare any guards or tuskers to protect you," he said looking around the room with a big smile on his face as if he held a great secret.

"Especially you," he said whirling around and pointing his long bony finger at me. Turning quickly he exited the room. The tuskers had to be dragged away from Nafuka. The lights went out.

"Go back to sleep," Nafuka said.

"Yeah, right," I responded the adrenalin flowing through my veins and keeping me wide awake. "We have quite an alliance. Why were those tuskers so interested in you?"

"I guess they have a long memory. Get some sleep. You'll need your energy."

"I don't think I'll be able to sleep peacefully until I get off this planet," I said wondering about Nafuka's comment about the tuskers. What else didn't I know about him?

Nothing else happened during the night and early the next morning all the men ate lightly. I stuffed some dried meat in my pocket as I headed toward the big gates. The Warder came forward flanked by guards and tuskers. One of them drew his sword and made a line in the dirt. In anticipation, we all lined up.

"Oh this is good, very good. You're ready to go and I haven't even told you that we are starting a day earlier. The course is quite simple. Just follow the orange flags. I'll see most of you tomorrow. It gets cold out there at night, but you know that already. Night can be very dangerous, so be vigilant. Open the gates!" he shouted.

The big wooden gates slowly creaked open and two guards with tuskers immediately went outside and took up their positions on either side.

"In the past years, I've seen sniffers show up at the start, waiting for the competition to begin. I don't know how they know. Maybe they're just hungry. Oh, I see you're getting jumpy," the Warder said as one of the competitors edged forward, stepping over the line.

"Wait for my command," he yelled as he snatched the whip out of one of the guard's hands and snapped it laying the leather on the back of the man who had tried to get a head start.

"When I crack my whip again, then you may go, not before. Any questions?" he asked.

The Warder lifted the whip and looked over the men, hunting for his next victim. He turned his arm and snapped the whip, hitting me in the back the sudden pain searing through my back dropping me to my knees. I quickly got back up and ran out.

Immediately I sprinted off the line, getting away from most of the competitors so I wouldn't get tripped, knifed, or thrown to the ground. The race was supposed to be a footrace, but the deadly competition had already begun. I knew some sort of trap awaited me. The Warder had confirmed it. A couple of the men were ahead of me, but I kept my distance content with the pace.

The first large incline came quickly and I could see those in front of me falter. I used short choppy steps and quickly ascended. I lengthened my strides, gliding down the backside of the slope. Soon, I was all alone and out in front. It wasn't what I'd planned, but I felt strong. If something was attacking me, it would come at me from the front where I'd have plenty of time to see the attack. The distant mountain range was much farther away than the one we had trained for, but I knew it didn't matter. My training was sufficient; even though this course was much longer, I had built the endurance to complete it.

After a while my second wind kicked in and I began the monotonous process of putting one foot in front of the other. I took a pull from the water I carried on my back and continued running, but the mountain range and the distant orange flags didn't seem to be getting any closer.

Pain racked my sides and I fought through it, not slowing down. I turned to either side to see if anyone was near me, but they weren't. I was free and clear and my mind began to wander as I maintained the grueling pace. The sun beat down and I took another drink of water. I'd settled into a steady rhythm for the next two hours and then looked behind. No one was moving up on me. I'd always been a superior runner and that talent gave me a huge advantage both mentally and physically.

For a long time I kept my eyes on the ground directly in front of me, never daring to see how far I'd traveled. I knew that in conquering distance the last thing that I wanted to do was keep my eyes fixed on the mountain range. I could easily slip if my mind drifted.

Something darted ahead of me. Immediately, I slowed down and looked all around, but couldn't spot anything unusual. Whatever it was, it was gone. I looked back, but shouldn't have. Something flashed in front of my face. Immediately, I hit the ground as it whizzed by. I couldn't see where the arrows landed. Off to the right were a bunch of smooth, weather beaten boulders. I kept my eyes fixed on them, waiting in case I needed to dive for protection from another onslaught. To my left a trail descended into a slight valley and offered protection from any more arrows.

I looked back and the other runners were strung out in a single file with many leeds between them. I was losing my advantage and thought I'd wait for them to pass, but they must have seen something because they veered off to the right, away from me.

I was on my own. Either I stayed the course or took my chances using the walls of the ravine as a way of cover. I jumped to my feet and immediately slipped down into the canyon. Starting again my pace was choppy.

Something was wrong! I felt it in my spirit. I accelerated to put the rocks behind me then looked back at the boulders. I hadn't noticed the trip wire strung between the walls. It caught my lead foot and I tumbled down. As I was falling, something told me to dive to higher ground on the left.

Figure 28: A Sword Trap

Five swords shot up from the sand. One was so close; its edge cut my side, drawing blood. I looked at the cut and noticed it wasn't very deep. The Almighty had protected me. Carefully, I got up and moved to the left, out of the ravine. I saw that I was now behind four runners. My hard fought advantage was lost, but at least I'd avoided the sword trap. I wondered if that was the only one as I followed behind the others. If something else happened I'd wait to see if it affected them first.

My pace settled out and I looked ahead at the mountain range. I wondered how far up we would go before we headed back to the compound. Midday soon passed and I was gaining on the front runners.

Then a thought popped into my mind. *"That trap had been set recently because they couldn't have known at the start where I would end up, so they must still be out there. I wondered when they would strike again."* .

Chapter Twenty-Nine

Dark shadows enslaved the desert sands as the sun released its control and slipped behind the towering mountain peaks. Florescent orange flags marked the incline. One of the runners stopped, drank a bit of water and pulled out something to eat. He looked at me and laughed, mocking my troubles in the sand. I powered up the pass keeping my head down, being refreshed by the cool mountain air. I had no intention of stopping and pulled a piece of dried clarion from under my belt and stuck it in my mouth.

Darkness smothered me, but I continued up the trail. A stab of pain lanced my side, my legs afire, begging me to stop, but I refused. I'd passed up three other competitors. Suddenly the man ahead of me tripped and fell.

"Are you okay?" I asked as I helped him up.

"What do you care?" he snapped as he shook off my hand and straightened up.

"Do you need something for your knee?" I asked pointing to the blood running down his legs.

"I'm fine," he said.

I couldn't help but notice the intensity of his grey eyes. "When we get in the battle ring, it'll be your blood flowing."

"Just trying to help. Don't worry about the battle ring. We have to make it out of here alive and then we'll meet."

"Count on it! I'll be waiting to grind you up. Some of the others think the Crown Champion is something special, but I don't."

"You're right. I'm just like any other man, but the difference in me is I've got Jesus in my heart. He's my strength."

"Go talk your Jesus to somebody else, fool!"

"Oh I will, just as soon as I'm done talking to you about Him. If you don't have Him in your life, you'll go to the Lake of Fire for all eternity."

"I'm outta here," he said running off.

"What's your name?" I shouted, but didn't get a response.

I followed him for a couple of hours until he stopped to drink water and eat. He glared at me as I passed him. It was getting late, but I had no intention of stopping.

The night air got much colder and solar markers barely lit the path. My eyes adjusted to the reduced light as dark clouds blocked the moon's rays. I slowed my pace because I couldn't see very well. I rounded a bend in the uphill path. The pain in my legs was unbearable. But, I knew my strength was in the Almighty and His Book.

A scripture floated into my mind, *"The race is not to the swift or to the strong, but to those who endure."* Then another one came, *"They shall mount up on wings of eagles, they shall run and not grow weary."*

"Okay Almighty Father, I know what you're telling me. I'm not stopping!" I said aloud pushing myself up the next incline. Suddenly I was over the top of the mountainside and airborne.

"Whoa," I yelled through my freefall before crashing hard against a rock. I bounced off the boulder jarring my teeth and biting my tongue. I kept my balance and danced down the side of the mountain going faster than I could ever have imagined, barely staying on my feet. I didn't know how I made it down the mountain at this speed, but the thought about being *'carried on the wings of eagles,'* came true. I knew the Almighty had saved me again. The taste of copper filled my mouth and I spit out the blood.

The next set of declines were slight and rolling. My heart slowed, my pace settling down. The path was like a jogging trail through a canyon. I rounded the bend for a long stretch downhill and started to relax my pace, but shouldn't have. The moment I relaxed, my enemy struck!

Heavy rocks slammed right in front of me. Instantly, I spun around. The next one hit directly behind me and I dodged it as it came right at me. Just then the clouds opened and the moon shone brightly. There they were! Four of them. Waiting! Swords drawn. Nowhere to run!

I skidded to a halt. My only escape was back uphill. I wondered if I had the strength to outrun them. I turned around.

"I wouldn't do that if I were you, Vying," Scarface said as two tuskers came out from behind a rock being pulled by two more Hoons. "They'd tear you apart before you got ten leeds."

Escaping both Hoons and tuskers was impossible, unless the angel with the flaming swords showed up. "What do you want?"

Scarface hesitantly looked all around as if expecting to see another flaming angel. "What do you think? You. Emperor Og thinks you're very special. He's giving you a free pass off Zartex. You should be grateful."

"Yeah, right."

"Put him in chains," Scarface growled as the four Hoons and the two tuskers descended upon me.

I took my chances and launched a forward kick, landing squarely in the chest of the lead Hoon. He fell backward and I squared myself for the first Hoon, but another grabbed me in a bear hug, lifting me off my feet. He began squeezing the life out of me. I struggled with all my might, but the Hoon was much more powerful. He held me tight against his body and continued to squeeze. I tried my best to move, but couldn't.

"Lord, help me," I cried out with my last breath. I started to get dizzy. I struggled for air, but none came. His grip was too tight.

Scarface laughed. "Without your big partner and the fiery angel throwing flaming spears, you're just an ordinary man."

"Why, Lord?" I asked as my mind slipped into darkness...

I don't know how much time passed as I started to regain consciousness. I was no longer on the running path. The Hoons had bound my hands and legs and I watched as they were perched on a ledge looking down. Scarface turned around.

"I'll bet you didn't expect to wake up," he laughed in a gravely voice. "Rok knew what he was doing. The emperor is sending a special ship for us and we'll be gone soon."

I couldn't believe it. Even though I'd been warned, their ambush was in the perfect place. There was no way to avoid it. Scarface turned away from me as I heard footsteps and rocks being kicked away as some of the competitors ran past on the mountain trail.

Then it was quiet again. Still I couldn't understand the Almighty. How could He have let me get captured by the Hoons after He carried me down the sheer incline of the mountainside?

I heard a high whining sound and looked into the sky. A shuttle was descending from the sky and it looked very familiar. It was the same prison shuttle that had brought me to Zartex. It landed nearby and I saw a couple people disembark and walk over to us.

"Good work, Scarface," the Warder said as he nodded to the Hoon. "Your plan was flawless."

The Warder looked at me and then at his tuskers.

"Were my pets helpful?"

"Oh indeed. It made his escape impossible."

"Now for you, Vying. I tried to warn you there was danger on this run, but you wouldn't listen to me," the Warder said smiling from ear to ear. A crazed look of delight filled his face. "My dear friend, Og, for some reason, wants to take you alive. So we shall accommodate the Emperor's wishes."

"Bring the prisoner out."

Two more prison guards came out of the shuttle with a man that was my size. He was dressed exactly as I was. I looked again and an eerie feeling swept over me. The man looked exactly like me.

"What do you think about his surgery? What are we going to do with two Vyings?" the Warder asked proud of my double.

I stood there amazed.

"Attach Vying's collar to his leg," the Warder ordered. Two guards walked toward me and took off my anklet and put it on the other man. The Hoons looked on as the tuskers strained at their leashes. I knew what would happen next. The Warder went over to the prisoner.

"I think every man deserves a chance to live. I'm going to give you a opportunity to finish the race and fight for your freedom. Who knows, you might win the Crucible while Vying pays a visit to Emperor Og. You will need water, so strap this bag on, but before you do, take a good long drink. A man can die of thirst out here," the Warder said thoroughly enjoying this moment his face framed with a sadistic smile.

"Do you know why the tuskers are pulling so hard at their leashes? Do you know what drives them crazy?"

The man shook his head afraid to answer.

"It's your fear. They can smell it oozing from you. It excites them like nothing else. Oh, did I forget to mention that these two have been fasting and haven't eaten in four days?" the Warder said, his eyes brows raised as if he were imparting a great truth to some young child. Then he laughed again.

"I believe in fairness. I've given you water and the advantage of not having to do the first part of the Crucible. The real Vying has done it for you. Now I give you the opportunity to finish the race, make it to the compound alive, and enter the battle ring competition. What do you say? Am I not a generous soul?"

The frightened man couldn't raise his head to look at the Warder.

"Now take another long drink of water because you must hydrate before the run. The sun will be hot today, but you will have a great advantage over the competition. Now go!"

But the man just stood there.

"Did you hear me? I said go. Run or I'll let my tuskers rip you to shreds right here."

As if on cue, the animals lunged forward, dragging the Hoons with them.

"You better go. They're quite hungry."

The tuskers lunged again and the man quickly took off running without looking back.

"Oh this will be so good," the Warder said smiling. "Let's give him a good fighting chance. Who knows, maybe he can outrun my tuskers?...That's enough. Let 'um go!"

The armored animals bolted across the plain, quickly attacking the helpless man. Blood flew everywhere as they tore him to pieces and gorged on his flesh. When the Hoons arrived they pulled the blood splattered tuskers off.

"Put the remains in a body bag and send it to Micron. They'll want proof that Vying is dead."

The guards went down and put the torn body in a black bag and carried it back to the Warder's shuttle. The tuskers were licking their blood splattered snouts as they were brought back aboard leaving the four Hoons on the ground.

"Give my best to Og, Scarface."

Figure 29: Scarface

The Hoon grunted as the Warder entered the shuttle and the hatch closed. I didn't know what was going to happen next, but I watched as the Warder's shuttle took off.

"Put the prisoner on the ground," Scarface said as they pushed me down. Something alerted Scarface as he walked off with sword in hand. I saw the movement of a clarion. One of the other Hoons followed Scarface.

I looked again and two spears flew right at me. I couldn't move!

Chapter Thirty

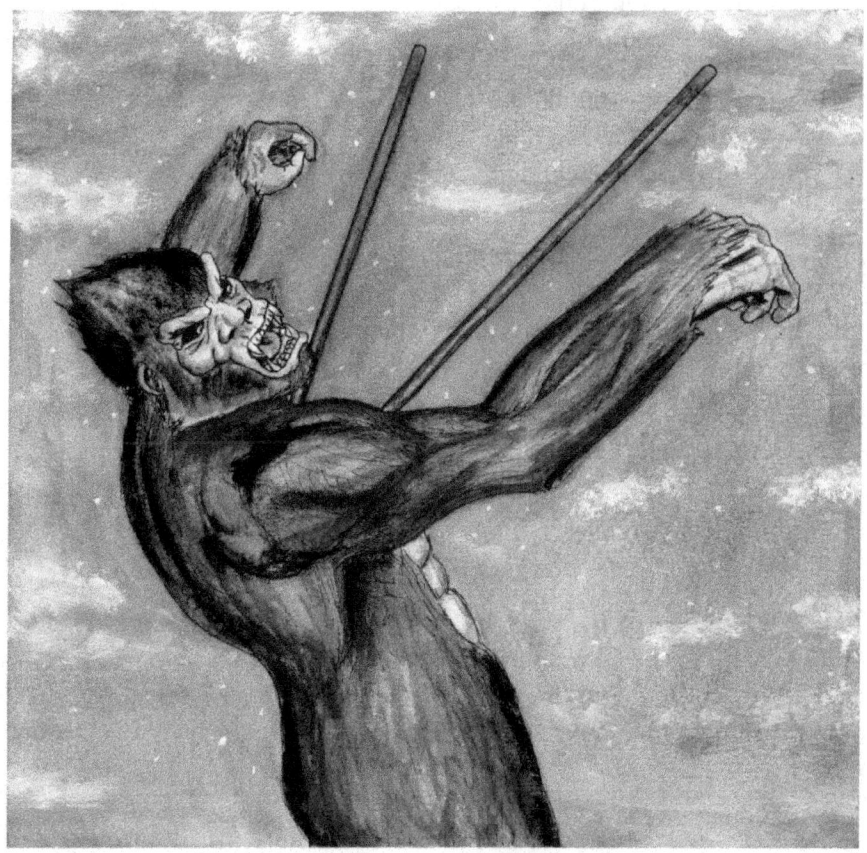

Figure 30: A Hoon Killed

Two hands jerked me aside as spears shot by my face impaling both Hoons. I looked around and saw twenty armed Che-Wa guarding the rim when we moved out through the canyon.

"That was too close, Nafuka. I could have been killed."

"What do you mean? Peen timed her throw perfectly."

"If you hadn't snatched me, I would've caught one of the spears."

"All part of the plan, my friend. We needed cover and you were just perfect. We better hurry! Scarface will be back in a moment."

"You two get going! We'll distract Scarface. We have a few more tricks for him before we leave."

"Peen, how did you know?"

"We were in the mountains hunting clarion when I saw you were in a bit of trouble. I kept an eye on your progress as you began your ascent up the mountain. Then I had a thought that you might not make it, so we followed you. That's when we saw the Hoons. You were too close to them, so we just waited. Then we saw Nafuka running down the slope and signaled him."

"Remember the alliance. We're a team and teammates help each other out. Now we've got to get going before Scarface returns and they catch us in the open," Nafuka said.

We ran as fast as we could before the Hoons returned and their shuttle arrived.

Finally, we reached the last downhill mountain trail leading back to the compound. We'd lost a lot of ground and could see many competitors ahead of us. In the distance the gates were wide open. This was the most difficult part of the Crucible. Not only was your body tired and worn, but you had to pick up two large canisters filled with rocks and carry them four hundred leeds to the finish line. The distance was long and the heavy canisters evened up the race, giving a distinct advantage to the bigger stronger men.

The morning sun baked the desert sand and I could see Nafuka faltering. I didn't know how many competitors were ahead of us, but I decided to stay with him. "Come on, Nafuka, keep up! We're almost there."

"Leave me, Vying. You have a shot at winning this, even now."

"I know, but I've made this mistake once before and I won't repeat it. We have an alliance. Now pick it up!"

Nafuka looked at me puzzled. "Are you crazy? The Realm needs you on Micron."

"Are you part of the Realm?"

"I'd like to be," Nafuka said.

"Then pick it up and get moving!"

Nafuka lifted his head and I could see he'd gotten a burst of energy.

"Looking good!" I encouraged in an upbeat tone.

We ran to the canisters and stopped. Both of us reached for our water and took long drinks. We picked up the weights and began carrying them toward the gates. As we toiled toward the gates, we came upon a competitor who was trying to move forward dragging his right leg. As we went by him, I said a prayer that the Almighty would help him. Even though he was an enemy, I wanted the Almighty's best for him.

The gates were getting closer, but every joint in my neck, back, shoulders, and arms were ready to explode. The pain was excruciating! I looked over at Nafuka. Agony etched his face. He was grimacing and swearing profusely. We passed a large fighter who was staggering towards the gates.

"If we pass one more competitor, I think we'll be alright," Nafuka uttered. My heart began to swell with pride as Nafuka was giving all he had to finish the run competitively.

Finally the gates were ten leeds away. My shoulders felt like they were being ripped off. Searing pain attacked every joint in my body. I wanted to drop the weights, but I knew if I did, I'd never pick them up again. Strangely, Nafuka picked up the pace. I did my best, but he surged ahead of me. I thought how ironic it would be if he got into the competition and I didn't. Together we stumbled through the gates dropping the canisters.

"Nineteen, twenty," the watchman called out and the gates cruelly closed to the competitors still out there.

I couldn't believe it. We made the competition. Nafuka dropped to his knees. He looked like he was praying, thanking the Almighty.

"Let's get some water!"

"Leave me alone! My feet are on fire."

I lifted the big man to his feet. He put an arm over my shoulder as we maneuvered to the table of food and water. We drank water, leaving the food for later. Our bodies hadn't slowed down as Nafuka dropped to the ground again.

"Nafuka, you've got to get up."

"I can't! My feet are a mess."

I walked around the compound slowly drinking water. Finally, I grabbed some fruit. The Crucible had taken its toll on Nafuka and I knew he had to recover in time for the bouts that would start in a few days. I brought more water over to Nafuka as the Warder was out checking on the competitors who had finished the run.

He looked at us and his jaw dropped. The look of sheer surprise on the Warder's face was priceless.

Quickly recovering, he said, "Well, well, I guess the reports about your demise were premature. You're still very much alive. Strange, there's an uncanny resemblance to the mangled body we sent back to Micron. I wonder how he got your bracelet?"

The Warder leaned close to my face. "I'm surprised you made it, Vying. No doubt Nafuka helped you."

I looked over at the Warder and shook my head.

"I'm sure Og will be upset when Scarface returns without you. What happened out there?"

"I really don't know," I answered.

The Warder laughed. "Oh, I'll find out. I always do and then I will punish all who helped you!"

Chapter Thirty-One

Over the next two days I trained lightly, replenishing my fluids and eating as much as I could. My muscles needed nutrients and recovery time, so I concentrated on stretching and throwing punches with speed. Nafuka was still hobbling, so I brought him food and drink. The balls and heels of his feet were rubbed raw and had holes in them where they had been eaten away by the constant pounding on the Crucible. Trenchfoot had set in. Painfully he stood up and I wondered if he could fight.

"Tonight begins single elimination. If you lose, you're out. Are you ready, Vying?"

"I feel good, but what about you?"

"Don't worry about me. Put these moleskins on the bottoms of my feet and I'll be able to fight," he said handing me two skins from a rodent he killed. I glued them to his feet and hoped they would help.

"Because we were the last two competitors to finish the Crucible, we must fight the top two finishers," Nafuka added.

"Maybe that's a blessing in disguise."

"Why?"

"I don't think anyone expected us to be so far down on the list of fighters," I said as we walked over to the outdoor arena. Excitement filled the air as the fighters gathered at the entrance to the battle ring.

Bright lights and a cool evening breeze greeted us as we were ushered inside the canvas tent that covered the battle ring and stands. The boisterous crowd filled the arena as noblemen and their advisors from Coralia began filing into their seats. All the fighters lined up and were given numbers as they were introduced to the crowd so that bets could be collected for each of the competitors before the tournament began. Hawkers circulated through the crowd, collecting money and keeping a ledger as pairings were announced for the first fights of the night.

Figure 31: The Battle Ring

I drew Velongo for the fifth match of the evening, Mercifully, Nafuka had a first round bye. He couldn't have fought anyway. We walked back to the barracks. I began to stretch my leg muscles as I sat on the ground. They were sore and tight, but I knew when I entered the ring, the adrenalin would kick in and I wouldn't feel a thing.

Nafuka limped out of the barracks. "This isn't good. Velongo uses a lot of leg kicks and elbow strikes. You shouldn't have slowed down to run with me. Because of me, you have to fight him. He's strong and powerful with lightning speed. Watch his low leg kicks. They'll destroy your knees, if he lands four or five kicks. Don't let him get in close."

"I didn't come this far to lose. The Almighty will see to that."

"I hope so, because I've seen this guy fight. He brings the heat right from the beginning. So don't walk in there expecting to dance around. He'll be coming at you non-stop. Velongo catches people off guard. Let's warm up. I want you to practice defending low leg and knee kicks. I'll throw one and you block it," Nafuka instructed as we went to the warm-up area behind the stands.

Painfully, Nafuka kicked with his leg and I blocked it with my shin. It didn't hurt me because my leg met his in the air and the full brunt of the blow wasn't delivered.

"I'll be standing on the edge of the moat. Listen for my voice and do what I tell you," Nafuka said as I watched my opponent stretch. He looked serene, as if this first fight was of little concern.

The first three bouts of the evening were quickly over with one unconscious man being carried out. Nafuka and I made our way to the center of the arena.

The battle ring was surrounded by a water moat. I walked across an expanding steel bridge and wondered if I was ready to enter the battle ring again. It had been five years since I'd entered this arena of furious combat with no rules. I looked up. "Almighty, I need you. Help me to carry out Your plan."

Velongo was already waiting for me. A confident look blanketed his face as we faced each other in the center. The gong droned and he immediately charged and caught me square in the stomach with a solid push kick that knocked the wind out of me and propelled me to the far side of the ring.

"Vying, wake up!" Nafuka screamed.

I hit the ground and rolled to my left, springing to my feet. I couldn't breathe and circled to catch my wind. He came at me again.

"You can't stand there. You've got to attack!" shouted Nafuka.

The suddenness of Velongo's next blow surprised me and I danced around him, watching him move, cutting off my retreat, controlling the center, controlling the fight and pushing me toward the water. Velongo smiled at me as I neared the moat, as if he knew some secret.

"Vying!" Nafuka screamed. "What are you doing? I told you to attack. One kick and you're in the water!"

Velongo rushed me and we clinched at the edge of the moat. He pushed at me with all his might trying to topple me into the moat. Then he kneed me in the stomach and kidneys with his long legs. I pushed back, but still hadn't even thrown a punch.

"Get out of there! He's going to hurt you if you don't," Nafuka yelled.

I broke the clench and returned to the center of the battle ring waiting for Velongo.

Another mistake. He charged again and threw a left jab, then a right, then an uppercut. I defended his attack and countered with a punch combo to his head and body.

"Finally!" Nafuka exclaimed. "I thought you dancing with Zelestar."

Velongo blocked my knee kick and came back with an overhand right. I slipped under it and countered with a solid right hand, punishing his kidney followed by a combination of hard uppercuts to his body. I could hear the whistling of air from his lungs as he jerked from the blows, peddling backwards. Finally I felt I in sync. I was back!

With arms extended he shot a takedown, but instinctively I sprawled backwards and landed an elbow strike to his temple before he got up. I scrambled to my feet and saw he was a little dazed.

"ATTACK! ATTACK! ATTACK!" screamed Nafuka from the other side of the moat.

Velongo didn't hesitate and threw a flurry of punches, most of which I blocked, but one connected and stung my lower lip, filling my mouth with blood. Some spilled onto my chin.

Smiling again, Velongo commented quietly, "Remember the mountain trail, I told you, I'd have you bleeding. Now I'm going to break you in two."

"Don't listen to him. Get after him!"

He came at me again with fists flying, but I easily counterpunched, unloading a flurry of my own. Pulverizing his chin with a roundhouse right, I rocked him backwards. Immediately, I shot a double leg takedown, sending him to his back. He rolled to his stomach and scrambled to his feet before I could apply any submissions.

We circled again, staying away from each other. I looked for an opening. We both understood each other's strengths and looked to exploit the other's weaknesses.

"Quit playing out there. Finish him!" Nafuka yelled.

Moving swiftly to my right, I cut off his circling by stepping in with a flying scissors kick that connected with his chin. Sweat sprayed the ring and snapped his head back. He countered by quickly moving to his right.

I threw a left jab and immediately dropped to the ground. I came up and hit a double-leg takedown hammering him to his back. He scrambled to his hands and knees attempting to get back to his feet, but I jumped on his back and wrapped my legs around his stomach and grabbed under his elbows, flattening him out.

I clamped a triangle body lock around his waist and grabbed his right arm. He reached back to unhook my legs, leaving his neck wide open. I seized the opportunity and secured the rear-naked chokehold. His face turned dark purple from the lack of oxygen. I could feel his strength leaving him and his body going limp before he finally tapped the mat.

Walking out of the ring toward Nafuka, they announced me as the winner.

"What were you thinking out there? Didn't I tell you he was going to attack. You've got to listen to me, Vying, or you're going get beat. These guys are out for blood. Don't you get it? They wouldn't be here if they weren't stone-cold killers. "

Chapter Thirty-Two

I left the arena a first round victim. In spite of Nafuka yelling in my ear, I felt elated. I still had it. My body hurt from the various blows Velongo had landed, but none seemed really too bad. I'd know more tomorrow when the real pain set in. Although I hadn't been in the ring long, the intensity of the match wore me out more than I would have thought. I remembered my title bout for the Crown Championship. I wasn't as tired then, but that was five years ago.

"He was pretty tough," I said to Nafuka as we walked away.

"You bet he was. You looked old and tired out there when the match started."

"What do you expect? It's been five years since I've been in the battle ring."

"Vying, some of these guys could've fought for the Crown Championship and won. They've been fighting all their lives. They've had nothing to do in prison, but lift weights, eat and fight."

"Calm down, Nafuka. Did you miss it? I won."

Whirling around Nafuka glared at me. "You don't get it! The next round will be even tougher. You've got to come out of the past, out of your daydreams, and strike immediately. You can't let them come to you. Velongo hit you four times before you woke up."

"Alright, alright. I'll attack."

"Did you remember the prison shuttle? Some of these guys are juiced?"

"What are you talking about? Where would they get the roids?"

"The noblemen love to win too. They slip the juice to the guys they've bet on. They aren't going to feel the pain, so they might not tap out. Let's head back to see the last fight of the night. Bork is fighting you need to watch his style."

We walked back into the arena and sat in a section of the stands near the ring reserved for the competitors. A couple of noblemen came over to check me out and see if I was injured, so they could place their bets accordingly.

I looked at the lone fighter in the middle of the battle ring. His opponent hadn't come out. The crowd grew restless, noisy and impatient. Whistling and shouting, they started clapping in unison, protesting the delay.

"Bork! Bork! Bork!" they chanted.

I couldn't believe what I was seeing and hearing. When I fought Megog the same thing happened to me. They chanted his name before he entered the battle ring.

Finally, he appeared at the edge of the moat and the crowd erupted. Shedding his makeshift animal skins, I noticed his big belly and wondered how much he weighed. He looked like a big, out-of-shape blob, but I knew that in the fight game, body type didn't dictate skill and competence.

Bork looked around with a scowl on his face. They loved it. Robust applause broke out as he slowly walked across the bridge at his own slow pace, lifting his heavy undefined arms and stretching.

His opponent, Falco, was a lean muscled man with slanted eyes and a tall build. His chest and back were ripped. He looked up for the task of taking on the slower moving Bork. In these fights, weight could be a factor, if used correctly, but quickness reigned supreme.

The gong sounded and the two men walked to the center of the ring. With clenched fists they began to circle each other. Falco moved in, but to the surprise of many, Bork threw a blinding right jab, scoring heavily on his opponent's eye. Within seconds, Falco's eye swelled up. He threw a flurry of misguided punches that were easily blocked.

The crowd "ooohed," watching Bork's footwork, which was anything but slow and clumsy. Jab, jab, uppercut and a leg kick to the thigh, he hammered his opponent with various combinations. Falco grimaced and staggered out of Bork's range. I could see the big-bellied man was quite nimble and liked to slow his opponents down by disabling body punches and side leg shots. I knew the more damaging blows were delivered by the leg kicks.

Sensing victory, Bork attacked quickly throwing a combination of punches and kicks. I wondered if he would do any grappling. A thundering body punch to Falco's kidneys resonated across the arena.

Hurt and unable to see out of one eye, he again back peddled and Bork charged immediately crashing into him using his big belly as a weapon. Falco went sprawling to the ground, but quickly rolled away from the edge of the moat, avoiding another leg kick that would have sent him into the water. The big man looked like a brawler, but it was all an act.

Falco bounded to his feet and threw a couple of quick punches, but Bork blocked them, ducked, and counterpunched to the body. In desperation, Falco changed his strategy and lunged for Bork's feet. The big man brought his knee straight up and caught Falco squarely under the chin. The muscular fighter slumped to the ground and tried to get up as Bork hammered him with a low side kick to the temple, dropping him instantly, knocking him out. Slowly the big bellied man walked over to the fallen fighter, picked him up and threw him into the moat. Falco's muscle mass was dense, so he sank to the bottom like an anchor.

Two guards jumped into the water and pulled him out, but he wasn't breathing. I ran into the ring past Bork whose arms were lifted high as he was receiving the praise of the crowd. I pulled Falco's mouth to the side and emptied the water, held his nose shut and gave him ten quick breaths of air in an attempt to revive him.

He wasn't breathing. I looked over at Bork and the murderous scowl returned to his face. "Leave him! He deserves to die," he said walking over to me. "I said, leave him be!"

Figure 32: Falco

CHAPTER THIRTY-THREE

A meaty hand tossed me away from Falco. Nafuka ran across the bridge and jumped into the air, crashing into Bork and body slamming him to the ground. Guards rushed in from both sides and tried to separate the two fighters, but the big men kept fighting. I rushed back to Falco and pushed down on his chest fifteen times and gave him three quick breathes of air, but still no movement. He was dead.

It took ten guards to separate Bork and Nafuka.

"You're next!" he yelled pointing a finger at me. "And then you," he said, turning to Nafuka.

Bork looked up at the judges. "Put me against either of these two in the next round."

The guards picked up Falco and carried him out of the ring.

"Vying, you're crazy. This tournament is tough enough, but now you've really angered Bork."

"Big deal."

"Big deal! He kills most of his competitors in the battle ring. The noblemen are betting he'll do it again. Thanks to your chivalry, one of us will face him next round."

"Nafuka, it wasn't right. Falco was defeated."

"I admire your chivalry, but he doesn't follow the warrior's code," Nafuka said. Then a sly grin came over his face. "This may work to your advantage."

"How?"

"You've upset the gambling. The noblemen usually let Bork fight only one preliminary bout and then he's placed in the semi-finals. If they do it again, I'm sure one of us won't fight again until the semi's."

"That doesn't make sense. I thought this was a tournament."

"Wake up! This tournament doesn't have any rules! They do as they want. The Warder will please the noblemen anyway he can."

That night I couldn't sleep. The Almighty wanted me to pray for Falco, but he was dead. Finally I got up and went to the infirmary where they had taken his body. I looked all around, but couldn't spot his body. I wondered if the tuskers had been fed. I had to obey the leading of the Almighty's Spirit and I began to pray. I prayed for a long time when a thought came into my mind to go to the back of the infirmary.

I thought about it. I'd already been there and hadn't seen anything, but I obeyed and walked to the rear of the building. A shaft of light peeked out from a door and I eased it open. There on the table was Falco. I knew this door was closed before. I went into the room, closed the door and laid my hands on the body. It was cold and clammy and rigor mortis had already set in, but with blind faith, I began to pray speaking life into his body. I prayed all night and wondered if I had heard from the Almighty. As dawn broke I felt a release and went to the door and walked out.

"Hey, where are you going?"

I about jumped out of my clothes. I couldn't believe what I'd heard. I turned around and saw Falco was sitting up.

"I'm hungry. Let's get something to eat," he said as he got off the table and we headed to the mess hall. I was stunned, but praised the Almighty.

"Where have you been?" Nafuka asked before he saw Falco. "That's impossible. You're dead."

"Not anymore. Thanks Vying for praying for me and raising me from the dead. I was headed to the Lake of Fire. It was hot down there."

"It wasn't me. Only Jesus has the power to raise people from the dead."

"It may have been Him, but you were the one praying," Falco said looking at me. "We'll talk later."

"Hurry up and eat, so we don't feel heavy," Nafuka said as the morning sun blazed its way across the sky. I watched as Falco consumed twice the food and water as anyone else.

A stern faced guard walked over to us. "Nafuka, if you win your first bout this evening, you will have one more. Vying, eat hardy. You will need all the strength you have. The Warder has something special for you."

"Thanks," I said to the guard.

"I knew it. This is nothing but a show and the Warder loves drama. Don't sweat Bork. You beat Megog. You controlled that fight until he outsmarted you. I don't think Bork is much of a ground fighter. So we've got to figure out a way to get him down."

"What about you? You've got the first bout of the evening."

"Don't worry about me. Look, there's so much more at stake for you than me. Hey, if I win and go to Coralia, all I'm going to do is be free from this hellhole and probably get back in trouble."

"What about Darcel? Don't you love her?"

"Sure I do."

"So come back for her."

"I love Darcel, but coming back here isn't my idea of living."

"She's a good woman. Maybe you could take her off this planet and go to Milo. She'd be near her sister, Zelestar."

"We already talked and she doesn't want to leave her people behind. Darcel believes that the Almighty has her here for a purpose, so I don't know. Enough of that, let's loosen up."

We went over to the training area and I knew if the Almighty was going to help me, I had to get it right with Him. The Almighty hadn't intervened on my behalf during the trial and I couldn't understand that. Deep in my heart, Nafuka's words about the Almighty's purpose resonated within me and I walked off by myself to pray.

Chapter Thirty-Four

Nafuka's match against his shorter, compact opponent didn't go well. His ground movements were slow and labored. The moleskins peeled off, taking more skin with them. Every time he made a sharp pivot, he cut his feet even more, making them a bleeding mess. From the opening gong, Jimilica darted in and out hitting Nafuka with an assortment of jabs, punches, and leg kicks all over his body. Nafuka tried to counter, to follow his quicker opponent, but couldn't keep up with him. Blood seeped from his shoes. Jimilica pounded the big man relentlessly. He just couldn't move to mount an offensive. It was bitter to watch Nafuka go down, but without quicker motion, he was an easy target. Jimilica wore him down with body shots and finally took him out with a submission hold. The big man tapped the mat.

"I can't believe it."

"Vying, I couldn't move. My feet were on fire. I never got a chance to go on the offensive. Who was he?"

"I don't know, but I heard he almost won last year's championship. It looks like he could make it into the finals."

"He moved so quickly at the start that I couldn't counter with moves of my own. Come on, let's get out of here," Nafuka said his head hung in frustrating shame.

He placed a hand on my shoulder and hobbled out of the arena. We went back to the barracks.

"Are you ready for Bork?" he asked.

"Do I have a choice?"

"Whatever you do, don't stand and trade blows with him. He's a big powerful man. Use that to your advantage. Tire him out. Move in quickly and hammer his body with leg and elbow strikes. You're in better shape. The noblemen will yell and complain. They'll jeer and whistle at you, but don't change your strategy. When he tires, go on the offensive."

I drank some water and we walked back to the arena. We waited until the announcer called my name. I knew I'd be next in the ring.

While I waited for Bork, I loosened up and noticed a ripple in the moat that surrounded the battle ring, as if a guard had just thrown something into the water. I walked over to the edge and looked at the water. Suddenly a fish jumped out and landed at my feet. Its tail slapped my foot bouncing up and moving closer.

"MOVE! GET AWAY FROM IT!" Nafuka screamed.

I moved back just as the fish opened its mouth, exposing rows of razor sharp teeth. In a flash, it snapped at my ankle, just missing it.

"What is it?" I yelled to Nafuka as Bork came across the bridge.

"I should have told you. The noblemen like to make some of the matches more interesting, so they bring flesh-eating fish from Coralia and put them in the moat. Usually they wait till the finals, but they want to make your match against Bork more interesting."

"Thanks for letting me know. What kind of friend are you?" I yelled angrily. Walking up to the fish I thought to myself, "Almighty Father, what were you thinking when you created this creature?" No answer came, but I knew His ways were perfect, even if it involved the creation of a flesh-eating fish.

Stepping back, I took careful aim and kicked the fish as hard as I could. It went flying into the air and landed in the moat on the other side of the ring right in front of Bork as he stepped into the arena.

He looked down at the fish, then at me. The fish snapped its jaws and he laughed. Then he pointed to me and then the fish as he glared at me. When he stepped into the battle ring, the bridges in the moat were quickly withdrawn, leaving us alone with no easy means of escape. The crowd roared in anticipation. I knew if Bork disabled me, he would take great pleasure in throwing me into the moat.

With a scowl, Bork looked across the ring. I looked at the moat again. If I was to win, the fish had to be the last thing on my mind.

Before introductions were made, the gong sounded, throwing another unexpected twist to the match.

Bork stared me down and began to circle. I stayed in a low crouch and kept my distance. Bork advanced and cut my angle of escape and threw his first punch. I ducked and moved speedily away. The crowd immediately began to boo. I circled around him and threw a low front kick that did little damage, but was impossible to defend.

Bork charged again and threw a quick jab. I slipped underneath it and pounded his sagging belly. I was surprised as my fist hit fat, but then hard muscle. I quickly moved away. He charged, but this time shot toward me for a takedown move. I sprawled backwards and pushed away going toward the edge of the moat. Quickly, I rolled away from the water and bounded to my feet. He closed the gap and threw a closed fisted haymaker, but I shifted my weight to the back of my feet and dodged the blow.

The crowd booed and whistled. They hadn't come for a dance. This wasn't what they wanted to see, but I didn't care. I wasn't going to trade punches with a brawler to satisfy the crowd. Sweat broke out over Bork's forehead and I continued to circle. I noticed the expression on his face had changed slightly. Frustration crept across his face as I continued to run away from him, making him chase me around the ring.

Suddenly Bork stopped. He stood in the center of the ring, and beckoned me with his hand to stand and fight him.

The unruly crowd agreed with him and cried out, "Action. What are you afraid of? Quit running away."

I slowly approached Bork and faked a shot at his knees, touching them and then rolled to my right, ending up near the edge of the ring. Bork immediately charged and thew a punch. He connected with a devastating right jab. I felt all of his power, but stood my ground. Nafuka yelled to move, but I threw a side kick to his upper thigh. He countered with a swift upper cut to my head that I barely deflected with my right hand. With his size, he could easily push me into the moat.

The crowd burst into excitement and cheered for Bork.

"Stop brawling with him. You're playing his game. He'll kill you! Vying get away from him," Nafuka yelled, but I had him right where I wanted him.

Bork seized the moment and lunged at me with both hands extended. I hooked over his left arm and under his right arm and using his momentum, I threw him into the moat.

Water cascaded everywhere. A flesh eating fish soared into the front row, sending the guards and noblemen into pandemonium. They jumped to their feet trying to get away from the razor sharp teeth as drinks and food flew everywhere. The carnivorous fish leaped up and sunk its jaw into a nobleman's thigh. He screamed in pain!

A guard with a sword rushed over and slashed the fish in two, creating a grotesque spectacle of human blood and fish guts splattering those who couldn't get out of the way. But the head of the fish refused to release its grip. A tusker tore its tie down from the ground and attacked. He bit the fish's head and ripped it from the nobleman's leg. Blood sprayed everywhere and the nobleman fainted from the loss of fluid. Guards rushed into the stands and put a huge bandage on the leg and carried the nobleman to the infirmary. This was the first time a nobleman had suffered injury, throwing the tournament in disarray.

Figure 34: Bork

The gong should have sounded, ending the match long before the fish incident, but it hadn't. Bork surged out of the moat. Scorching eyes lit his reddened face as a fish hung from his right forearm. Grabbing it by the head, Bork crushed its skull. Tearing it from his arm, he threw it back into the moat as if it were nothing more than a mosquito that had been dealt a death blow with a simple swat. Climbing back into the battle ring with rivulets of blood pulsating from his arm, he slipped on the edge of the moat and stumbled into the ring. He tried to lunge at me as he fell, but I dodged the move and hammered him under the chin with a powerful uppercut.

The crowd returned to their seats and cheered at the flow of action.

My punch had solidly connected, snapping his head back. Dazed, he rolled to the left and came up swinging wildly. In a flash, he leapt into the air trying to knock me to the ground with a flying leg kick. I rolled to my back and with both legs up, took the force of his body and tossed him back into the water.

The excited crowd cheered louder. The gong should have sounded again ending the match, but it didn't. I quickly realized the Warder had no intention of stopping this fight.

Bork scrambled out of the moat, leaving the water tinged red with his blood. I leapt to my feet as he regained his footing.

Pure hatred shot out of his bloodshot eyes. He rushed me and I knew I had to knock him senseless or put him in a submission hold. With all my strength, I hammered him with a hard right cross. Pain shot the length of my arm to my shoulder. Bork staggered and crashed to the ground. I jumped on his back and put him in a submission hold, but he rolled away before I could really apply the pressure. I didn't want to get caught under his body weight and we both bounded to our feet. Blood ran down his lips and I knew I'd hurt him.

Leaping into the air, I launched a flying scissor's kick and hit him squarely in the chin. He staggered again. Immediately, I hit him with a forward knee kick to his upper thigh trying to hit his nerve. Unprotected, Bork went down on one knee. I jumped on his back and drove him to the mat before he rolled to his stomach and got into a defensive position to fight me. I scooped under his armpits and flattened him out. I grabbed his head and applied the rear-naked choke hold and squeezed with all my might. Bork's neck was thick and muscular. I knew he wouldn't tap out and I squeezed with all my might until my arms burned. He thrashed about, but I controlled his head and knew he couldn't get up. Air was slowly being cut off and finally he collapsed, motionless. I knew he wasn't dead and carefully got off him, watching him the whole time. But he never moved.

The gong finally sounded ending the match. For the first time, the noblemen clapped and cheered for me. This by far was the most exciting match of the tournament.

With my back to the unconscious Bork, I looked for Nafuka and saw the bridges over the moat being extending. I couldn't understand why Nafuka was hobbling forward dragging one leg. I knew I'd fought a great match and was happy to see that he was excited over my victory. I wanted to thank him for his strategy. It had changed the match completely and provided me the opportunity to defeat Bork.

"Turn around!" he shouted pointing at me.

I thought he wanted me to turn toward the crowd and bow. Maybe the Warder wanted to come out and raise my hand, so I turned toward the audience and lowered my head.

A rushing wind blew over the top of my head as Bork's right hand grazed me knocking me down. Jumping on my back, he grabbed my neck with both hands and began to squeeze. His body weight was so great, I couldn't move or even squirm.

His powerful hands continued suffocating the life out of me. I tried to roll away or break his death grip, but my strength left my body and I drifted into a sea of darkness.

Chapter Thirty-Five

I felt a warm glow, surrounded by the sweetest love I'd ever experienced, His Love. I knew I had passed to life's final dimension. Finally, I rested. My life had been a constant battle and I was glad it was over. I looked for my mom and dad as I was bathed in the warm glow of His Light. I didn't want to move a muscle. I felt so good, so peaceful. I didn't want to open my eyes. I heard a deep, but gentle masculine voice calling my name. I knew it was the Almighty. I looked for Him, but couldn't see Him. Where was He?

"Vying, everything will be alright, just get up," the gentle voice said encouraging me.

I wanted to rest in His presence and laying in this safe warm place. I was finally away from the life's warfare and safely in the eternal kingdom. I didn't want to leave. I didn't want to return to Zartex. Then I saw the Son of the Almighty, Jesus, standing before me. I knelt down before Him and worshipped Him. He reached down and lifted me up smiling at me. It was the most gentle and loving smile I'd ever seen. I felt His love come into my heart, a love so deep it took my breath away.

He looked into my eyes. "You have a choice. Stay here or return and complete your mission."

Deep in my heart my desire was to serve Him and to do that, I knew I had to enter the battle ring. It was my destiny, established before the foundation of time. I looked once more into His eyes and saw the pleasure my obedience gave Him. Then I felt myself falling, falling back to Zartex.

"Vying! Wake up!" Nafuka yelled and my eyes popped open .

"What are you doing here?" I asked in disbelief.

"Are you alright?" asked Nafuka in disbelief. "I carried you here to the infirmary so they could check you out. You've been unconscious since Bork jumped you."

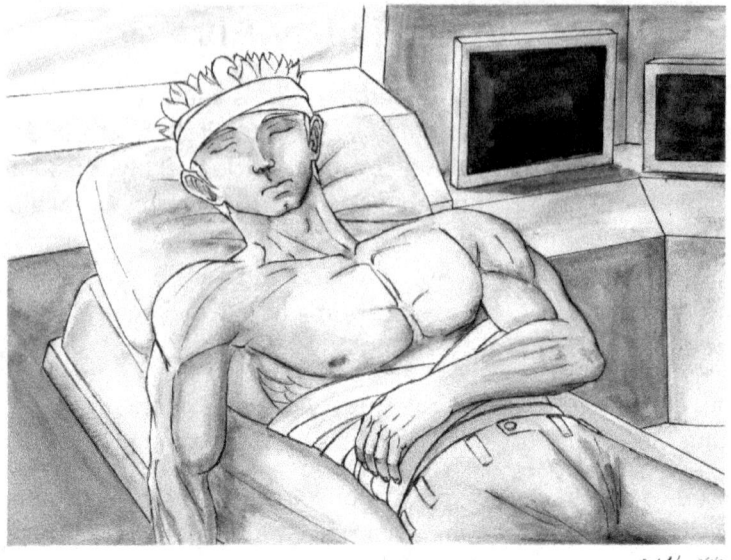

Figure 35: Vying in the Infirmary

"Really! What happened?"

"You blacked out."

"Ooh, my stomach."

"I hope nothing's broken. Bork's pretty heavy."

"You're telling me!"

"Can you get up?"

"Why?"

"I don't trust the Warder. He might send somebody in here to drug you, just to see you lose in the finals."

"You mean I won?"

"It was a wild finish. The Warder tried to declare Bork the winner because he knocked you out, but the gong had sounded and the noblemen wouldn't allow it. Now, let's get out of here."

Nafuka helped me to my feet and we walked out of the infirmary just as an orderly came in with a tray filled with needles, small brown vials and little cups of fluid.

"He can't leave. I must examine him. I've got pain medication."

"Save it for the next victim. I'm done here," I said as my mind instantly cleared. Nafuka and I went back to the barracks where the fighters had gathered.

"You fought well, Vying. You can win this thing," Falco said extending his hand as we walked past his bunk. He was looking much better.

"Thanks," I said as I rolled onto my bed. Pain shot through all parts of my crushed and broken body. I wondered how I'd be ready for the finals. Bork was a heavy man and when he jumped on me, I heard something snap.

The next day, I awoke with a splitting headache, but couldn't remember the blow to the head that caused the pain.

"How do you feel?" Nafuka asked.

"Beat up. What happened last night?"

"The gong sounded and the match was over, but Bork jumped you."

"I remember that. What happened next?"

"He knocked you to the ground and choked you until you passed out. I jumped into the ring and hammered him in the head with a board from the stands. He fell over. I picked you up and took you to the infirmary. As I was leaving, Bork pulled himself together to appeal the decision, but all the noblemen turned their thumbs down and the Warder had to announce you as the winner. This is much more than a tournament for them. The want the toughest competitor to go on "the run," so they have a huge say in who wins."

"Is there any ice? I sure could use some."

"On this planet? Are you kidding? Try and drink this soup. You're going to need to eat food later."

Nafuka went out and I thanked the Almighty for Nafuka's friendship before I realized that I had fully accepted him. Once again Nafuka had saved me from certain death. I wondered why I ever doubted him. I picked up the soup and began to sip it. When I was finished I prayed. "Dear Lord Jesus, please heal me and get me ready for the championship bout. Help me get off this planet so that I can return to Micron and free my friends. If it was just about me, I'd go to Milo and be with Zelestar, but not my will, but Yours."

I sat with my back against the wall, but I was still in pain. As I lifted my arm, a shot of pain raced the length of it. In excruciating agony, I tried to raise my arm above my head, but couldn't get it above my shoulder.

Over the years, I'd dealt with pain. I remembered the championship fight with Megog many years ago and how the Almighty had delivered me. I took confidence that He would deliver me again. I didn't sense His presence this time, but I had a knowing thought that He was always with me, no matter what happened.

I went into the showers and turned the valve to the coldest setting it would go. I put my head under the running water and my throbbing headache finally went away. How long I stood under the water, I didn't know, but the frigid water stopped the pounding pain.

"Come on out, Vying," Nafuka yelled. "We need to discuss your strategy against Jimilica.

Reluctantly I left the cold relief and my headache instantly returned.

"Jimilica's style is deceptive. He loves to box and has an assortment of jabs, punches, and leg kicks, but he's a superb grappler. I saw him win his last match by taking his opponent to the mat. He's a complete fighter."

"I'd sure like another day to heal up."

"The Warder knows that and has declared that tonight he will stage the championship bout. Usually they wait a day so both fighters can heal, but he wants you to lose. There's been something else going on here since we arrived. Let's take a walk and get your blood flowing. It might make you feel better. Keep drinking lots of water. It helps the healing process."

"Get the blood flowing? I can barely move and you want me up and walking. What's wrong with you?"

"Look Vying, if I wasn't your friend, I'd let you wallow in your pain. Sure, I know you're hurt, but I've got to get you ready for tonight."

"What's in it for you?" I demanded.

Nafuka didn't say anything for a moment. "I'm not going to lie to you. Sometimes the nobleman will take both members of the alliance."

"What? Is that what this alliance is all about. Every time I think I can trust you and that you're my friend, you hit me with a new wrinkle of truth."

"Initially, yes, you were my ticket outta here. I knew you had a great shot at winning and I wanted off this planet, but I've grown to like and respect you."

"Nafuka, you never cease to amaze me."

I spent the rest of the day putting on compresses and walking around. It was no secret that I'd taken a beating, but then anyone entering the ring was bound to be hurt, even if they won. The question was, How much pain could you withstand?

Evening quietly arrived.

"Let's go, Vying," Nafuka said as he waited at the door of the barracks.

All of the fighters had gone to watch the final bout, so I had a moment to pray alone. "Dear Almighty Father, please help me tonight. Please give me the strength to fight hard and win, in Jesus name."

As I walked up toward the noisy arena, the excitement of a finals match had everyone bubbling. I heard my name being shouted and people pointing at me. The gambling hawkers took bets on the final bout. I visualized my first seven moves. Walking into the arena, my adrenalin instantly spiked to overload. Despite my injuries, I felt ready to go. I knew that I had no other choice, but to trust in the Almighty.

Walking across the moat, I heard the announcer say, "Tonight we have a most excellent finals match. In the far corner we have Jimilica, last year's finalist. Maybe this year he will be the victor." The boisterous crowd cheered.

After it became quiet again, he began, "In the other part of the ring, we have a former Crown Champion of the Blue Ring Galaxy, convicted of murder and serving a life sentence for the death of a young knight on Micron — Commander Vying!" A chorus of boos erupted. Clearly Jimilica was tonight's favorite. "He defeated Megog in the battle ring on planet Mercus five years ago. Indeed, this will be a good match."

Jimilica was already stretching his legs, arms, and midsection. I walked to the center of the ring and looked directly into his eyes. Unmistakable rage filled them, but then he slightly tipped his head to me.

I was surprised. No one on Zartex had shown a shred of honor to anyone. Jimilica backed up and we waited for the gong. With both hands he grabbed his head and rotated it, cracking his neck. The crowd had been drinking Milo wine and were restless as the betting continued. They came for violence and to gamble.

The gong sounded and we came at each other. Immediately, I launched a round house kick and threw a quick right jab. The kick landed on the side of his thigh and Jimilica winced slightly as I pounded the jab into his chin. He counterpunched with three quick jabs as we closed the gap between us.

The fight fans went wild. They'd come for an all-out slugfest and weren't disappointed. We clenched in the center of the ring, throwing leg kicks and looking for an opening to shoot a takedown. I broke the clench and began circling. Cutting the circles short, I moved closer. Dipping my right shoulder in a slight faint, I threw an overhand punch that landed hard. Jimilica winched for a moment, but quickly recovered with a smirk on his face, almost laughing.

My temper flared as I threw an elbow strike to his head. He ducked and came up with a knee in my groin and I doubled over. Jimilica saw the weakness and attacked. I was trying to straighten up when he threw a flurry of punches followed by a side kick to my knee. Then, he shot a takedown.

I sprawled backwards and jumped to my feet. I lunged at him with an elbow strike to his forehead. He ducked and rolled to his right. Both of us bounded to our feet in the same instant. He came at me and I met him in the center of the ring. We locked arms in another clench as each of us tried to score blows with our knees and legs. I wrapped one of my legs around him and pushed backwards, toppling him over. As soon as he hit, he rolled out of my hold and we scrambled back to our feet.

Sucking a huge gulp of air, I knew I was in trouble. My endurance just wasn't there. I looked over at a smiling Jimilica. He wasn't even winded. Usually I out-trained my opponents and could count on superior conditioning at the end of a bout, but the injuries I sustained last night were taking their toll.

Without giving me a chance to think or catch my breath, Jimilica charged forward and threw an explosion of fists and elbow strikes. I defended his onslaught and launched a knee to his solar plexus, but it was half-hearted and he grabbed my knee and twisted it before letting go. Pain ripped through my leg.

Circling to buy recovery time, my knee was on fire. He countered by cutting off my escape and threw a vicious combination of elbow strikes, legs kicks, and knees to the midsection. I broke away, but he'd caused more damage. I could feel the fight quickly slipping away from me. Jimilica was initiating all the moves and carrying the battle to me.

"The crowd began to shout, "JIMILICA! JIMILICA!"

We came together and he threw a brutal right cross. Another side kick and a devastating body punch hit my sore ribs. Pain shot across my side. He lunged at my legs and I was barely able sprawl toward the edge of the ring.

"Watch out!" Nafuka yelled. I knew the carnivorous fish would rip at my feet if I stayed on the ground near the moat. Painly I got to my feet just as Jimilica shot another takedown. I let him grab my right leg and delivered a punishing right hook to his unprotected kidney. He winced, but he locked up my other wrist with an arm bar behind my back. I struggled to get free and pulled his arm with all my strength. We tumbled to the ground, grabbling. I gained superiority, but he continued to roll. Reversing me, he regained the advantage and grabbed my forearm. Turning my wrist against his thumb, I broke his wrist lock and we both surged to our feet.

I could see a trickle of blood from his left eye. Every part of my back and sides hurt. Every time I threw a kick or a punch, my sides exploded in pain. We began to circle again and the crowd cheered. The quick pace drained me and Jimilica was looking to strike for the victory. In the bright lights, beads of sweat glistened off his back. I knew he'd be slippery and difficult to throw into the water.

Jimilica shot across the mat, faked a jab and threw a left knee to my groin. I dodged the blow, but he followed with a round house kick to my ribs with his leg. It felt like someone had taken a hammer to my side. I pushed through the pain and shot a takedown, hoping to grapple with him and get the advantage on the ground. He sprawled out and we both returned to our feet.

My body was beat up, I was sucking wind and if I didn't score a knockout or submission hold, it would all be over. My ribs ached from the punishment, but I couldn't give up. I shot a prayer to the Almighty, hoping His power would fill me up and rescue me, but nothing happened.

A thought came to my mind, to let him come at me. Disregarding it, I circled and prayed again hoping the Almighty would answer my request. Again, the thought came to my mind to turn around and let him come at me. That was insane. I'd never turned my back on any fighter and this was not the time, especially in a championship bout.

But then, I just did it. Jimilica came at me and locked his arms around my chest. Immediately, I lowered my level and grabbed his right foot. I pulled with all my might and he fell. I wrapped my body around his arm and pulled upward. With the triangle arm bar fully engaged, I looked down at Jimilica. He had the choice of tapping out or I would pull with all my might, hyper extending his socket. We locked eyes. He knew what was happening as I waited for him to tap out. But he wouldn't. I increased the pressure twisting his arm even more. Like a fish out of water, he flopped around on the ground in great pain, but still he wouldn't tap out. I waited kept stretching his arm. He grabbed for my head, but I ducked. I hoped he would tap out, but then suddenly it popped.

His face turned white, but still he wouldn't signal the end. The last thing I wanted to do was to completely destroy his arm and shoulder, but he left me no option. I pulled harder and I knew it wouldn't be long before the arm and shoulder were completely destroyed.

"Tap out, before I break it!" I yelled at him as I increased the pressure and his face went to bright red.

Finally, he tapped the mat and I released his the hold.

"Why did you wait so long?" I asked as the crowd cheered my victory.

"I had to know if you'd really do it. I wasn't going to give up if you weren't going to finish me. I had to know," Jimilica said as he grabbed his shoulder wincing in pain.

"You almost found out the hard way," I said reaching down and helping him up. The guards extended the bridge to the battle ring as I helped Jimilica to his feet. We walked out of the ring. Unexpectantly, his knee buckled. I grabbed his good arm before he hit the ground. We continued walking as the crowd booed and jeered us.

"I've watched you. You're different than the others," he said through clenched teeth as a bolt of pain raced up his leg.

"What do you mean?"

"I don't know, but I can feel it. You have an inner strength. Even when you're on the verge of defeat, you radiate light from within. When Megog knocked you out, you glowed even more. I was at that match when you won the Crown Championship on Mercus. I saw how badly beaten and bloody you were, like tonight. Just when it looked as if you were finished and Megog was about to pound you senseless, you deflected his blows with unbelievable power."

"It was the Almighty's Son who gave me His power."

"I want what you've got. I want the Almighty's Son."

Chapter Thirty-Six

A tall powerfully built man with deep blue eyes flanked by four guards met me at the edge of the arena. Wisps of steel grey hair around his ears gave him a look of authority and wisdom.

"You're the nobleman's property now," he said, his unforgiving eyes captivating all he observed. "Shackle and escort the prisoner to the ship immediately."

I lowered my head in disappointment. I thought I'd be able to quietly reflect on the victory, but cold metal bit into my wrists and ankles again, snapping me back to reality. I couldn't see through my right eye and sharp pain gripped my lower back and wouldn't let go.

"Move it," the one of the guards ordered.

They led me to the Sapphire Star, a deep space clipper ship and I walked up a ramp and into an open cargo bay. The sleek merchant had huge holds being filled with ore from the wastelands of Zartex. Hovercraft front end loaders with deep buckets were moving in and out of the ship dumping the black rock. The ship's long interior passageways were bright and colorful in sharp contrast to the dingy grey of the prison shuttle, fighters, and battle carriers I'd flown on. A small, but efficient crew was aboard and I could see they were getting ready for the voyage to Coralia.

Ship's stores were being loaded and secured in air tight compartments. The busy crew was running extensive diagnostic checks using electron scanners on all the equipment. Fuel rods and water capacities were verified, atmospheric pressure recorded, and temperature readings were taken throughout the ship. Hull integrity was checked and the electromagnetic force field on the outside plating of the ship tested. It would be energized when the ship accelerated to critical frequency and burst into the dimension of plasma energy.

A bulkhead mounted screen displayed visuals of the eight cargo holds. As we walked by, I could see the ship's computer constantly calculating and posting the tonnage for each of the holds, so that the Chief Mate could balance the cargo.

Walking toward the bow of the ship, I noticed a couple of laser turrets on the starboard side next to portholes. Moving forward, the guards suddenly stopped at a door as it slid open.

"This is your room. Sit on the bed and we'll take off your shackles. We may be a small merchant crew, but we know what we're doing. You will be monitored at all times, so don't think of trying anything stupid."

"Trust me, I'm more than happy to leave Zartex," I said welcoming the sound of steel shackles clinking on the deck. I rubbed my wrists and ankles.

"The nobleman wants to get home quickly and get you ready for the run, so rest and recuperate. We'll bring you anything you need or want. Just ask."

"Thanks, I could use some food, water and ice."

The older man nodded to the other guard and he left immediately. When the door closed, he smiled at me. "I thought you were the best fighter in the tournament, but then I've seen you fight before, so I wasn't surprised. I told the nobleman you were a Crown Champion so he bid heavily for you. He thought Bork was going to beat you, but you took care of him as well. Jimilica almost beat you. Turning your back on him was bizarre! I thought you had given up. He was winning, you know."

"Turning my back on him was the Almighty's idea."

"Well, whatever you want to call it. I've never seen anything like it in my life."

"Follow the Almighty and He'll reveal all kinds of creative thoughts, visions and dreams."

"Right," he said coldly, ending the conversation. "I'll be checking on you throughout the voyage."

"Thanks for everything."

"No need to thank me."

"What's the nobleman's name?"

"I'm surprised you don't know, Og."

My heart stopped! I couldn't believe my ears. How was it possible? What strange turn of events had occurred? I needed to escape this ship immediately. I looked around, my mind racing wildly, trying to find an escape. Surely I would have seen him in the crowd during the competition.

The old guard laughed. "Relax, Vying. I was just kidding. I wish you could have seen the look on your face."

"I'm not amused."

"Sorry, but I couldn't help it. I was there when you took the Crown Championship from Megog. That too was a most extraordinary fight. Long ago, I once trained for the Crown Championship, but my right knee blew out. I was never the same again. If you had pushed harder, Jimilica wouldn't be walking today."

"I know. What's your name?"

"Normally slaves are not permitted to know my name, let alone talk to me, but in your case having won two championships in the battle ring, I will grant you the liberty. My name is Kryil and I'm very curious to know how the Crown Champion of the Blue Ring Galaxy ended up here."

A female crew member entered the room carrying a bowl of fruit, a jar, water and towels. She placed them on the side table.

"Would you like me to put some cream on your swollen eye?" she asked.

"Please," I said.

Gently she began applying the cream as the guard went to the door and stepped out, but then he poked his head back in. "I don't know why, but the nobleman bought the rights to your training partner as well. He'll be making the trip with us."

"Nafuka?"

"I don't know the brute's name. He's a strong one. I'm using him to shovel cargo in the holds, evening it out. We'll talk later," he said as he left me with the attendant. She finished and put the top on the jar.

249

"If you want anything else, just push this button," she said exiting the room.

"Thank you." I stood up and walked to the table. I drank some water and ate the fruit. I lay down in my bunk and thanked the Almighty Father for delivering me from the prison planet - Zartex. As I was about to close my eyes, I heard a distant hum and felt a slight throbbing vibration.

The ship was testing its engines and powering up its gravity thrusters. I knew we'd be lifting off soon. The fusion turbines whined louder and louder. I felt a tremor as the engines howled as we left the the surface. With a sudden jolt we broke free from Zartex's gravitational pull. The thrusters howled even louder as we accelerated to critical frequency and burst into the dimension of plasma energy approaching the speed of light. Seconds later, the ship stopped vibrating and became very quiet. Finally, I closed my eyes and went to sleep as the inter-space clipper ship sailed through the dimension of plasma energy on its way to Coralia.

Figure 36: SS Sapphire Star

Suddenly I was lifted off my bunk and thrown to the deck. A violent energy wave must have crashed into the ship, altering the vessel's magnetic field and throwing the ship around. Climbing back into my bunk, I grabbed the side rails. Every time the ship slipped to port or starboard my body hit the sides of the bunk. Every injury I'd sustained in the battle ring ignited in pain. I'd been hurt more than I initially thought. My stomach violently rebelled at the fruit I'd eaten and bile raced up in my throat. A raging skull-splitting headache erupted in my head as I staggered to the commode.

The ship surged to the right and again I was lifted off the deck and I grabbed the side rails with all my strength. Every joint in my body exploded in pain and for a moment I felt like I was back in the battle ring fighting Bork. I'd been in the dimension of energy before, but this was the most turbulent storm I'd ever experienced. I wondered if we were under attack.

I grabbed the side of the bunk and pulled myself to my feet. Slowly, I walked to the door. It opened instantly.

The ship suddenly pitched down, as if the bottom had fallen out and then it violently slid to starboard. I grabbed the handrail in the passageway and pulled myself forward. I had to get to the bridge.

Lights blinked on and off in the corridors and then total darkness engulfed me.

A glow light shined in the passageway. "Hey, what are you doing out of your stateroom?"

"I wanted to see what was going on."

"We encountered an energy storm and a photon wave hit us pretty hard, momentarily knocking out our electrical control circuits out. Get back in your room," Kyril ordered.

"Maybe I can help."

"I doubt it. It's pretty complicated."

"I've designed a scintilla, including its electrical control circuits. I might be able to help."

"Really," Kyril said with raised eyebrows, but then the ship hogged to the starboard again. "It's worth a try. Come on, I'll take you to the

Engineering Control Station."

Kyril walked aft and I followed him down two ladders. Five men and two women were viewing a three dimensional hologram that showed a nest of multi-colored fiber optic circuits feeding the ship's fusion reactor with electronic packages. They held glow lights to examine the hologram.

"The audio commands aren't responding," the white haired man in charge said.

"Hue, can't we bypass this circuitry and operate in manual?" one of his assistants asked pointing to a blue colored circuit.

"I wish it were that easy. The bean counters wanted to save money during the last overhaul and refurbished the old controls instead of replacing them."

"Didn't you design a backup system?" another asked.

"Of course, I did, but they said we didn't need it and cut if from the budget."

"The captain said we need power immediately," Kryil said.

"Jimmy boy, do you think I don't know that!" Hue snapped not even looking at Kryil.

"Maybe something is blocking the signals," I offered.

"Well now, who in the world might you be?" Hue asked taking his eyes off the hologram and focusing his frustration on me.

"He's the fighter from the battle ring the nobleman just purchased."

"Jimmy boy, do you think a convicted criminal, a murderer, can tell me how to repair a command control system?" the old man questioned and then laughed. "Jimmy boy, I've been a Chief Engineer since you were the gleam in your daddy's eyes. Get him out of here and let me get back to work!"

I reached up to the hologram and began to page through the virtual manual. I accessed different fiber optic circuits on the hologram, scanning them as they flashed. Putting my finger on a yellow circuits in the hologram, I said, "Pull this portal apart. It looks like your signals are blocked from being transmitted to the engine controls."

With raised eyes, Hue looked at me and scratched his head. Reluctantly he said, "Do what this jimmy boy convict says."

The ship's engineers began pulling a panel apart in the bulkhead adjacent to the hologram when they noticed a blinking light coming from a small box with leads on both ends.

"Jumping Jimmy boy, what's that?" Hue exclaimed.

One of the technicians reached down to pull it off.

"Don't!" I shouted. "I've seen these before. If you pull that cable, you'll trip a fusion charge that will ignite and fry the electrical controls."

"Slave, are you sure?" Hue asked promoting me from convict.

"Someone is jamming your control signals. Get me a small portable power supply, a signal generator and two jumper cables."

"Go get what this Jimmy boy wants and be quick about it." He turned to me as they brought the equipment, "You better be right about this, Jimmy boy."

I took the fiber optic jumper cables and fused a circuit around the portal. Then, I carefully cut the wires that were imbedded into the ship's controls. The lights came on immediately and power was restored to the engines. The ship suddenly surged forward.

"Somebody planted a ghost wave generator on your controls and activated it so they could control your ship," I said, looking at Hue.

Chapter Thirty-Seven

"Kyril, take me to the bridge! Quickly!" I demanded. We raced to the bridge of the Sapphire Star. The ship's captain was there sitting in a prominent chair looking into the huge view finder to see when the next photon wave from the energy storm would hit.

"Slave, Hue tells me you fixed the controls. How did you manage that?" He asked calmly now that power had been restored to the ship.

"We found a phantom controller that was blocking the control signals to the engines. Someone is using it to control your ship."

"What! Are you out of your mind? Why would anyone want to disable my ship?"

"Because of the cargo," I offered.

"Black ore isn't exotic. I just load it so I don't waste the trip."

"It might not be the black ore they're after."

"Meaning?" the captain inquired.

"They could be after me."

The Captain laughed. "Why would anyone attack my ship for one slave? You're going to make the run on Coralia and maybe return with your life and the fruit. If you make it, you'll get your freedom. Why would anyone care about you?"

I looked into the view finder and noticed another wave of energy coming our way.

"Captain, cut the power to the engines. Let them think we're disabled."

"What? Who are you talking about. I don't see any ships out there."

"Unless I miss the mark, standby for heavy rolls. These aren't normal energy waves. Check their frequency. Have you ever seen energy waves operating on that frequency?" I asked.

Kryil, second in command of the ship, ran a pulse check of the wave's frequency.

"He's right, Captain."

"Slow the engines to half-speed," ordered the captain over the command system.

"That's a good idea, but anyone who's out there is going to know that you're not disabled and that their signal generator has been discovered," I said.

"Slave, if you're wrong, I'll have you go on the run twice. Stop the engines."

A streak of light flashed across the view screen.

"What was that?" the nobleman asked.

The viewer blinked, went blank, and came alive. "Hailing the Sapphire Star, I see you are disabled. Do you need assistance?" the man looming in the shadows of the view finder asked. His bridge was empty and he wasn't wearing a uniform.

A small distant dot appeared on the screen.

"What's the name of your ship?" the captain of the Sapphire Star asked.

"For a ship that's floundering in the dimension of plasma energy, I would think you would be more than happy to receive help from another vessel," the man replied.

"Forgive me, I appreciate your offer of help, but we're currently restoring our systems."

"Do you think your hull can sustain any more damage? I see a large burn mark on your port bow."

"Sir, could I have your name and your ship's name for my log?"

Somehow the voice sounded familiar, but I couldn't place it. I accessed the power panel and tripped the power to the view finder.

"Slave, what are you doing?" the captain exclaimed.

"Captain, that's a pirate ship from Mercus. I've seen that man before. If he tells you anything different, he's lying. Look at his laser cannons. They're all aimed at us. Tell him you lost power to the bridge momentarily."

I reached over and re-energized the power circuits. The view finder surged to life.

"Ah, there you are Sapphire Star, for a moment there I thought I'd lost you. Again I say, do you want my team to come aboard. I've got some very skilled technicians."

"I'm sorry, Captain. As you can see we are experiencing conductivity problems with our ship wide electronics network, but I think our thrusters can handle it."

I reached over and tripped the view screen again. "Captain man your laser cannons and get ready to fire. This ship isn't going to leave our quadrant without a fight. Be sure of that. If you let him bring his team over here, just be ready to fight them in the transport room." I quickly flipped the breaker back on and the view screen came alive.

"Captain of the Sapphire Star, my technicians are standing by, ready to come over."

"Thank you, Captain. The name of your ship, for the log, please."

"This is the deep space vessel, Aladar and I, a free merchant, am Captain Daal."

I reached over and shut off the screen again. "This is worse than I thought. He's one of Og's best captains and I would guess that is a new ship of the line, which means it's armed for battle and carries veteran troops. We have only one chance. Drift closer to it and fire on the stern. Try to disable his directional thrusters when they let down their shields to send their team over here. Fire your laser cannons the moment they come."

"Slave, how do you know battle tactics?"

"I was not always been a slave, sir."

"Who are you?"

"He is Vying. He commanded the forces of the Realm during the interplanetary war. They defeated Og and Megog in the interplanetary war," Kryil said.

"I've heard of you. You're a hero. What are you doing here?"

"It's a long story. The Almighty has sent me here for His purpose."

"Well, I hope that He has a way out for us, because the Aladar has just launched two shuttles from their landing bay."

"Fire on those shuttles. They're probably drones. Daal always kept his pilots aboard the mother ship," I advised.

"But that will give away our element of surprise! Hold your fire," the captain ordered.

"I think Daal already suspects something. Those drones are back-up for the team he's sending over here. Wait till he opens his shields and then fire on his ship."

"Hail the Aladar. This is the Captain of the Sapphire Star. You may send your team over now."

They watched the view screen as the huge ship released its electronic shields and came into full view. It was much bigger than the Sapphire Star. Looming on the view screen was an enormous battle carrier!

"Fire on the drones and thrusters and bring the ship to full speed. If we can disable their ship even slightly, we've got a chance to outrun them to dimensional space."

Laser beams brightened the atmosphere, destroying the drones. As the Sapphire Star flew by the Aladar, they fired at their thrusters doing little damage. The gigantic warship accelerated in an arc, pursuing the cargo carrier.

"Vying, I hope you're right. The Aladar is completing its arc and coming at us full speed," the captain said as he redirected the view finder to the stern so he could observe the movement of the Aladar.

The view screen suddenly came alive with Daal's face on it. "Fool! You can't escape."

"What's that?" the captain asked as they saw a thick slow moving green beam coming at them from the Aladar.

"It's a tractor beam. They're going to try and pull us in to their ship. Full speed, sir."

"We're going full speed! I don't know if we'll make it to dimensional space."

"Praise the Almighty, look over there," Vying said pointing to the starboard quarter.

"What's that?" Kryil asked.

"It's a black hole. It'll take us to dimensional space."

"I don't think we're going to make it," the captain said.

"Jettison the black ore," I replied.

"What? That cargo will be very valuable on Coralia."

"Not if you don't make it. The tractor beam will grab the black ore, allowing us to escape."

"Hue, divert all power to the laser cannons and fire on that ship."

"I can't sir. That tractor beam would suck us up the moment I shut power off the engines. It's the only thing keeping us from being pulled into their ship."

"Alright, jettison the cargo," the captain said reluctantly with bitter disappointment in his heart. He loved money and he knew he was losing a great deal. Even though his ship was saved, the loss of the income from the ore was precious to him.

The men and women on the bridge watched as the black ore was scuttled from their ship and sucked into Aladar's hanger bay allowing the Sapphire Star to escape. The deep space clipper ship entered the black hole and burst into dimensional space.

For the rest of the trip to Coralia, I stayed away from the bridge. Nafuka came and visited me. My body began healing and I felt much better. After traveling for several days, I heard the engines slowing. I headed to the observation deck above the bridge. As we descended through the clouds, I got my first look at Coralia.

The planet was covered with green trees and jungles, except for a strange floating structure surrounded by a river. Intrigued, I adjusted the telefinder and looked at the sheer cliffs on the mainland.

"I'm glad that you're studying the Beast's home."

Surprised, I whirled around and saw a man dressed in fine white linen robes. A golden sash was tied around his waist. His face looked drawn out, as if life had taxed him heavily.

"That's where we'll be going soon after we land," the nobleman said pointing to the structures in the middle of a river.

"What's that circular island?"

"The floating city. I built it after the Beast arrived."

"Why is it so dark around the island?"

"You'll find out, Vying. Are you ready for the run?" he said with intense expectation on his face.

"Almost."

I wanted to say something about the lost cargo, but decided not to. I looked again at the structure and saw many buildings on it.

Figure 37: The Floating City

Chapter Thirty-Eight

The Sapphire Star splashed down in the ocean near the outlet of the river. The big ship deployed its props and we motored up stream to the floating city. I saw succulent green vegetation hanging from both banks on the mainland and shook my head. Why were the people stuck on this man-made island? It didn't make sense. Why wouldn't they move to the land mass across from the river?

The inter-space clipper ship pulled up to a dock where there were vessels of all shapes and sizes tied to the pier. I looked up above and noticed a palace on the hill. Houses were jammed one on top of the other and in every possible place. It was a wonder that the floating city actually floated. People were walking everywhere and as I disembarked the Sapphire Star, Nafuka joined me.

"Have you been here before?" I asked.

"Not here, but another part of the city where the lesser noblemen live."

"There's so many buildings here, I wonder how this city stays afloat."

"Most of the city is anchored to a small island."

Kryil came up to us as we were admiring the houses where green plants grew in glass containers hanging from balconies. "The nobleman wants to see you immediately. Follow me to his palace."

"We just got here," Nafuka pleaded.

"Immediately!" Kryril repeated sharply.

We walked behind him like two slaves as we were led up a winding labyrinth where thousands of homes were built. Balconies extended over the paved pathway. We arrived at a large black iron gate. Looking beyond the iron bars were leafy trees, birds chirping and many lush plants. Walking through the cool garden reminded me of Che-Wa village in the mountains on Zartex, except no children greeted our arrival. Sparkling white stone steps led to an cream-colored archway in the middle of the palace. Stepping through an open door, we arrived in an ornate receiving room. Honey brown marble columns stood at attention supporting the cathedral glass archway. Colored light flowed through the stained glass overhead windows from different angles to form rainbows on the flowing white marble flooring leading to a doorway. I could have stayed for hours just enjoying the divine beauty of this room.

Kryil waited a few moments and then led us through the doors down a hallway lined with windows six leeds tall, extending to the ceiling and overlooking the floating city and the distant mainland. We got to the end of the hallway and stood before two geometrically sculpted dark wooden doors Gold inlay highlighted the interconnected circular designs on the paneling. As we approached, the two large doors opened as if on cue.

"The nobleman will receive you now," the waiting attendant dressed in a long white silk gown announced as she opened the doors and the three of us walked into the room. Her flowing black hair lifted as a crisp breeze slipped through the doorway refreshing us with a succulent citrus aroma.

"Thank you, Yolee," Kryil said with a lingering smile admiring her comeliness, accented by her crystal blue eyes.

We walked across azure marble sprinkled with embedded gold flakes that glistened in the sunlight. The nobleman sat on his chair on the dais. He was dressed in a purple robe with a gold sash on his waist. In his hand was a bowl. There were two pieces of fruit glowing, one red, the other orange.

"Yolee, bring my guests something to drink," he said as the enchanting beauty elegantly strolled across the room.

"Vying, Nafuka, step forward. Normally slaves are not allowed in this room, but you have demonstrated noble qualities. I need to discuss your assignment. Vying, do you know why I purchased you?"

"To go on the run, I've been told."

"Correct. Nafuka, Do you know why I purchased you?"

Just then, Yolee re-entered, carrying a gold platter with glasses of refreshment. The nobleman drank in her beauty as he took the beverage from her hand. She gave the others their glasses and quietly left the room, taking our breath with her.

262

"Because I've been on the run before?" Nafuka said after the pleasant interruption passed.

"Excellent Nafuka, you have a keen wit. You went on the run before and successfully returned with more fruit than anyone else."

Nafuka stood there and didn't respond.

"Don't worry, Nafuka. You fulfilled your contract and did something no one ever expected of a slave. You brought back extra fruit, but it also brought you trouble."

"That's true," he answered looking down.

"You successfully completed the run and I want you to train Vying. Tell him all your tricks so that he can bring enough back to free you as well."

"That would be most generous, sir."

"Trust me, I'm not generous, but I'm willing to spend a little extra to improve the odds of success. You are also the only one who has returned to Zartex after successfully getting your freedom. You must thank the Warder the next time you see him. It was his idea to sell you and of course you are now in my debt."

"Thank you, sir."

"Don't thank me with words, Nafuka. Train Vying. Train him so he gets what I want and you get your freedom. Do you understand?"

"Absolutely," he said.

"Good. You'll make the run within the next moon. Go when you think the time is right," the nobleman said pointing to the last two pieces of fruit in the bowl, "I cannot wait much longer. I leave the exact day up to you. Choose wisely. You're dismissed. Don't disappoint me Nafuka or you'll be sent back to Zartex."

Bowing to the nobleman, Yolee silently reappeared and led us out of the opulent room. Kryil took us out of the palace and showed us where we would be staying.

"Vying, do you need any further medical attention?" Kyril asked.

"No, I feel much better."

"Good."

"Can you find out if it has rained lately?" Nafuka asked.

"I'll let you know and by the way there are a few boats down at the waterfront. You might want to use one of them."

"Thanks," Nafuka said. "Let's get our things put away and then I'll take you for a walk through the floating city. It's quite interesting."

We walked back to the Sapphire Star, got our meager personal belongings and stowed them in our rooms on the palace grounds. After living in the barracks of the prison planet, these rooms were very comfortable. We walked down the hill to the gate that separated the nobleman from the floating city.

"Things are a little strange here. The commoners believe that evil spirits fly about on air currents, so they keep their windows closed. Look over there!" Nafuka said pointing to a house with heavy batons secured over their windows and frames.

"What about outside? Aren't they afraid of the evil spirits then?" I asked watching young boys laughing and running by us in their game of tag. The city was bustling with people walking along the streets.

"No, when you're outside, it's okay. It's when you're in a house and especially at night that the locals are concerned about the evil spirits flying into their homes on air currents."

"What about those beautiful open air homes?" I said pointing to some buildings.

"Those aren't homes. They're worship centers to the spirits."

"You've got to be kidding. How many gods do they worship on Coralia?"

"I don't know. I never went into the temple to worship. I just know they are very spiritual."

"If they're not worshipping the Almighty, His Son, and the Spirit, they're all going to go to the Lake of Fire for all eternity," I stated.

As we approached the river docks of the floating city, I examined the weathered structures secured to one another with corded hemp. The homes didn't look very substantial and were crowded tightly together. It was amazing to watch as the river houses independently shifted and bobbed up and down with the river waves. Many of the houses were large and painted with shiny blues, greens, and reds.

"Why so colorful?"

"They believe the color scares off the evil spirits."

"Does anyone live on the mainland? There's plenty of land."

"They did, before the Beast came."

"The Beast?"

"Many years ago, a fisherman snagged a huge sea monster from the deep. He feared that his boat would capsize and headed to shore. Others saw the huge beast thrashing about behind his boat and they came alongside and tried to kill it with their spears. One of them wounded it. Blood gushed everywhere, but then before their very eyes the Beast's wound magically healed."

Figure 38: The Beast from the Deep

"That's unbelievable. Who told you this?"

"One night I was drinking wine with one of the locals and she told me that all the other boats came in to help against the Beast because the fisherman couldn't get his boat to the beach. Others came with sharp poles and tried to spear it, but it went berserk and attacked the fishermen. Some were sliced in half by the Beast's tail. The others on the boat got scared at his awesome power and jumped overboard, swimming ashore. The Beast attacked the rest of the fisherman and they headed upriver in their boats, but strangely the Beast didn't follow."

"This is unbelievable."

"Hold on, it gets better," Nafuka said. "At the mouth of the river, fresh and salt water mix, but when the Beast swam upriver he suddenly screamed in agony and swam back to the ocean."

"Why?"

"Near as anyone could tell, he can't stand the fresh water. The Beast fled downriver and into the ocean where he swam alongside the mainland shores and terrorized the beach communities. Once he left the ocean, no one on land could stop him. He attacked everywhere on the mainland and the lucky ones escaped in boats to the river of pure water. After awhile, the noblemen built his palace on the island and began building the floating city. It's anchored to the island and protected by the fresh water."

"How long has this been going on?"

"Maybe twenty years."

"Twenty years! So where did they get the wood to build the floating city?"

"People crossed to the mainland and chopped trees on the shoreline. Two people would always stand guard watching for the Beast. The others did the work."

"And if he came?"

"As soon as the Beast came, they jumped back in their boats and paddled out to the safety of the river. They shot up a flare when they saw him, warning the others, but that's not the really interesting part."

"There's more?"

"You'll see tonight."

"What do they call this river?"

"Oh you'll really like this. Because it protects them from the Beast, they call it 'The River of Life.'"

"I'm surprised they don't worship the river if it protects them from the Beast."

"Don't be foolish. It's just water."

"But it saves them from the Beast and provides so much for them."

"That makes sense to me, Vying, but I'm telling you these people think a little different than most. Come on, let's go down and drink some Milo wine and celebrate your victory and our freedom from Zartex."

"I'm not drinking the wine."

"That's fine with me, you're the one in training."

"Take it easy with the wine, Nafuka. I wouldn't want to see you get in trouble and end up back on Zartex."

"I'm never going back to Zartex as a prisoner. I miss Darcel already. I can't believe it."

"Maybe you're growing soft."

Nafuka scowled at me, but let the comment slide. "No, maybe I'm just growing older. Besides, if I don't prepare you for the run, I'll be shipped back to Zartex anyway."

We continued walking on the floating gangways through the river houses as the wooden planking rose and fell. I noticed a man in a small boat tending some wooden cages half submerged in the river. One of them was tied up to the pier.

"Look a little closer. What do you see?"

I walked over to the gage and looked in. A finned brown fish broke the surface and flapped its tail. Instantly I jumped back remembering the moat around the battle ring.

Nafuka laughed. "Don't worry, he can't get out of his cage. Those fish are very valuable."

We headed down the wooden walkway when a massive three-story building painted bright red appeared outside of the houses. Two couples walked toward us hanging onto the rope rails that hung from the bridge that led to the building.

"What's that?"

"Glad you asked. That's where the Milo wine flows freely. Come on, let's walk over."

We walked over the wooden bridge. "I suppose it would be easy to fall in the water if you drank too much."

"When the wind picks up, it makes it especially difficult to return, but somehow they make it."

We arrived at the anchored floating structure which was much bigger and steadier than all the others. Its big bulky timbers withstood the motion of the river. We entered the wooden building and walked through a bunch of people sitting at small round tables. We found an empty one and sat down. A waitress with dark circles under her eyes slammed two glasses of wine on the table. She waited for payment.

"This is the nobleman's runner and I'm his trainer," Nafuka said. She nodded her head and left.

"How are you going to pay?" I asked.

"I just did. They don't get many visitors here on Coralia, so they know we're the new runners."

Two beautiful women came up to our table and looked at us, smiling eagerly.

"Are these seats taken?" one of them asked.

"Be out guests," Nafuka volunteered, pulling one of the chairs back like a gentleman.

They were bold, but Nafuka seemed in paradise and grinned from ear to ear. I wanted to learn all I could so I asked, "Have you ever seen the Beast?"

The dark haired woman gave a deep hard look and said, "No, but at night you can see the colored fruit glowing from the trees on the mainland."

"Have you eaten the fruit?"

"At first I didn't, it was forbidden, but then I became curious. One of the men from the island made the run and returned with fruits of all colors. It was incredible. When you eat the fruit, it takes you away from this dreary life. You dream and become anything you desire. If I were a man, I'd make the run to the mainland and get as much as I could," she said, her eyes drawn toward the mainland and her countenance filled with an unquenchable desire.

"Did you ever try the fruit?" I asked the blonde.

She pushed her dazed friend aside. "What do you think? Have you ever consumed anything like it? Oh, it will take you on a journey where anything is possible. I love the golden fruit. It makes me feel regal and powerful. I dream that I'm a queen and everyone serves me. I wear the finest clothes, live in a royal palace, and have male and female slaves to wait on my every whim. I'd give anything for another taste of the golden fruit."

The other begged, "When you go, remember me. Please bring back a green one. It makes me feel rich when I eat it. I can buy anything I want, go anywhere I want, do anything I want. People look up to me. I have all that I need when I eat the green fruit. I'll do anything in exchange for the green fruit— anything," she said with a wink, pressing her body against me.

"Has anyone journeyed to the source of the River of Life?" I asked turning away from her.

The question jolted her thinking away from the fruit.

"Some have tried. They paddled upstream, but had to stop. The stream gets very narrow. They heard the Beast howling and got scared. Somehow the Beast always knows when someone goes ashore. Long ago, one of the men tried to go to the source, but the Beast found him and killed him."

The blonde spoke up, "There's a legend about the source. It's a small clear pool where water bubbles up, forming a pool. The outlet from the pool flows down a rocky slope and widens into a rushing river. We believe that if you are submerged in the River of Life at the source, you will be victorious over the Beast. That's why he attacks anyone who gets near the source. He can't allow anyone to get too close to the pure water that flows from it."

"Before the Beast took over the mainland, there wasn't any forbidden fruit on the mainland, but now it's plentiful. However, there's a steep price to pay to get it. Few make it back alive. That's why the nobleman bought you two convicts," the brunette added.

"You know who we are?"

"Of course, you're not the first to go on the run for a noblemen. They crave the fruit just like anyone else and pay handsomely. Anyone can go over there, but it takes a special person to return."

"Have many done it?"

"At first many went. It was a way to quick riches, but the temptation of the forbidden fruit can turn your life upside down. I've seen some who made it back. The noblemen gave them great riches for their treasure, but their lives completely changed. Everything was good for a while," she said, again escaping reality. "If you taste it, you'll want more and more, never satisfied. Eventually the fruit controls all their thoughts and drives them to the mainland for more. Few ever return from the mainland a second time."

A distinguished looking gentleman approached our table and waited patiently for a break in our conversation. He looked at the two women. "Hello Necai, Samita. I see you've beaten me to the table. Whatever offer they have made to you, including themselves, I can double it if you bring me the blue fruit."

Then, he looked over at Nafuka. "You're back. You remember the blue fruit, don't you?"

"Sure Aswani," Nafuka replied.

With delight, he looked happily at Nafuka. "Have you come to make me happy again? It'll be like old times. Remember? Bring back the blue fruit. When I eat it, it makes me feel so happy. The nobleman will never know if you slip me a piece. You brought so much the last time."

Chapter Thirty-Nine

Like old friends meeting again after a long absence, Aswani, the girls, Nafuaka and I sat, talked and ordered dinner. The fresh fish served in an mango coconut sauce was scrumptious. Everyone was having a grand time as laughter filled the room powered by the Milo wine. The sun had completed its work for the day and the darkened sky displayed the distant stars and galaxies. Nafuka, like a bright nova, was the returning comet of the evening.

He retold his story about tricking the Beast and getting two loads of the forbidden fruit. Aswani and the girls were pleasant enough, but their insatiable hunger for another taste of the forbidden fruit brought the conversation back to the colored produce from across the river.

The stylish Yolee entered the bar and Nafuka's head swiveled to gaze at her. She was no longer dressed in her flowing white silk gown, but instead was dressed in a sleeveless wrap-around teal green dress.

"Nafuka, I thought you were in love with Darcel."

"I am, but a man can look."

Suddenly a low sounding roar erupted shaking the glasses on the wall behind the bar. All heads turned toward the mainland in dead silence. The malevolent howl roared again, paralyzing everyone's conversation.

"Someone didn't make it," one of the girls said softly.

"What do you mean?" I asked.

"They'll find his broken body on the rocks. The beast likes to gloat over his kill to remind all that he's the god of this world."

"Hasn't an army fought him?"

"Over the years, the noblemen have tried. They've hired bands of fighters to come and kill the Beast, but he has turned them all back. The Beast is very powerful and hides so well in the jungle that no one can see him. He has supernatural powers. Look! Off in the distance. The colors of the night!"

Deep darkness cloaked the mainland. I looked and saw the

forbidden fruit hanging from the trees. Some were bright orange, fiery red, luminescent yellow, a reddish pink, azure, a soft but visible green, deep violet, magenta, amber, fuchsia, carnelian, and a barely visible brown. It was a colorful sight.

"You can hardly see the violet fruit. They're hard to spot and are the ones most sought after. Even though the Beast has killed again, I wouldn't be surprised if someone makes the run tonight. Just seeing the colors of the night provokes a hunger from those who have tasted the forbidden fruit. Don't forget us when you come back."

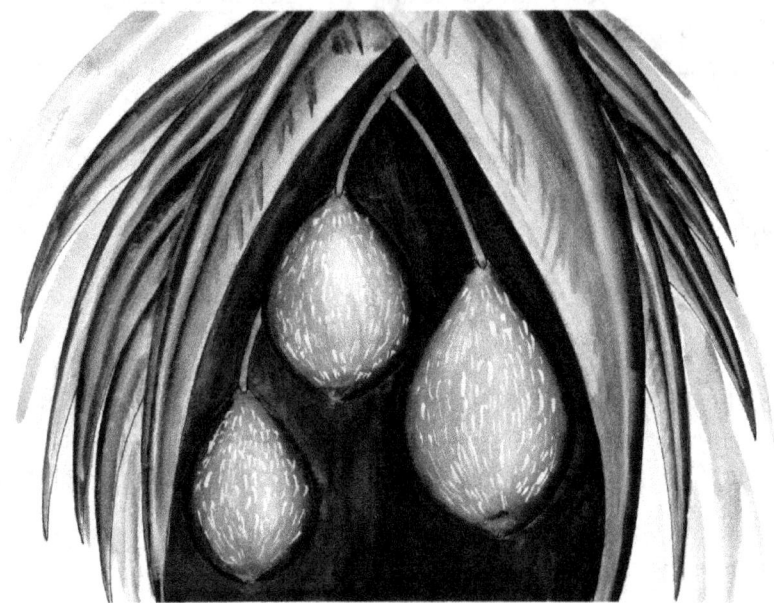

Figure 39: Forbidden Fruit

"Is there a way to trick the Beast or is it sheer speed that defeats him?"

"Trickery is the only way to defeat the Beast," Nafuka interjected. "That's how I was able to make it back alive. Sheer speed is an advantage, but that only goes so far. You've got to use your brains to outsmart him. After I returned that night, four more made the run and came back with fruit. They ate their booty, but it weakened all of them. After consuming the fruit, the hunger for more drove them back. They never returned."

"What about the nobleman? Does the forbidden fruit weaken him as well?"

"Of course, but they crave it, just like anyone. That's why the bidding is so strong on Zartex to get the prisoners from the Warder. Most prisoners want their freedom more than the fruit."

"Why?"

"Because they haven't tasted the fruit."

"What about you, Nafuka. Will you make the run again?" the blond asked.

"Before I met Vying, I was trying to get back here to make another run, but now that the Almighty is in my heart, I have no desire for the fruit. He has delivered me from my craving," Nafuka said softly, leaning over to me. "Look at these people. I used to be one of them. Their every thought is about the fruit. I made a huge mistake. I was free after I made the run, but I ate the fruit and could never get enough of it. I'm free now. I want to go back to Zartex and take Darcel to Milo. She will be near her sister and perhaps we can live a normal life."

"What are you talking about?" one of the girls asked interrupting our conversation.

I looked at her with pity. "The floating city is filled with evil spirits. You've been driven from your homeland by the Beast. When will you rise up and defeat this evil creature?"

"How? We've tried. The beast is crafty. He was the one who began planting the trees with the colorful fruit on the cliffs beckoning us to come over. Until the trees appeared we were content to be fisherman and live in the floating city away from him. Initially, we thought the trees and the fruit were a gift from the Beast," the dark haired woman said.

"A gift? You can't be serious?" Nafuka exclaimed.

"The Almighty has a greater gift, the gift of eternal life with Him," I added.

"What are you talking about? Who is the Almighty?" the blonde asked.

I looked at her and the epiphany of why I'd been sent to Zartex manifested in my mind. It was my mission to come here and tell these people about the Almighty's Son, Jesus, who has set free all those who are tormented by evil spirits. With stunning realization, I knew why I had come to Coralia. The Almighty had been guiding my every step and a sense of urgency overcame me.

"Let's go, Nafuka. I need to begin training for the battle ahead."

He looked at me in bewilderment. "Now? Vying, you're ready. We've sweated and trained hard. You defeated all in the battle ring. Relax, enjoy the night, you've earned it. Don't worry, you'll be successful at making the run. I'm confident of that."

"I know I can complete the run, but that's not why I'm here."

"What do you mean?"

"I've got to go back and study the Almighty's Book if I'm going to have any chance of using His Son's power to defeat the Beast. Let's go."

"No, please don't go. Wouldn't you like to stay with me?" the blonde pleaded touching my forearm lightly. At that moment I could see clearly that they had no idea how the Beast and the evil spirits controlled them. The words they spoke were a hindrance to prevent me from completing the Almighty's mission.

"Vying, please, this is our first night off the prison planet. Surely we can celebrate tonight and you can begin tomorrow," pleaded Nafuka.

"Nafuka, tomorrow is not promised to any man. You can stay if you want, but I must be about the Almighty's business. I have no time to waste. This Beast is very powerful and I've got to spend time in His presence and study His Book if I'm going to use the His power to defeat the Beast."

"You go ahead. There's someone I want to talk to," Nafuka said as he got up and walked over to Yolee.

I left the bar and walked across the bridge to the floating village and retraced my steps to the nobleman's palace. It wasn't hard, because the nobleman's house perched on a hill.

Once in my room, I pulled out the hologram and began studying.

After a while, I spent time in prayer, asking the Almighty to help me on this mission. Then, I sat silently in His Presence, picturing the Almighty in my mind. I had to refocus my mind several times as I waited on Him. Stealing the forbidden fruit was a mighty task, but to defeat and destroy the Beast was something humanly impossible. I knew my life would be in great danger, but I remembered how the Almighty had saved me in the battle ring not once, but twice. I understood that I needed His power now more than ever.

For a long time, I sat and studied His Word. I read the scripture; *"These kind only come out through prayer and fasting."* I paused, wondering why fasting was so important. Just then the revelation burst into my mind. My flesh had to be put down for me to walk as a spirit warrior with a deeper intimacy with the great Holy Spirit, if I was going succeed at this difficult challenge. Success would only come as He showed me what I to do. I prayed and vowed not to eat again until the Almighty showed me how to destroy the Beast.

As the sun rose, I heard Nafuka stumble into his room and crash on his bed. I got up from my knees after praying for everyone I knew, then crawled into my bed and instantly fell asleep.

Chapter Forty

The next morning, I was awakened by the wooden window shutters beating against the house. A pounding monsoon storm was ripping across the island unabated. For three days, the high winds and torrential downpour were unrelenting. I was left alone to study and pray, awaiting the Almighty's direction.

"Vying," Nafuka said knocking on my door. I got up from my knees and opened it. "Are you ready?"

"In this weather?"

"It's a perfect cover. If you go now, the Beast won't see or smell you. That's one of the tricks I used. Remember, if you are to defeat him, you must be wise," Nafuka advised.

"Then let's go," I said not wanting to miss this opportunity.

"The climb will be much more dangerous, but the Beast won't expect anyone to come in this storm."

"The rocks will be slippery."

"You're right, but I think the storm is letting up," Nafuka said.

"I hope you're right. The Almighty will be with me to the top."

"Then let's go."

I grabbed my climbing gear; gloves, chalk, a hammer, a knife and buckles I shoved them all in a backpack with a couple of water bottles.

"Once you get to the top, eat off the jungle, sleep in the jungle, become one with the jungle and he won't be able to smell you. Then, you pick your time to attack. Here's some special food to take with you."

I looked at the loaves in his hands. "I won't be eating."

"What! Are you crazy? You're going to need all the strength you've got."

"The Almighty's Spirit has led me to fast. How long, I don't know."

Nafuka just shook his head as I put on climbing boots and slid the backpack over my shoulders. We headed down to the nobleman's pier and checked out the various boats tied up in the boathouse. We saw a small narrow kayak with one seat in the middle and covering for the front and the back.

"Because of the monsoon, this is the only one that won't get swamped water. Once you cross, you've got to hide it for the return trip. If the Beast spots it, he'll destroy it. Some have gotten the fruit only to discover the Beast had found their boat and was waiting on the beach for them."

"Did they make it?"

"A couple did by jumping into the river and swimming back over. But the point is that you don't want to give the Beast any indication that you've arrived."

"Thanks Nafuka, you're a true friend."

"I'll be praying for you and don't worry, I won't be going back to the floating village to get any social lubricants. I know there is nothing down there for me. I want to get out of here too."

We clasped hands as we prayed. I slipped into the slender boat and pushed away from the pier into the open water. Like red hot pokers, the driving rain drilled my face continuously. I looked back and Nafuka confidently nodded. The frenzied wind snapped and swirled. I put my head down and continued paddling on the choppy river into a strong cross wind.

My trek across the river was slow and arduous. I kept my paddle on the port side of the boat because the wind was pushing so hard against on the starboard side. Like any endurance test, I faced the trial with fervor, never letting up continuing to row. It didn't take long for my arms to become enflamed, and instead of holding a pity party, I got angry with my body and pushed harder. The fasting had sapped some of my strength and I stopped for a brief moment to catch my breath, but quickly drifted backwards, downstream. The last thing I wanted was to make up any distance because of rest. Pushing myself even harder, I resumed paddling. A scripture came to my mind, *"When I am weak, He is strong."*

Figure 40-1: Crossing the River

The night crossing dragged on. Slowly and steadily, I made it to the middle of the river. The relentless wind was wearing me down, but I didn't give up nor stop. The distant shore grudgingly came closer and closer. Finally I got into the lee of the mainland and with a fresh burst of adrenaline picked up the pace.

Slamming up against the bank, I jumped out of the boat and pulled it ashore. I looked for some trees or brush to the cover the boat, but there weren't any. Then I spotted a small opening at the base of the cliff and stowed the boat inside. I pushed a large stone in front of it and swept my footprints with a piece of deadwood.

The vertical mass of stone was intimidating. I jammed my fingers and toes into the cracks in the rocks and began climbing. I noticed an outcropping of rock and trees near the top. I fixed my eyes on it. The further I climbed, the more intense the swirling winds and driving rain got. I reached for a crack in a rock as a strong gust pushed my body away from the cliff. Desperately, I reached out for a hand hold while balancing on the balls of my feet, but the wind was too strong. Suddenly, my left foot slipped. For a moment I fought the wind while balancing on an edge. But the wind was stronger, pushing me out away from the rocks. I fought for my life trying to maintain balance. With every ounce of strength in me, I reached out and finally grabbed the edge of a stone, but it was too smooth.

My other foot slipped out from under me and I was airborne. Terror gripped my mind when a gust of wind slammed me against the stone wall and I began sliding down. I had to focus. Panicking would mean my death. Grabbing for anything with both hands, my feet cascaded over a small fissure. Instinctively I reached for it as I slid by. My shins banged against the cliff, rocketing pain up both legs, but I was able to hang on with my right hand. Using my left hand, I grabbed a small shrub growing out of the side of the rock.

"Dear Almighty, help me," I cried out as I carefully pulled myself up to a crevice. "Just a little more," I begged. With both hands I pulled myself and put my toes on the ragged edge. How long I stayed there, I didn't know.

My heart pounded so hard against my chest, I thought it would explode. Unbearable pain throbbed in both shins with an unquenchable vengeance, taking my breath away. Bone on rock has a way of doing that. Through it all, I was thankful to the Almighty that I hadn't fallen to the beach fifty leeds below. I waited until the pain subsided to a manageable level and realized that I had to be more careful.

Slowly and cautiously, I started again. I climbed with the hope of getting up and over the top while it was still dark. A faint glow on the horizon signaled a new dawn as the wind and rain slowly abated.

Going across the river in the heavy rainfall had taken more time than I'd figured. I stopped under a ledge. There was barely enough room, but I managed to sit down. What a relief. I prayed to the Almighty and asked Him for His guidance on whether to continue, but in my heart I knew I needed to rest.

Evil thoughts suddenly flooded my mind, unchecked. Resentment toward those who had framed me rose up. Anger raged against Zelestar. Why hadn't she visited me on Micron when I was in prison? Why had she abandoned me on Zartex. Life wasn't fair. Suddenly I felt like a hopeless failure. Lustful thoughts of Peen and other women filled my mind.

Remembering my Crown Championship and the battle ring on Zartex, I felt proud of my many achievements. I remembered people telling me how great a fighter I was and without me the Realm wouldn't have defeated Og and Megog in the Great War.

As I was reflecting on my greatness, an idea surfaced, *"Take every thought captive to the obedience of Christ."* Realizing the sins of lust and pride, I took those thoughts and cast them from my mind. I looked up to the Almighty and asked for His forgiveness for my thought sins and instantly my mind cleared.

A sudden shadow infiltrated my space from the ledge above. I wondered what it was. Glistening trees growing out from the rock provided me cover, but they also blocked my vision. Carefully I craned my neck around a branch.

Then I saw him!

Figure 40-2: The Beast's Perch

Fingered claws stretched out from each foot. Oozing pus blooms covered his horned head. Red eyes jammed together by a dented skull searched the river below.

I didn't move. I couldn't. Frozen with fear, I could hardly breathe. Did he see me? Did he know I was here?

Quietly I prayed that I wouldn't be seen. The Beast looked across the river, reared his grotesque head back as fluid shot from both sides of his mouth. The two streams crashed together igniting instantly and I remembered the dream I had in the prison cell on Micron.

The Beast stayed on his post for over an hour constantly searching the water below. I shook my head wondering how I could've picked this spot to climb to. But, then I realized the Almighty had guided me. It was the perfect lookout spot for the Beast. Huge boulders provided him with a post where he could see the cliff walls and the river. Straight beneath him I stood motionless.

Perverse thoughts continued bombarding my mind. Again, I took authority over them and cast them out. I looked up and saw the Beast moving his head back and forth scanning the river as if expecting someone. I couldn't believe he hadn't seen me. Burning pain from being in the same place for a long time racked my motionless body, but I wouldn't stretch a muscle to relieve the pain.

Maybe the battle was to begin here and now. I wondered if I should take authority over the Beast when the scripture came up in me, *"These do not come out but with prayer and fasting."*

I thought about that and knew my course for the next few days would be to continue fasting and praying, building my inner man up before engaging the Beast in spiritual combat.

Looking up again, I saw the Beast had moved off the edge, but just as quickly he reappeared. I sensed he was confused. I was sure the Beast would look down and either torch me with his vapor streams or reach down and pluck me off the ledge with his claws, but he never looked down toward me.

The Beast snorted, blew flaming gas into the air and walked off. Finally I collapsed on a rock, grateful that I could sit down. I looked behind in the darkness and saw an alcove. I pulled out the hologram, muted it, and began reading the Almighty's Book.

Day was coming into full bloom. I drank water and leaned back and began praying in the Spirit. Soon I was overcome with tiredness and succumbed to sleep.

Several hours later, I awoke. The sun was shining with warmth drying up the water. I felt lazy and just wanted to sit in the cave. I was safe, but then bizarre thoughts flooded my mind again and I wondered if I was going crazy. I'd never had such depressing, prideful, lustful, and angry thoughts in my life. I realized I was under attack again. I wondered if the Beast knew where I was. As I moved forward from the under hang, he reappeared. I was trapped. I couldn't move, not now. Again the Beast scanned the river, looking for something or someone.

Chapter Forty-One

Without the wind and rain, I smelled the hideous odor of sulfur spilling over the ledge. Somehow the Beast must have known I was coming. I wondered why he didn't know that I was already here, five leeds beneath him. My mind was flooded with thoughts of despair, suicide, and betrayal. Depressing spectulations besieged me and made me feel trapped under the ledge, that my life was going to end here. I wanted to climb back down the cliff, but I knew the noise would alert him.

Slowly, ever so slowly, I turned around and pulled out the hologram. A couple of verses came up, *"We wrestle not against flesh and blood, but against Principalities, Powers, Rulers, and wickedness in heavenly places... Our weapons are not carnal, but mighty in the Lord."*

Evil was lurking directly above me, seeking to hunt me down and devour me. Tormenting spirits had already attacked with all kinds of evil thoughts. I had to get away. This was too much. I was a fighter, but this mind battle was more than I'd anticipated.

I'd been sitting under the ledge for two days, praying and fasting. I wondered when I'd be ready to do battle with the Beast. But then a revelation came to me. *The battle began a long time ago.* I knew it wasn't my idea, so it had to be the Almighty's. If the tormenting spirits could put thoughts in my mind, so could the Almighty. I took hope.

Bright sunlight broke through the early morning cloud cover and the Beast lumbered away from his perch. I climbed up to the edge of the stone overhang. Listening intently for any kind of movement from the Beast, I heard the faint sound of foraging. Climbing the last leed to the top of the cliff, I peeked over the edge. The Beast trekked slowly to his cave. Naked white bones littered the blackened ground. Flame charred trees, like coffins waiting to be buried, lay on the ground. Scorched rocks formed the entrance to his lair.

I couldn't wait any longer. I needed to slip over the edge and run into the jungle. Fear immediately snatched my mind. *What if the Beast turned around? Would the brush give me enough cover? Could I run fast enough to escape his fire?*

"In Jesus name," I said, taking authority over these doubts and cast them from my mind. I took a giant leap of faith, believing the Almighty would protect me and pulled myself up over the edge of the cliff. I ran to the trees without looking back.

I felt victorious in my run. I had overcome my fears. Then I heard a strange wailing. I watched as the Beast stopped before entering his cave. He walked over to the opening, looked around slowly, and disappeared inside. I ran to the edge of the dense misty foliage. Without turning back, I ran into the jungle and hid under some large green leaves. I wondered how the others had successfully completed the run and the thought came to my mind that this was all a setup.

The Beast's game was deadly. He allowed some people to succeed at making the run to encourage others. If he didn't allow a few to succeed, others would never try. Those that ate the forbidden fruit would enter into a season of pleasure dreams, always wanting more, never satiated, never filled, never realizing that death's call was waiting at their doorstep. They would risk everything, even their lives, for another taste of the fruit.

I sat down and as the day wore on and fell asleep. Later, I woke up and listened for the Beast, but didn't hear anything. I took some mud and smeared my body with it as Nafuka had advised. I wondered if his advice made any difference. Maybe he was one of the few that were allowed to live to tell others about the run.

I knew I would have to kill the Beast and looked around at the moss laden trees to fashion a weapon. I saw some dried up bamboo and pulled them down, hoping to find a couple of good shoots. There were a few sturdy ones, so I took my knife and whittled one end. A pointed tip emerged. I was hungry, but I wouldn't give in to the hunger pains and drank water instead. I pulled out the hologram and began to read more of the Almighty's Words. Because I was fasting, I sensed a deeper, closer intimacy with the Almighty.

Night was approaching and the jungle got quiet. I knew the hologram would project light to make the words of the Almighty's Book visible, so I put it away. I wasn't ready to fight the Beast in his territory, so I sat down behind the brush and began praying. A sweet peace swept over me and I rested in it.

A deafening cry jarred me from my solitude. It sounded much

louder than before. Carefully, I parted the leaves and looked out. The Beast was staring straight into the jungle and me. Fear enveloped me. I froze as he roared again, but then a thought popped into my mind. *"I didn't give you a spirit of fear, but of power and a sound mind."*

I thought about the Almighty's Words and a picture popped into my mind. A naked woman was coming toward me. Sexual images danced in my head, but I resisted them.

"I bind you spirits of lust in the Name of Jesus and cast you from my mind," I declared aloud, fighting the spirit battle within my mind. The peace of the Almighty come over me and I realized I had to fight the spiritual battle first. The Beast had already declared war and was sending all kinds of evil and perverse thoughts my way to dissuade me from my mission.

The next tormenting spirit told me how I'd been cheated during my trial because the truth had been spun in a way to make me appear guilty. I wrestled with this thought, because I knew it was true. I'd been obedient to the leading of the Almighty's Spirit and yet I was pronounced guilty. Why had the Almighty allowed this to happen? The Council of Peers laughed at me when I told them about the Almighty and how He led me with His Spirit. No one wanted to hear that. The truth was buried, never told. I was judged guilty in man's court and became bitter.

I remembered another message from the hologram, *"Blessed are you when men revile you and persecute you and utter all kinds of evil against you falsely on my account. Rejoice and be glad, for great is your reward in heaven. For they persecuted the prophets who came before you."*

I realized the thoughts of injustice came from the evil one and were filled with revenge and spite. Then it dawned on me that if I served the Almighty, those that hated Him wouldn't treat me fairly. Again I began praying in the spirit and finally the peace of the Almighty descended upon me and I fell asleep. I dreamed that I was being led by chains to a den of sleeping lions. They opened their eyes, strained at their chains and roared at me. Suddenly their chains were released and they all came running toward me.

"Jesus save me!" I cried out in my dream. I began to sing praises to the Almighty, His Son – Jesus, and the Holy Spirit as they got ready to pounce on me.

A bloodcurdling roar jarred me from the dream. Was I still sleeping? Had the lions escaped my dream? The Beast roared again. He was returning to his cave as the sun's light pierced the darkness. I realized the Beast couldn't stay in the light, just like it couldn't swim in the fresh water of the river that protected the floating village. Maybe that's when Nafuka snatched the fruit.

I pulled the hologram out and continued to study the Almighty's Book. If I was going to be victorious in this spiritual battle, I had to know His Word. Something made me look up just before I turned it on. There, standing twenty leeds from me was a yeknom, the smaller cousin of a Hoon. With a raised a finger, he pointed straight at me.

Chapter Forty-Two

Grabbing a bamboo shaft, I readied to throw it. An uneasy quiet settled over the jungle as every living creature watched to see who would make the first move. A half empty bottle of Milo wine in one hand and a smoldering cigarette in the other, the yeknom walked toward me. I'd never seen an animal act so human and it was fearless of the light. I steadied my make shift spear and got ready to throw it. I wouldn't go down without a fight.

"Easy pardner," it slurred. "De Beast will soon be asleep. I came out for a liddle speaks before he captures you."

My spirit pounded within me and I knew I couldn't trust him or any word he said. I'd dealt with talking animals before and knew they were demon possessed.

With child-like curiosity, he looked me up and down as he walked closer. "So yous de ladest one do make de run. You lookin' do steal some of de Beast's fruit? Yeah know, he be waitin' for you. He knows you're here."

"What are you, the welcoming committee?'

The yeknom laughed a little too much. "Yeah, I guess you could say dat."

"If the Beast knows I'm here, why hasn't he attacked?"

"Oh, he be playing which you. You ever seen a predador and de prey? De Beast loves do play with his victim. He'll come when he's ready. You'll end up like de odders."

"So who are you?"

"His slave. Somebody's godda keep dings goin' around here."

"Why don't you leave?"

"I can't. Look ad him. He too powerful. Sides, he'd send someone to find me. It's not doo bad working for him and being part of de kingdom. I gets do drink plenty of Milo wine and smoke dees cigs. You wanna get high?"

"No thanks. I've got water."

Figure 42: The Yeknom

"How about a hit of dis stuff? It'll knock you zilly," he said offering the cigarette.

"I'm sure it will, but I don't need anything. I've been dining on the Almighty's Word."

292

"Ooh, de Almighty's Word. That's novel. I haven't heard de Almighty's Word in a long, long dime. I suppose you dink you can defeat de Beast wid it."

"I really don't know what's going to happen."

"Yeah, I can dell you don't. You're like all de odders. You'll make de run and de Beast will sdop you and frow you into de cave. You'll never come out, dil you're nothin' bud de bones."

"There's people in the cave?" I asked incredulously.

"He keeps dem locked up. Dey brings de Beast pleasure do see de Almighty's creation suffer. I'm de one dat's godda keep dem alive."

"But I thought he killed them and threw their bodies over the cliff."

The yeknom laughed some more. "I always wondered if de people dought dat. Oh he gets rid of a few, but dose are de ones dats been here a long time. De Beast likes to dorment dem."

He looked around suspiciousily. "I gots do go. I dold you doo much already. You're de second one do come up here and not immediately dry and steal de fruit. De odder one, a different color dan you. He took a lot of de fruit wid him. I don't dink de Beast got him."

Nafuka! Everywhere I went, he was always ahead of me. So he had been telling the truth. A thought came into my mind that I wasn't ready to face the Beast. I needed to study the Almighty's Word more, but I wasn't going to move until this creature left me. I couldn't trust a word the yeknom said and I knew that I better move before the Beast emerged from his cave.

As if reading my thoughts, he said, "Not do worry. De Beast sleeps in de day. Dell you what friend, I won't dell him about you. Give you a fightin chance. Besides, I have do have my fun do. Now, I've got do get some food for de guests. Good luck on de run."

"I don't need luck. The Almighty will protect me."

"Like I said, good luck. I don't know about dis Almighty protecting you. He sure didn't prodect de odders. Deys suffered a lot," he said as he wandered off. "Oh by de way, when de Beast flies into the air, for some reason he always banks do de left before he flies ad you."

"Really. Why would you tell me that?"

"Maybe you be de one. I wouldn't mind getting out of here. Change of scenery would do me good."

"What's your name?"

"I be Skeldor."

I waited until he had gone away before I relaxed my grip on the spear. Demons by nature lie, so I took all that was said with caution. I didn't want to fight the Beast until I was built up in the Spirit. I went off to read and listen to the Almighty's Word and pray. My stomach growled and I drank from a stream of cool water. The water filled my stomach and the pain went away for a while. I still hadn't eaten anything for several days. I knew that I had to put my flesh down, if I was to hear from the Almighty and conquer the Beast. I knew that the Almighty Father had to show me how to defeat this demon and set the captives of Coralia free.

Chapter Forty-Three

For the next two weeks, I kept fasting, praying and studying the word. I felt weak, but wasn't hungry. I realized that I had fasted for twenty-one days. Suddenly a powerful heavenly presence come over me. I felt a burning sensation in my body. For the first time since I'd climbed the mainland cliffs, I felt empowered to defeat the Beast. Because of the fast, my mind was centered on the Almighty. My flesh wasn't rising against my spirit. Strengthened in faith, impure thoughts were quickly deflected from my mind by the Almighty's invisible shield of faith. I knew all aspects of my life had to be as pure as possible, as I walked on the Highway of Holiness, going deeper into the secret place of the Most High. Led by the Holy Spirit, I grabbed my three bamboo spears and sharpened their points. I didn't know why I'd need spears in a spiritual battle, but I obeyed.

The Almighty overshadowed my every step. I could feel huge hands encompassing mine as I prayed. When I lifted them to Him and prayed, a slow moving fire, like warm oil, ran from my hands down my arms to the top of my head down my back. Looking up to heaven, I felt a hot sensation around my head and I knew I was being anointed to go into battle. I knelt down and waited on Him. As long as I felt His presence, I didn't move. I wanted all He had for me to defeat the Beast.

The sun went down and the cool evening air permeated the jungle around me. My legs had fallen asleep in the kneeling position. Streaks of pain shot through them as I got up. Even though it was a spiritual battle, I picked up my hand made weapons. I was ready for battle and moved toward the edge of the jungle. There I waited for the Almighty to show me what to do. With his head held high, the dragon prince of Coralia emerged from his cave, strutting to his perch overlooking the river. Rising up, he let out a thunderous roar, stopping all movement in the jungle.

Moving quickly through the underbrush to the clearing, I wondered if he'd notice me. I knew demonic beings could sense the presence of the Almighty. Without turning around, he said in a low tone of voice, "What took you so long? I've been waiting for you. Have you come to steal my forbidden fruit?"

"I didn't come for the fruit, but to destroy you!"

"Destroy me?" he roared and then laughed. "I am god of Coralia. Who are you that you think you can destroy me?"

"I, the Almighty's servant, come in the name of His Son, Jesus Christ."

Turning around he said, "I see you've brought three puny spears. Do you really think you can kill me like some little clarion?"

"In the Name of the Almighty Father, His Son - Jesus Christ, and the Holy Spirit, I come against you."

Enraged, the Beast flew at me with his deadly claws fully extended. I ducked behind a boulder at the last possible moment as he flew over me. His speed of flight and reaction time were extraordinary. This was no ordinary dragon. I felt something wet dripping down my back. It was blood, my blood. He'd cut me and I hadn't even felt it. Landing on his perch, he glared at me.

"It's lucky there was a boulder to protect you. How does your back feel?" the Beast asked proudly.

Words came flying out of my mouth. *"To suffer for His sake is gain,"* I said wondering where those words had come from.

"Oh, suffer you will!" The Beast laughed. "There's a whole army of sufferers inside my hell hole. You'll join them in a little while."

"I don't think so. Every knee shall bow to the Name of Jesus Christ."

"Bow? To who? By whose authority? Yours?"

"On my own, I can do nothing. It's through the authority and power of the Almighty's Son, Jesus, that I can do all things. He's already been victorious over your boss."

"Is that so? Where is He? Where is this Son of the Almighty – this Jesus? I see a puny man before me, a convicted murderer. You've been sent to me for punishment. You'll spend eternity being tormented for the murder of Cappy. You deserve it. I, the god of this world, have spoken!"

The fire of the Almighty stirred hotly in me. "Enough," I yelled. "In the name of Jesus Christ, I command you to come out of him."

Figure 43-1: Attacking the Beast

The Beast flew out of sight. I picked up one of the bamboo spears.

"Oh dis be so good!" the yeknom cheered. "You done bedder dan all de odders!"

I hadn't heard the yeknom coming and glanced his way for just a split second, but that was enough. The Beast instantly dove at me with tremendous speed, but I was ready. Without looking, I jammed one of my spears straight up into his right wing, knocking him off course. The wounded dragon screamed as he hit the ground, but got back up and struggled to fly to his perch.

"Oh dad was so good. Come on, Vying you can do id," the yeknom cheered.

"Good trick, but now you die!" the Beast said lifting up his right claw and holding it out toward me. Power shot out and knocked me to the ground. Dazed, I looked up as he flew at me. Instinctively I rolled to the right, just as fire came out of his mouth, burning the ground where I'd been.

"Ooh, a quick one," the yeknom cheered as the dragon circled above.

At first, I wondered why the Name of Jesus seemed to have little effect on him, but then I noticed his labored breathing. Trying to rise higher, I could see the strain in his face. His breath was labored as he rose higher, wilting under the power of the name of Jesus. I grabbed another spear and got ready.

"In the name of Jesus every knee must bow!" I shouted with authority as I hurled the spear at the flying dragon.

It caught him square in the chest. The Beast flew to his perch, holding on for all he had. Taking in a deep breath, he exhaled through his nose, but only a wisp of gaseous flames escaped. Flapping his wings, he flew away, trying to escape across the river. I ran towards the edge and threw the last bamboo spear with all the strength I had. It pierced his other wing and the Beast plummeted to the River of Life. Hitting the water, fire exploded into the darkened sky. I watched as a whirlpool of turbulent water sent him to the deep. Exhausted, I leaned back against a rock, knowing the people of Coralia were free from the Beast

who had manipulated and ruled their lives. Finally they could leave the floating island and return to the mainland and live a much better life, free from the evil oppression.

"Bwavo! Bwavo! You did wonderful. You're de only person ever do defead de Beasd."

I turned and noticed the yeknom slowly coming towards me. I wondered why he was still here. The Beast was defeated and he too was free. "It was Jesus Christ who defeated that demon, not me."

"On de condrary. You, Vying, a mighty warrior in de spirit, hero of de Blue Ring Galaxy have done a great deed. You are do be commended. You are do be praised! All of Coralia will exald your name."

It felt good to be victorious over the Beast, I thought, but quickly realized how he was giving me the credit for the victory. "It was the power and authority in the Name of Jesus Christ that defeated the Beast. You need to get your facts straight. Why are you here anyway?."

His face glowed red. "Why am I here? You ask why I'm here! Do you really dink dad de dragon is in charge around here? You, like all de odders, have focused on de wrong beast. I am de god of Coralia and you will bow do me!" the yeknom demanded. The battle of spiritual authority and dominion had just begun.

Figure 43-2: The god of Coralia

Chapter Forty-Four

The Yeknom's body elongated and turned into a hideous two headed creature, towering above me. He was twice the size of the dragon. I had no more spears. What good would they have done? Instinctively, I lifted my right hand to the Lord, bowed my head, extending my left hand outward, palm facing the yeknom. I closed my eyes and fervently began to pray in the spirit.

"Oh Vying, you don't need to do that," a gentle voice said warmly.

Zelestar! I quickly opened my eyes. Where had she come from? She was radiant, glowing white with a shimmering colorful rainbow above her head, more beautiful than I had ever remembered, and a welcomed sight after this battle. She glowed and I looked around for the two-headed monster, but it was gone.

"The Holy Spirit told me to come. I rebuked that demonic spirit for you. Oh Vying, how I've wanted to be with you, but the war, Emperor Og, and my leadership on Milo has kept us apart too long. I think of you often and love you very very much. You are so wonderful, so brave. I saw the Beast hit the River of Life as I climbed the cliffs. Come," she said extending her hand, "let's go to the cave and free those trapped by the Beast."

Her loving words were so intoxicating. Eagerly, joyfully I followed her to the cave. She looked like an angel who had just left the presence of the Almighty. I wanted to hold her in my arms again. I relaxed, knowing the battle was over and Zelestar had once again appeared in my life. I couldn't be happier and I couldn't wait to hold her in my arms, but first we had to free the prisoners in the cave. I wondered how she had destroyed the yeknom, but I knew deep in my heart that the Almighty's power flowed through those who truly believed.

Love struck, by her beauty, both inside and out, I followed her. As we neared the cave she turned around and handed me some chains. "Here, put these on. Those inside will be frightened if they see you walking in here without restraints."

How could she know that? I wondered. My spirit was tingling, jumping up and down inside of me, but I wanted to be with Zelestar, to please her more than anything. I'd do whatever she asked.

"Remember when you were frightened in the tunnel on Za-Kar and I held your hand? Let me help you now, darling," she said sweetly. As I got closer to her a horrible foul stench filled the air. I wondered what it was and realized it must be the stench from the cave. I gagged, holding my breath so the vomit wouldn't escape. I wondered how many dead or decaying were inside.

"You can do this Vying, but like before. The Almighty has sent me to help you. I'll follow you in," she said, holding the chains, the manacles open, ready to snap them on my wrists.

The Almighty was a little late in sending her, but at least she came and was with me, I thought as I willingly extended my wrists, looking deeply into her lovely eyes.

The Holy Spirit screamed inside of me and I heard an audible voice yell, "RUN!"

Just as the cold chains kissed my wrists I dropped my arms, running away as fast as I could.

"Don't be afraid, my love. Please, come back," she called sweetly.

At the edge of the cliff, I turned around and saw a giant snake shoot out of her mouth. Her body grew twice its size, the huge snake continued to pour out. It hit the ground and with its mouth open and fangs showing, it shot straight at me! I dove for the rock that had protected me before and looked up. The giant snake curled up above me, exposing its deadly fangs, waiting to strike as it grew larger and larger. I was no match for this viper, but a thought spoke to my heart.

"I take authority over this evil spirit. In the name of Jesus Christ, I command you to stop." But the gigantic snake kept coming toward me.

What was I going to do? Hadn't I been trained in spiritual warfare? I looked over the side of the cliff and thought of jumping. Maybe I could survive the fall if I landed in the river. Acidic saliva dripping from the serpent's mouth burned my skin. I had to decide. Would I stand my ground spiritually or jump? Quickly, I decided to place my life in the hands of the Almighty.

"In the name of Jesus the Christ, I rebuke you foul spirit and command you to leave Coralia, never to return!" I said with all the faith I had. Either I was going to die here or this demon was going to be bound for all eternity.

"Oh please don't do that," the snake said, turning back into the lovely Zelestar, the woman I loved, now scantily clad. In a low seductive voice she said, "Let's make love tonight, darling. You've been waiting to have me for a long time. Tonight you'll be amply rewarded, just come to me."

I knew this wasn't right. Somehow this foul spirit had the ability to change into something beautiful, even the woman I loved. But I wasn't falling for his tricks again and with inner authority I declared, "Be gone in the name of Jesus Christ of Nazareth!"

Zelestar disappeared and the yeknom reappeared.

"In the Name that's above every name, the name of Jesus Christ. I cast you, Skeldor, from this planet!"

Immediately, the demon Skeldor disappeared. Peace engulfed me as I dropped to my knees, thanking the Almighty for His deliverance. I felt his hot presence around my head and focused on Him as I kneeled there, my head bowed to Him. After awhile the hot sensation left and I got up and ran to the cave. The fires had gone out and many emaciated people began stumbling out as if they had just awakened from a nightmare. Their faces were gaunt and sickly.

"Please heal them, Almighty," I declared as I lifted my right hand to heaven and extended my left hand to them. My body became His conduit as His power flowed through me as I prayed in the spirit.

As they made their way to the cliffs, I tied off my climbing rope so they could descend to the River of Life. Joy and hope, the inner strength of heaven, returned to their eyes as they lifted their heads up.

"Look at the sky," one of them cried out, "it's not grey."

He was right. A shift in atmosphere over Coralia had occurred and the sky for the first time was a brilliant blue. With anger, I looked at the colored fruit trees growing on the banks and cut off their branches. When I threw the forbidden fruit over the cliff, they ignited in flames as it hit the surface of the River of Life. Furiously I began cutting and pulling the trees up by their roots and threw them over the side. It took several exhausting hours, but I was filled with a supernatural strength. I had to make sure that the people of Coralia would never be tempted by the fruit again. Physically and emotionally spent, I sat down near the jungle under the cool green plants. I was very hungry and thirsty. The cave was empty and the people gone. I lifted my arms in triumph. Finally Coralia was free!

I heard stones cascading down the cliff. When I looked toward the cliff, I couldn't believe my eyes! A sick feeling of dread came over me.

Not again! My battle wasn't finished. How could he have survived? How could this demon have returned? I picked up my knife. Just as she appeared, I took careful aim. I wanted the force of impact to kill this demonic spirit who was manifesting again in the form of Zelestar.

I raised my hand high over my head and threw the knife.

"No," the Holy Spirit cried out, but it was too late.

Zelestar screamed.

Instantly, I knew my mistake and tried to alter my throw, but it was too late. I couldn't bear to look. I dropped my head as I heard the fleshly impact, instantly killing the woman I loved.

I dropped to my knees in anguish. "Kill me now, Almighty! I deserve to die."

But nothing happened to me. I waited. Slowly, I looked up afraid to see what I had done. Nafuka was on the ground, a knife sticking out of his chest. The demon had manifested again into Nafuka and I was relieved. Then I saw Zelestar. What was going on?

"Get over here, Vying!" he yelled gasping for breath.

I rushed over to him. I couldn't believe it. He was still alive.

"Don't stand there. Pull it out!"

"You'll die, if I pull it out."

"Don't be a fool. The Almighty hasn't brought me this far for me to die. Besides, I've been knifed several times before. If you'd hit my heart, I'd be coughing blood. Now pull it out."

Figure 44: Vying's Mistake

I was stunned and couldn't move. Zelestar reached down and pulled the knife out. Using the bloody weapon, she cut off a piece of her skirt and wrapped it around Nafuka's chest stopping the flow of blood. Then a bewildered look came over her face.

"Why would you try to kill me? I thought you loved me."

"I do love you with all my heart, but I thought you were the demon Skeldor manifesting again."

She thought about it for a moment and nodded her head. "It must

304

have been tough up here. We saw the Beast fall into the River of Life, but then we heard another growl and knew you were still in battle. We prayed and climbed even faster."

"I knew I should have obeyed the Spirit when He told me to call out to you before we came over the top," Nafuka said from behind me.

"I thought Skeldor had returned. He'd transformed into Zelestar, then a huge snake. I thought he'd come back. I'm so sorry. Please forgive me, Zelestar."

"Let me get this right," Nafuka droned. "You're apologizing to Zelestar and I'm the one with blood pouring out of my chest."

I laughed at my own foolishness. "I'm sorry, Nafuka. With all my heart, thanks for saving Zelestar."

"You're incredibly brave, Nafuka. Why did you jump in front of me?" she asked.

"One day, I listened to the hologram, waiting for Vying to come and train with me. It talked about laying down your life for your friend. All I could see was my friend making a terrible mistake. I had to stop him the only way I knew. Now do you believe me that I'm your friend?"

"Yes, Nafuka. The Almighty works in mysterious ways, but you, Nafuka, are by far the most mysterious. Forgive me for all the doubt and disbelief I had about you. You have been my friend from the time we sat together on the prison shuttle."

"I forgive you, but don't just stand there, can you help me up."

I helped him up and Zelestar wrapped her arms around him and kissed him.

What? Not again! The woman I loved was in the arms of another man.

With a twinkle in her eye, Zelestar laughed. "I couldn't resist."

"I can't take any more of this. I love you, Zelestar. Will you please marry me?"

"Of course, Vying. There's never been any other man but you."

"Let's get out of here and return to Zartex?"

"Zartex? Whoa. What are talking about?" Nafuka asked.

"We're going to have a wedding there and then we're going to Milo," I said.

"Are you and Zelestar getting married on Zartex?"

"Nafuka, I've seen the way you look at my sister. She's waiting for you."

"You and I both know what trouble you'll get into if you remain a single man," I said.

"This time you won't be alone," Zelestar added.

Nafuka didn't say anything as we climbed down the cliff and headed to the floating city. There was rejoicing everywhere. The nobleman met us on the pier. He looked much younger and very handsome. The lovely Yolee was at his side.

"Thank you, Vying, for rescuing my planet. How can I ever repay you?"

"It wasn't me. It was the Almighty, His Son — Lord Jesus, and the Holy Spirit. Lead your people by following Him all the days of your life or you'll be a slave to an evil spirit seven times worse than Skeldor and spend eternity in the Lake of Fire."

"I shall follow the Almighty."

We got into Zelestar's ship and left Coralia. I held her in my arms, but as I looked down at the planet, my mind drifted and I wondered what battle awaited me in the *City Beneath the Sea*.

ABOUT THE AUTHOR

Peter H. Zindler is an awarding winning author who has written, directed and produced several stage plays, edited Praise the Lord newspaper, has written screen plays, and has written and directed two TV pilots. For a year he wrote, produced and directed a radio show for KTYM in LA. He had a small part in the movie *Rain Man* in the opening scenes with Tom Cruise.

He is mentor to several writers and has a passion to see others succeed at the craft he loves. He heads up a critique group for the San Diego Christian Writers Guild and has started a critique group for Teen Writers at the Ramona Library.

Pete was a wrestler in high school and college and has been a wrestling coach at Ramona High School for 13 years helping the team win many championships. He has trained as a UFC fighter at Ken Shamrock's gym - the Lions Den and has coached against him on the high school level.

As a long time member of Kiwanis, he partnering with the Ramona Kiwanis Club using the proceeds from the first printing of "Spirit Warrior" to build a trade school in Romania for orphans.

www.ingramcontent.com/pod-product-compliance
Lightning Source LLC
Chambersburg PA
CBHW071231250626
47163CB00001B/140